Having left school at 15, education was not a priority until it was a requirement for Andy's role as an apprentice carpenter. He went on to complete his trade and subsequent post-trade qualifications.

Being pronounced a failure at school, his new love for post education earned him a pilot's license at 27, eventually building his own 2-seater aircraft. Construction in his blood, he travelled Asia and refined his experience and eventually a career change to property management, at 42.

With computers skills in both 2 and 3D building software, he needed to attest one last thing to those that said he couldn't, and wrote a book, completing it before turning 57.

As hard as it is to truly dedicate everyone and everything that has allowed me to place words on a piece of paper, ultimately, I must dedicate this book to my parents, Valerie and Reginald James [Jim]. Hope I have made them both proud. Mum, especially to you, this book is for the one that you never were able to finish and trust you are able to read it, be it in this life or the next.

Andy Gaunt

IMPROBABLE DREAM

AUSTIN MACAULEY PUBLISHERS™
LONDON • CAMBRIDGE • NEW YORK • SHARJAH

Copyright © Andy Gaunt (2020)

The right of Andy Gaunt to be identified as author of this work has been asserted by him in accordance with section 77 and 78 of the Copyright, Designs and Patents Act 1988.

All rights reserved. No part of this publication may be reproduced, stored in a retrieval system, or transmitted in any form or by any means, electronic, mechanical, photocopying, recording, or otherwise, without the prior permission of the publishers.

Any person who commits any unauthorised act in relation to this publication may be liable to criminal prosecution and civil claims for damages.

Austin Macauley is committed to publishing works of quality and integrity. In this spirit, we are proud to offer this book to our readers; however, the story, the experiences, and the words are the author's alone.

A CIP catalogue record for this title is available from the British Library.

ISBN 9781528918077 (Paperback)
ISBN 9781528918084 (Hardback)
ISBN 9781528962179 (ePub e-book)

www.austinmacauley.com

First Published (2020)
Austin Macauley Publishers Ltd
25 Canada Square
Canary Wharf
London
E14 5LQ

I would like to acknowledge those who have helped me in my life up to now, albeit possibly long overdue for some, and regrettable to others that have since passed on.

Thank you, Jan, for a munificent appraisal and honest sentiment for this book. You listened, remained impartial and most importantly true to who you are.

I want to take the time in acknowledging Austin Macauley Publishers, for believing in me enough to publish this book. I had a lull in my life and a half-completed manuscript and could not find the words to fill the pages, so Jitka to you who provided me a little zest when I needed it most. Thank you, it is much appreciated.

'Don't be guided in life from any of the misfortunes of complacency, awaken from that anxiety and don't let it be your destiny, turn your dream into an actuality.'

Chapter 1

Norwich England 1953, August 14:
The young man just sat there seemingly not looking at anything in particular. His sombre gaze harmonised precisely with his statue-like exterior, with almost his entire body shape devoid of any movement. His only change from his deceptive sculptured form, was the tiny lowering of an eyelid perhaps hindering his ogle, yet his eyes where fixed on an object only known to him. You would be exonerated of any felony charge if in fact it were a crime and you had to explain in twenty words or less, his purpose. You would not be condemned if you had chosen the pigeon only metres in front of him, dipping and bobbing its head in search of food, like one of those silly plastic birds with the red or blue bowler hats that you have in a bar, relentlessly consuming coloured water from a cup.

A young boy, who was playing on a small section of grass close to the young man's wooden bench seat, was now more interested in him, than his ball. The seat, in which the young man sat, was "cupped" inform, precisely contoured to his body shape, unerringly moulded to that of his profile. With legs crossed, he was nestled comfortably back into the seat, one hand on his waist, the other somewhat firmly placed over a russet coloured leather satchel bag at his side. He appeared oblivious to anything – his surroundings, the noise of passers-by, even the pigeon, yet his hand clutched the strap of the haversack as if it were his very last possession on this earth. Given the young man's motionless existence if indeed he was a statue, he and the bench would have convincingly been carved from the one piece of oak tree.

The boy was playing ball with his mother and not paying any attention to his game, not that it needed much when it was just throwing back and forth without any formality. Sometimes hitting the ground or sometimes just bouncing two or three times as it fell precisely into her outstretched hands. His mother making sure her son's aim was the sole reason she was just able to catch it, by giving one of those big 'yeeeahs' mothers always did. The boy's impatience in not being able to quite understand the games reasoning, spent more time staring at his newly found statuette of the young man, and every now and then she reminded him not to gawk, it was impolite after all, but without understanding why, boys of his age simply did this without meaning.

The park where they were, adjoined "Old Morley Hall", a 16th century manor, built after the great plague of Tutor England, circa 1509. The mansion was constructed around an old Anglo-Saxon moat probably built around 700 years earlier and had most likely unchanged for decades. Even after successfully surviving the war, it would undoubtedly look as it did when first built. It was now a gathering place for families with children, a place of peace after the great conflict, where they would feed the waterfowl or walk about the manicured lawns. They would spend hours strolling the cobblestone paths, just to view the innumerable varieties of vegetation, and plant life. The cobbled walkways unpredictable in both shape and form provided the onlooker the disbelief they were in fact man made. You would clearly believe they must have formed this way by nature had it not been for neatly cut conifer hedges and pencil pines which mimicked the paths twisted and bent shapes.

The park or better "common" surrounded the village of Saint Peter and was made up of mostly small farms and pastoral grounds, almost certainly servicing the needs of the nobleman who once lived here decades ago. Families now days, generally the local farmers came here on a weekend; they would bring a picnic lunch with cut sandwiches and freshly made buttered scones with dates and homemade jam, and copious dollops of whipped cream followed by a traditional cup of tea. They had all worked in unison rebuilding the damaged farmlands that where handed back to them from the war office at the end of the battle. The rebuilding had taken many years and was nearing its end with the runway of "Old Buckenham Airfield" now barely visible apart from the purple flowers of the "spear thistle" making a home in the cracking tarmac, and outbuildings now milking stations and meeting points for farmers who once leased these lands.

It was not long before the boy was kicking his ball in the direction of the young man, perhaps to attract his attention and to see if he was real, only again being disciplined by his mother. The young man unexpectedly looked up from his seemingly devoid stare, briefly startling the boy. The boy now knew in an instant that he was not a sculpture or somehow not fixed to the park bench or in fact cut from the same tree. The young man stood then looked around as if he had suddenly woken from an unconscious nothingness. It was as if programmed to happen at that specific moment in time, and without delay acknowledged the boy and his mother with a resolute yet gentle wave.

The woman now able to guess his age at around twenty-two somewhat her junior of thirty and without thinking she spoke to him.

'I am sorry that my son is pestering you,' she exclaimed to the young man, 'he can be a bit bothersome at times but…' she paused, 'He means no harm.'

The young man gave a kind-hearted nod then smiled. This instantly provided the woman perhaps the assurance he was moral and pondered over as to why she would even think that he was not in the first place.

The woman had noticed a figure standing off to one side of the young man. She turned toward the silhouette and saw it was plainly just a man. Why she even considered anything else at the time she never quite worked that out, other than he was quite handsome and around 40. She thought it very strange that he had on clothing that was a little confusing to her as it seemed imaginary, and he represented someone or something that was perhaps fictional. Had it not been for his reading glasses in his jacket pocket she might have simply assumed that.

The strange impression she had fashioned of him, was gone as quick as it had entered into her head.

She looked back at the young man who had now taken on a fresh new characteristic. He had gone from this unresponsive human shape with a stare into emptiness, to as alert as her son now was. His motionless gaze was now a tilted head facing upwards as every now and then he would cast his eye at an overflying aircraft, then strangely back into his frozen state. She watched intently at him as he religiously looked up as if programmed each and every time an aircraft flew above him.

The boy soon tossed his ball at the young man's feet, perhaps purposely, or by chance, he would never quite recall doing this, nor would his mother have any recollection in seeing the strange standing man leave. They both felt drawn toward the young man, feeling compelled to now talk to him.

The boy soon whispered out a long drawn out, 'H-e-l-l-o' and with that passed he continued with a, 'What are you doing?'

The young man smiled at the boy, then answered back with a calming quality.

'Well to be truthful I don't really know exactly why, except I am here pretty much every day and do much of the same, look at the birds and planes and people who enjoy the park as I do.'

'Why do you look at the aeroplanes?' asked the boy.

'Oh, they were a part of my life once!' exclaimed the young man, 'and I miss them, as I do other parts of my life.'

The boy continued with his noticeable questioning, questioning the young man instantly remembered he did as a boy.

'I am going to fly them when I get older,' said the boy, 'Just like my father did in the war.'

The boy's mother moved in closer, perhaps by instinct or just because of a mother's likely impulse to protect her own offspring. With all the eagerness and purity that comes from being a boy, the young man instantly remembered his youth and went on to tell the boy and his mother how he too had the gusto equal to that of the youngster. They both noticed his delight in talking, and how his past rigid state was replaced with hand movements and pointing and waving gestures. He almost immediately let his consciousness unwind and think of when he was a young boy. He painted a luminous picture in his mind how this place was not that much different, the ponds still had waterfowl, and the mansion looked much as it did today. He recalled the kites that where made from tree twigs, fixed into cross-like shapes, held together with newspaper, hemp twine and flour paste. His mind then drifted back to the old airfield not too far from here when the bombers flew their night missions. He went on to explain how he was just a causality of the war, an expendable item as he recalled in his flight briefing.

The young man abruptly stopped his story sat back down onto his bench seat to once again fall back into his torpid shape. He briefly glanced back to the boy then lowered his head and again went back into his rigid form. The mother confused by his anomalous appearance from motionless to invigorated, felt compelled to ask him if he needed help. She took a deep breath and tried her very best to ask without sounding presumptuous and assuming he was in fact in need of a doctor.

'I am sorry to ask you, but please don't think it bad of me, but was wondering if I can help you or do you need help I, I mean sorry but…'

The young man looked at her and smiled. He slightly shook his head from side to side then apologised.

'I am very sorry for my confusing state of appearance and must come across as someone in need of help, but I can assure you I am fine, it's just that I…' he again stopped short, and lowered his head briefly, then continued after taking a deep breath, followed by a fatigued yet relieved sigh.

'If you have the time, perhaps, I could tell you my story, I need to start from a beginning that I can remember, but afraid you as others have done will find my story rather implausible, I mean to the point rather disbelieving.'

The mother feeling a little concerned for her safety and that of her son mindfully questioned the thought to stay and all but convinced herself to leave him in peace, but something told her she needed to hear his story no matter what it was. Something had drawn her to his apparent needs and unsure if it was the fact, she was lonely after the death of a loved one from the consequences of war, and the young man would perhaps comfort her with his memories. Would it be of battle, death or loss of a loved one, she would never truly understand the reasoning of war and this may give her some piece of mind that it was all worth her loss. She needed to find out and gave the young man a smile of assurance, one he probably sounded like he was looking for. The mother now fully relaxed sat intently on the ground with her son as the young man then began.

He let his mind drift back to the pastoral grounds around the airfield that were not that much different than today. His thoughts were soon able to draw images and visualise the meadows in which he once stood, a time he soon remembered as if it were just yesterday. His surroundings seemed to lose their vivid colour, becoming almost pallid and allowing a coldness to exhume and swallow the now depleting warmness of the day's air. The nearby noises soon amplified to a surreal silence, the distance rapidly turning wraithlike; his mind was able drift back when he once stood in this very countryside. He stood in both picture and place he repudiated to disregard. He began to tell a story with all the effortlessness and with meticulousness facts as if he had returned to that very moment in time. His words were to be a re-count of a period in which he once lived, spoken as if written with the costliest of "quills" using the finest of black inks, and printed on the most exorbitant of handpicked opulent paper.

Old Buckenham Airfield England 1943, August 9

The runway was located neatly between two adjoining farms. The aerodrome had carefully positioned "silver birch" trees, which aligned the boundary in neat rows, their amber leaves and the stiff breeze was the onset of approaching cooler weather. Surrounding the airfield was open pastoral ground, with the odd scattered "Red Polls" and "Sussex" Cows eating the abundant grasses; there were a small number of them looking skyward trying to pinpoint the approaching noise. The airfield blended in nicely with the surrounding vegetation, and had it not been for the airstrip patch of tarmac stretching north south, and the white painted threshold markers numbering "zero seven" and "two five", one could easily have missed it. There were few scattered buildings of little meaning and to a passer-by, they would have just merged in with the vegetation making the airfield, look very much insignificant. The hill-less almost flat rural grounds about the field allowed aircraft to approach low, and from almost any direction.

The cows continued their chewing of the lush grasslands while farmers were maintaining fences and tending to the herds. A few cows were leisurely walking in procession following one farmer perhaps getting ready for milking. Machinery was being driven systematically up and down the fields preparing them for cooler weather crops. Everything that day seemingly had a chore, well almost everything apart from a young man who stood in the middle of one of the fields amongst the cows, looking skyward, head tilted upward, eyes firmly fixed in the distance. The cows' heads where soon looking about in every direction too, trying to pinpoint an area from which the contradictory of noises of the approaching aircraft where coming from. The young man around 20, stood unmoving, his belongings at his feet, eyes fixed on the planes that where arriving in non-formation and by any means and speeds and from different flight paths. Some propellers he knew where "feathered", others where providing minimal thrust power from damaged engines, their exhaust system exuded both flame and blooms of black grey smoke. He knew it was not logical for the planes to be flying, yet as if held up by giant strings they remained aloft. He understood each pilot knew his duty and order for landing, like patients in the emergency room of a hospital, the sickest where seen to first, those who could wait, waited.

From the flight operations office, Marks had a clear view to most of the approaching planes, his field glasses allowing him to see the majority of the aircraft in detail. He was able to confirm aircraft type and in particular "nose art", the planes painted on individuality of pilot and crew. The aircrew would choose something of importance, a wife, a girlfriend, something that would boost their moral, and have it hand painted on the aircrafts nose, usually on the port side, a mark of respect to the pilot. Marks spoke in a sobering tone to the Chief Flight Operations Officer, Tomas Walker he preferred Tommy, but Marks just called him Chief. Marks had this silly tendency, call it an idiosyncrasy if you will to practically label all those close to him, as chief, something he had done since for as long as he could remember.

'Chief, that's twenty-four, confirm two four in the log at 14:21 hours.'

Tommy knew this was good, 24 aircraft returning was first-rate, a blessing for them, the war effort and mostly for pilot moral.

Tommy and Marks stepped out of flight operations in time to see the last B-24 nose wheel set down safely on home soil. It was only an inconsequential bombing run into enemy soil with the 24 aircraft; you could even propose a preparation run, tuition of sorts as this base was hinting to become covert. Marks knew in around three or four months their inventory would increase to an additional 25 to that of the current 24, B-24 aircraft and an unknown amount and type of light bomber. The bases 25th Liberator was yet to arrive, and it was to be a newer model. Marks was told it was a 'J' version, and was meant to be here already, and could arrive any day, he hoped today. The delays were due to a paint shortage and lack of pilots to ferry it to the base, so it was just a waiting game and knew he needed to be patient. The new 'J' model aircrafts' exterior would be left in its raw aluminium form, from the paint shortage and Marks would leave it to the men to make up their minds on how it was to be finished off-well with its nose art of course.

Back at the field, the young man picked up his duffle bag, placed his cap neatly on his head, tilted it just at the right angle and looked down at his boots. He needed to ensure each lace had an equal sized loop so bend down and used his thumb as a guide, it was his way of being thorough, even though he was known to be rebellious at times. It was probably at the right time to do so having bend down just as one of the cows ran in the direction of a woman waving some grasses in the air, and calling out, his first thought was to him.

He headed toward the base entry after having a meaningless conversation with the woman over the cow and trekked the two miles up the narrow path. It too was lined with trees, not deciduous like the "birch", but pine conifers, tall, pencil like, and a pea green, their tips tilting sideways as if acknowledging the gentle breeze. Almost out of nowhere, he saw a silvery bomber fly low very nearly colliding into the treetops, as did the cow with him. He had seen the bomber before he had heard the deafening drone of its engines. It had approached from a northeasterly direction, possibly towards "St Peter", and a further 10 or so minutes behind the squadron. The plane had no markings that he could make out, nor the customary nose art, so the young man shrugged it off, regained his composure and continued back along a track toward the base entry.

The curved path leading up the entry point, had been shaped with a type of crushed granite, and was partially overgrown with grasses, thistle and lavender. Either way it did not seem to be a path often used, perhaps hidden or simply just forgotten. His long walk up the track allowed him to continue to listen for any late arriving aircraft. The soundless tranquillity of his stride provided him the awareness there were going to be no more safe arrivals of planes that day. They had either ditched from lack of fuel or had become part of the causality of war. He had time to think of his past and how it may have moulded him into who he was and why he was now walking toward an airfield.

His life before now like the path, had journeyed some interesting times. They were not now in his mind, and not even evident, yet would in turn would become recognised, be it confusing as to what was real, and what was an imagination, yet his life had been moulded the way it was now for a very good reason.

He soon arrived at the end of the track, which opened to an adjoining road also of crushed granite. The road must have been a thoroughfare used by the farms before the airfield was built as it clearly intersected the entry to the aerodrome then simply stopped. He could see in the distance the road start again as if it where the remaining piece of a pie having had a big chunk taken out of it. In the distance there was an entry point to the airfield, he knew that in just a few moments all of his training was about to provide him with some meaning, and all of his efforts would soon be rewarded, and he too would be helping the war effort. He stood motionless, as his mind briefly drifted back to his youth, he then gave a gentle sigh, and walked the final leg of his journey.

The entrance point to the airfield had a single gate. Its guards station was a small building, door-less and just big enough for a person to stand in out of the weather. It had a timber-lined wall painted in a sickly yellow colour, and a silvery grey partially rusting iron roof, which matched precisely the adjoining buildings. The guard who was now standing a little taller than before, perhaps marking authority looked at the young man with intent. The young man not knowing protocol continued his walk up to the guard and handed him his papers. The brown envelope was addressed to "The Commander and Chief" and had a "Confidential" red in colour stamp on it. The guard's stance now a little relaxed picked up a green telephone hand piece placed it to next to his ear, and then turned a handle just below the hand pieces cradle, four or five times in a clockwise rotation. A crackly sound came through a speaker followed by a deep resonating voice,

'Yes Corporal.'

The guard gave a little cough just to clear his throat and to perhaps ensure his words came out that little bit clearer.

'Good afternoon Sergeant, I am sorry to bother you sir but there is a civilian here to see the Field Marshal.'

'Thank you Corporal, I will send a vehicle.'

The guard replaced the handset into its metal holder and relayed the message to the young man, who had one last time looked down at his laces to ensure they were tied correctly. Satisfied his boot laces where precisely tied his focus soon changed to the sound of an approaching vehicle. A jeep with driver and passenger stopped near the gate and the guard anxiously walked over and opened the single passenger's door.

A tall man perhaps six-foot-three clambered out of the passenger seat. He wasn't in uniform and the young man didn't have much time to assess him apart from a pair of silver coloured aviation sunglasses he was wearing, the ones that had that mirror refection. He didn't have any insignia other than a pair of flight wings pinned to his jacket and pistol stowed into its holster.

Marks acknowledged the guards salute, and then removed his glasses and cap. The guard handed Marks the envelope, while the young man simply stood not knowing what the procedure was. Marks turned and faced the young man who immediately saluted, Marks acknowledged, then opened the envelope and briefly skipped over the papers.

Marks, then in soft tone; a character very much unexpected from his status began to talk to the young man.

'Hello son, I hope you have a safe trip, and here we don't do things that formal, so at ease.'

The young man not quite understanding the intent of "formal" still went by the book. 'Yes sir, my trip was fine in fact my home is not that far away sir.'

Marks answered again in a soft tone, 'Please son, not so official, you have come to me as a volunteered citizen, and I am not much for formality, so putting that aside guess we might go for a quick tour of this facility to settle you in.'

Marks and the young man climbed into the jeep, just as it lightly started to rain, bringing a chill instantly to the air. The drive to the main facility was only short, and Marks took the time to point out a few of the buildings to the young man.

Marks again spoke in a soft tone, 'Being a civilian military trained pilot, they don't tell us who we are getting, so I guess a name would be good.'

The young man looked with confusion and quickly spoke, 'Sorry sir, I didn't know, I am Ben Walters well Benjamin Walters.'

'Nice to meet you Ben, I'm Field Marshal Harold Marks, Commander and Chief of Home Land Security at this facility, people round here just call me Marks, so I am happy with that.'

'Nice to meet you sir and my mother had once given me strict instructions to be polite, so if you don't mind, can I still call you sir?'

'That's fine,' Marks answered in a relaxing manner, 'Your mother is a real gem for instilling that in you, in respect to her, I will let you decide.'

'Thank you, sir, very much for your support,' Ben acknowledged. 'I think my mother would have considered you, and as silly as it sounds, a requirement of war.'

'Yes,' Marks replied in a much deeper tone than before, perhaps showing his formal side.

The main facility building had a domed roof, again in iron, matching the adjoining buildings. The entry door that they were now parked in front of was neatly moulded into the arched roofline of the structure, with a small flat roof section in a mixture of iron and a type of "ship lap" timber board lining the walls, in that awful yellow colour. Marks and Ben climbed out of the jeep, the driver insisting on carrying Ben's, duffel bag and leather satchel. Ben, quickly grabbed at the satchel, entwining his palms firmly about the strap.

'If it's OK, I will carry this,' Ben pleaded, he was referring to his small threadbare looking brown leather haversack.

Marks looked over at Ben as his head was turning in every direction, trying to analyse his surroundings.

The pair walked up to the door, the driver stood to one side allowing the two to enter. Marks looked at Ben one last time before they entered the building and spoke in a gentle manner, hoping this would settle Ben's probable anxiety.

'Ben, what was your mother's name?'

Ben wanted to speak, but instantly his throat tightened, and with a small tear starting to well in his eye, answered in a sombre tone, 'Charlotte, it was Charlotte but she liked me to call her "Charlie", not Mum; she said Charlotte made her feel old.'

'You are a very lucky young man Ben, your mother has provided you with a level head,' Marks announced with conviction.

The two, followed by the driver entered the building. Marks proceeded with his seemingly formal side and gave Ben a brief of the facility.

'This base was set up initially as an airport training facility. As the war progressed, we added the hospital then research facility later, which is independent to the war effort. It is regarded as a covert base as most of the public are not sure of what we operate from here, apart from the odd formation of aircraft and the one or two that fly in and out of here mostly on night operations.'

Ben spoke this time a little less formal. 'I knew of this place a few years ago and just thought it was a basic aerodrome, little more than a training facility and often wondered why I went to another flight school so far away and not this one?'

'Now that you are here son, I can give you a bit more information about what we do,' Marks confessed, still looking very informal.

'The Chief, who you will soon meet son, is my number two, his name is Dr Steven Halverson, and he is responsible and for RDF. It's a technology we are working on, with other allies that will save this war effort. It basically allows us to pinpoint approaching enemy aircraft before they arrive, giving us a very small window in which to prepare? The combined effort of our allies in advancing this technology has provided us with some improvement in our research. Our Navy boys use the acronym of just "Radar" shortened down from "Radio Detection and Ranging" we still call it, "Range and Detection Finding" or RDF as I just mentioned. Well that's not all of its pluses, we have also discovered what we think is a way of removing a magnetic field that surrounds steel or any metal for that matter but more of that later, we better carry on and meet the crew.'

Marks and Ben continued past the entry inside to the main facility, Marks went on explaining most of what they did in brief not detailing too much as he said to Ben it may just confuse him or provide too much information in one day. They walked down a narrow corridor; the floors had gone from a plain polished concrete finish to a patterned linoleum floor covering, in largish black and white square patterns. Marks stopped at a door sign posted "laboratory".

'Ben, would you like to continue the tour or get settled into your barracks?' questioned Marks. 'The barracks are that way,' Marks pointed to the left, 'right is the mess hall and hospital wing.'

Ben, looking a little tired did not want to disappoint the Field Marshal with his tour brief and elected to continue regardless. Marks asked the driver to take Bens duffel bag to his barracks as they walked off to the laboratory.

'I see, you are fond of the haversack, Ben,' said Marks, 'a little worn though, I bet it has some stories?'

'It does, sir,' replayed Ben, 'it truly does.'

The laboratory had many individual workstations, most of which were occupied by men in white uniform overcoats not looking that formal though. A small number of woman where there too but had bleached coloured caps that sort of looked like nuns Cornett's, Ben assumed they must have been nursing staff. To his count, Ben could see about fifteen or so people working at stations no bigger than six-foot square to his reckoning. Some stations had laboratory flasks and beakers with long winding out of shape adjoining tubes, and what he considered where little ovens with very small glass viewing panels in the doors.

Suddenly over the buildings intercom system came a short announcement;

'General Marks, you are needed in your office, you have a call from General Dickson, sir.'

'Excuse me Ben, I need to take this call I will be back in no time; I will send the Chief if am going to be a while.'

Ben looked around, taking it all in and eventually cast his eyes on another section of the laboratory that was separated by two doors with a keypad arrangement on the outer door, possibly a locking device of some sort? Ben only noticed one person in the room, a man around 40 and appeared to be a civilian. He was dressed in normal clothing, well as normal as you would if you were a civilian, a sort of casual suit without the tie. In all accounts, he was elegantly dressed and had noticed Ben to the point he removed his reading glasses bringing them down to chest height. The man stared at Ben with direct eye contact as he walked out of the separated room, and towards him. Ben felt a little unconformable which was only amplified as he now noticed most of the others had stopped what they were doing and where looking at him with interest. They looked at Ben with confusion as he stood as if he were addressing someone, yet to them he stared into nothingness, a devoid space. But to Ben, he stood almost mirrored to an image of an older man who was the exact same height, similar in posture and remarkably analogous in looks, had it not been for a blemish across the top of the civilian's left eye one would suggest Ben was now looking at his older self.

'Hello' he said, 'Ben, you appear to have a question for me, ask away but will guess you already know the answer to it.'

Confused by the civilian's line of interrogation, Ben looked around the room, remaining silent. He had noticed the others were still looking at him, which only confused him more?

'I am Marshall, Marshall Hartley, the resident civilian scientist; well, resident as I reside nearby over at "Old Morley Hall".' So Ben, I hope your short stay here "is" as you expect,' whispered Marshall as if he were trying to imply otherwise.

Ben not quite knowing or even understanding Marshall's odd response, made an effort to avoid the sudden interest in him by the others in the room, who had now quickly dropped their heads and continued their work as Marks re-entered the room. Ben, striving to look and act as nothing out of the ordinary just happened, avoided their curiosity by turning his attention to Marks asking inquisitively, 'What is all this stuff, it sort of looks very much like my school's science room?'

Marks replied, 'You know scientists, it makes them feel important to have beakers and test tubes and graphs that make no sense to us. But briefly the ones here in these stations are looking at developing better bomb fuses and time delays in the different technologies we are working on. Those,' Marks pointed to the room where Marshall came from but by now had different people there in overcoats, 'are developing a metallic blocking system, which will work together with the RDF, the US Government is trying some sort of system, that dare I say it, make a ship invisible.'

'What?' said Ben in disbelief.

'Well, not exactly invisible, more so undistinguishable to the RDF, I mean the object is still there, the RDF just can't see it.'

Marks gave one of those answers you give when you probably don't really know the answer to, and with that Marks suggested they would discuss it later at the Bar that evening.

'So what does Marshall do?' enquired Ben.

'Well my boy, that's about as silly of a question as my answer of "invisible", the only Marshall we have here is for the movement of aircraft, let's move on.'

Ben appeared more confused now than he was just moments ago when talking to the strange man, who not only knew his name, but had now appeared to have suddenly gone.

One of the nurses in the room caught Ben's eye, smiling and blushing at the very same time. Around Ben's age, she tried not to continue the eye contact by pretending to read a folder she had in her hand, Marks had noticed and took away Ben's attention from her and suggested he be shown his barracks, complete his medical examination, shower then off to the Bar. Ben looked at the nurse and instantly his entire body had a coldness to it. He looked at her face, it was one of those if you had met, you would most definitely not forget. Her ruby lipstick matched perfectly her long curly scarlet hair, and petite frame made her look almost fragile. Ben's chilliness soon warmed, he went to speak to her as if he knew her, but the name just didn't come out. She looked at him, smile now fading as if she too had met him, eventually persuading herself perhaps not. Ben looked one last time as Marks went over to the microphone that was sitting on one of the workstations and called for the Chief; Ben could hear the request reverberate from the speakers within the room.

'Chief, Marks here, can you come and meet our newest of recruits, we're in the lab.'

The young nurse looked up from her ruse of reading the folder, and cheekily grinned perhaps at the thought she knew the young man was here to stay. Moments later, a heavily built man, wearing black rimmed glasses and rather casual attire, still military in appearance but nonetheless informal, walked into the lab. He partially smiled as he entered the room, he carried a small hardback clipboard, probably nothing meaningful on it, and he stopped and with outstretched hand introduced himself to the young man standing in front of him.

'Hello, I'm Dr Steven Halverson, or just Chief if you like, it could be a little confusing at first as Marks calls a few of us round here Chief, you'll get used to it'.

'Hello sir, I'm Ben Walters.'

The Chief looked at Marks then back at Ben and to ease his obvious nervousness denounced his formality by making a little joke about Marks calling him and few others Chief diplomatically of course, then in almost word for word to that of Marks leaned forward to Ben and quietly spoke in his ear.

'Ben, we are not that formal, just Chief please, it takes away the required regimented procedure of this horrible war and offers us all with a little relief.'

Ben nodded and with those comments from the Chief, agreed he would be less formal despite his mother's insistent request

Ben saluted to Marks and thanked him for his hospitality so far, then followed the Chief out of the lab.

The barracks where just as expected with bunks aligned each side of the room, stacked two high and neatly placed between windows giving an unrestricted view out to the airfield. There were 10 in the room and the Chief explained there were 25 barracks in use at the moment and 50 in total. Each barrack housed the crew of each bomber; the remaining 25 were for the base's expansion in a few months. The Chief smiled absorbedly as he looked out of the window toward the field, then spoke to Ben with a little eagerness in his breath.

'Ben, I probably expect you are keen to meet the crew members of the base but first we need to get yourself passed to fly and sitting in the left seat as soon as you are capable.'

'Yes Chief, that would great,' Ben had replied with an informal tone coupled with total zest.

The Chief noticed this and although he didn't show it, was happy that Ben had enlisted. Ben stowed his belongs in the chest at the foot of his bunk bed, gave a casual nod of acceptance of his newfound home then followed the Chief out of the barracks, brown satchel slung over his shoulder.

The hospital wing was close to the lab, and the pair of swinging doors that joined the two rooms together had large round glass viewing panels in them. Although each door swung in both directions, they clearly had marked on them an "enter" and "exit" plaque. The Chief left Ben sitting on one the beds in the ward, as he made his way over to the nurses' station. He gave one of the nurses in the ward his file after briefly having read a few of the unimportant lines. As Ben looked around the room he could see some flight crew being treated, some were patiently standing while others were sitting at bunks having nurses attend to wounds and changing dressings. A few hospital doctors were helping some of the crew still wearing flight gear, perhaps the injured who had just returned. Ben soon became aware of a nurse standing in front of him. His eyes made instant contact with the young carer who he had seen earlier in the lab. Her bottle-green-coloured eyes now visible, matched perfectly with her auburn hair, she blushed as she tried to be professional in her behaviour.

'Please stand and face this wall Corporal,' she spoke in a soft tone while pointing at the eye chart. 'Cover your left eye, and read the second row from the bottom, right to left.'

Ben swallowed, smiled at her and quickly rattled off the letters, 'B R S O X T L,' each letter flowing into the next making it sound almost like one big word.

She focussed on her clipboard, and without looking up kept her poise and spoke again in a supple tone,

'Please try that again Corporal, this time a little slower,' she demanded.

Ben feeling a little intimidated from her obvious professionalism then spoke with a little more composure.

'B-R-S-O-X-T-L,' he said while trying to keep his smirk to himself.

'Cover your right eye, read from the bottom line and the middle letter only,' requested the young nurse, again with professionalism.

Before Ben read it, he glanced in her direction just as he caught her looking at him, she dropped her head in embarrassment, only to look up again as he turned his head to read off the chart.

'That's fine Corporal, we just have your vaccinations to go so can you please loosen your belt and remove your pants off your waist,' the young nurse now sounding a little more skilled.

Ben smiled and as he had his back to her, loosening his pants preparing himself for the jab he was about to get. Pulling his trousers aside exposing a piece of hip, he started questioning her to take his mind of the needle he so much did not want to get.

'So, my name is Ben, have you a name I call you by?'

'I don't fraternise with the pilots or flight crew Corporal, so please refrain from being so forward,' the young nurse retorted, yet sneakily smiled whilst plunging the air from the syringe.

'Well, I was just wondering as I am well new here, I just thought perhaps you could, well sort of show me round, well I, I don't mean show me exactly, I mean introduce me to —'

Ben felt the onset of her vengeance of sorts by way of a deep jab in his buttock, gritting his teeth and swallowing he let out a load moan in his voice, and yelled out without thinking.

'That went all the way in,' half expelling what air he had in his lungs at the very same time.

'Sorry Corporal did that hurt?' she replied and without warning, jabbed him again with his second shot.

'Woo,' Ben yelped like a small puppy, but held his dignity with elegance.

'Did that hurt too, Corporal?' she asked.

'No, no nurse that's fine just, just an old football injury, that's all,' Ben whispered.

'That's funny,' said the nurse, 'your background history says you didn't play sport at school as you preferred reading. Anyway, you are done so you may get yourself dressed as the Chief will be back soon.'

The Chief arrived back at the ward just as Ben was tightening his belt.

'All done, son?' he asked smiling at knowing just what had happened.

'Yes,' replied the young nurse, 'we are all done, unless the Corporal has any further questions.'

Ben looked over at her as she stamped on his file, "approved" and replied in a wounded tone.

'No, I, am no I don't believe I do, thank, thank you nurse.'

The Chief and Ben walked off, Ben limping slightly when the young nurse called out.

'Excuse me Corporal, you have forgotten your notes on the post vaccination symptoms.'

Ben walked back, took the note from her hand, tried not to smile, nodded and thanked her again. She grinned back and with her head slightly tilted to one side, spoke softly to him, 'I will see around the base, Corporal, and don't forget to read those notes.'

'Yes Nurse,' Ben replied, showing his formal side.

The Chief looked over at Ben as they walked off and explained that it's not very often a recruit gets special attention from a nurse, that is, unless he had made an impression on her, especially when it's the daughter of the Commander and Chief.

'What?' enquired Ben, 'She is his daughter, well that's just great, I am here only one day and I all but asked the commander's daughter for a date, well I didn't really, I mean I just asked her name, oh boy, that's going to go down well.'

The Chief then looked at Ben and provided him a little comfort.

'Ben, I think you are looking too much into this, she was just doing her job by ensuring you read your notes, don't make too much of it, it will be fine.'

'I hope so,' replied Ben as they continued their walk to the mess hall.

The canteen had a similar door plaque to that of the laboratory but other than words denoting something to do with food, someone had fixed a plate with knife and fork ether side just above the doorframe. Ben guessed it was a continuation of the less formal side to the base. Ben followed the Chief into the mess hall; the room having many tables with stools that were not in any logical fashion. At the end of the room and opposite to the entry door, was the food station; some men still dressed in flying jackets with plate in hand were being served what closely resembled a grandmothers old fashioned roast dinner and Yorkshire pudding, with copious amounts of a thick dark brown gravy. The room did not seem to be divided in rank or squadron, there were no groups of men, and everyone seemed to be chatting to everyone. Ben was unsure if this was the norm or perhaps he had a presumption things would be very much disciplined.

The men in the room eventually noticed the Chief who was standing there with a new recruit. The Chief never pushed his rank on the men as he had clearly showed that to Ben, nor did Marks. Both the clatter of plates being stacked and natter of men soon ceased as each man stopped what they were doing and with almost perfect choreography stood at attention.

'At ease men,' the Chief spoke in an incomplete tone of authority. I would like you all to welcome our newest recruit Ben Walters; he has been sent to us and he is one of our youngest pilots we have had through here, so please welcome him.'

The men continued standing at attention, then saluted, and with a long "whoop" "whoop" sound followed by progressive "hoot" "hoot" "hoots", picked up what was ever in their reach from their plates and in an almost well-rehearsed fashion threw it in Ben's direction, then instantly stopped their torment of food throwing and eased into a well-practised poem;

Welcome Ben, to Buckenham, a place you'll now call home;
We will fly together, so rest assured, you will never be alone;
Misfits we are, and titles are out, so let us
Make that clear;
We are all brothers here and equal now, no rank
Or saluting here;
The war will soon end, and we will be,
A nation free of harm;
Our bombers are safe so don't feel despair, and forever remain calm;
The squadron will fight a sacred battle, so don't feel like you are cursed;
Welcome again Ben, your home is here, we call it the 451st

Ben now covered in food scraps and the Chief smiling at the traditional welcome by the men, gradually walked Ben about the room and introduced him very briefly to the those that were in the cafeteria.

'Tonight, Ben, you will meet your crew over a cold ale at the bar, so perhaps get yourself cleaned up and I will see you at 21:00 hours in the saloon, it's just through those doors,' the Chief pointing at two doors adjacent the kitchen. Ben acknowledged all of their hospitality with a candid nod as he made his way back to the barracks for a shower and change of clothes.

At the barracks, Ben shuffled through his leather haversack then concealed it under some clothing at the base of his footlocker. He looked for something casual to wear and amongst his clothing, he found an old book he read as a child. He placed his soiled cloths in a laundry bag, luckily noticing his notes on the post vaccination where in his shirt pocket. Partially covered in food scraps, he cleaned what he could from the face then opened it up to ensure no food had sandwiched between the pages as he did a note fell out. It was a small piece of lavender paper, neatly folded in half, then half again and in carefully written handwriting were the words:

My name is Emily,
I am pleased to meet you, Flying officer Benjamin Walters.

Ben instantly felt a chill come over his body, Benjamin was a name his mother called him when he was in trouble as a child, although it bought up his past, he felt comfort in it, he felt a certain ease that this woman, the young nurse had chosen this name in which to call him. Ben's mind raced back to his youth; it forged its way through many good and bad memories. Today, he was reminded of his mother's preferred name, "Charlie", after Marks had asked about her, and now with Emily calling him Benjamin, he felt comfort, he felt purpose, he felt as if he belonged here and truly hoped he could make a difference. Ben was excited to be part of this squadron and would try his very best to become the best pilot he could be. First, he needed to be accepted by the crew; he wanted so much to be a part of what so far, he had seen. Ben was happy to be here, he sighed, opened up his footlocker, grabbed his dowdy coloured towel, toiletry bag and headed for the showers.

The bar was probably just like any other you would find at an air force base; well, that is to say it had a single barman, aka the Chief and probably there just to keep order. Bottles of differing spirits and mixers lined the shelf behind the Chief, with a mirror background and trashy coloured red and green lights that flashed all out of sequence. A cooler chest filled with ice, and four different types of beer were within easy reach of the Chief as was the bucket which he tossed the beer caps into after opening. On the bar top, was what looked like grandma's homemade lemon aid in a large fruit bowl; it had an oversized glass ladle and handwritten sign next to it, with the words "free". Some of the nurses and doctors were drinking from it, they were probably still on duty? Below the lemonade, was a single font offering a draft beer from the tap. Typically, about the room were white painted signs with black lettering posting country names and flight mile distances similar to the ones he had seen about the base, a sort of keepsake he guessed perhaps for sanity. Each were pointing in different directions to that supposedly of its destination, mostly for show, but putting it simply, it added to the air of ambience. Little toy planes and old wooden propellers, photos and paintings of aircraft also lined the walls.

There were groups of people at the tables, some dancing and others were at a jukebox playing records, also free. He could see Marks in the distance with a group of men he assumed were flight crew. Taking it all in, he soon became aware he was searching for Emily. Looking about the room for her, he noticed the Chief looking across at him holding up a beer, waiting for an acknowledgment of sorts, Ben politely nodded as the Chief opened it in his usual fashion, then handed him the beer.

'5p, thanks Ben, the second ones free,' said the Chief.

Ben tossed him a shilling and yelled out over the noise, 'That's your tip Chief.'

'Hey Ben, give this to Marks, will you,' pleaded the Chief, as he held up a pint of beer.

Ben grabbed the ale and made his way through the crowd towards Marks.

'Excuse me, sir,' Ben said to Marks not wanting to barge in on his conversation.

Marks turned to Ben; his cheeks had a glow to them not from the cold outside but more so from the few pints he most likely had by now.

'Ben my boy, good to see you, settled in I take it,' Marks asked whilst placing one hand on Ben's shoulder. 'I would like to take this opportunity to introduce you the boys you will be flying with,' continued Marks.

Ben took a sip of his beer, wiped the excess froth from his lips and partially smiled in anticipation as Marks prepared his address of introduction.

'Ben, please meet Ball Turret Gunner-Peter Murphy of Irish descent, we just call him Murph.'

Ben smiled, shook his hand and acknowledged he probably had some Irish blood in him somewhere also, well, most likely anyway, he would have thought?

Marks continued, 'The Right and Left Waist Gunners, ironically they are both brothers, Samuel "Sparky" and Michael "Mickey" McClain, also Irish, Sparky doubles as our radioman.'

Ben nodded at the two, too far around the table to shake their hands but gave a small wave hoping this would suffice.

Marks walked around a group not in Ben's squadron, and then stopped at a small number of men about one of the smallish round timber coffee tables.

'Top Turret Gunner and Engineer, Anthony Marks, no relationship to me of course, we call him Chips, every meal including breakfast, he has them. Over here is the Tail and Nose Gunners, Henry R Wilson is the Tail Gunner, Henry is from the posh side of London and hates his middle name, so we use it anyway. Ben meet Roger.'

'Is it OK if I call you Roger?' enquired Ben, thinking it polite to ask.

Henry smiled at Ben and said, 'We will get on just fine, so long as you don't call me Roger,' he did so with the cheekiest of grins.

'And this is Nose Gunner, Alexander Dunstan, we call him Spot, and yes just like the dog,' explained Marks, before Ben could say anything.

Marks and Ben continued around the room and stopped at the bar, where three men where drinking pints of beer. The pitchers looking almost undrinkable, flat, bubble-less and without the white froth on top. Marks looking at the navigator still wearing his headphones around his neck, Ben had found out later that he even slept with them. The Navigator, as was with the pilot were considered just as important, the quicker they got to the target, the quicker they turned and headed home.

'Ben this is our Navigator, Martin Hensley,' before the Chief even finished, Ben recognised the surname, he spoke with conviction.

'Hensley as in the department store, Hensley's?' Ben enquired.

'Yes,' Martin replied, 'but don't tell my wife.'

Ben unsure if it was a joke, looked confused so enquired anyway. 'Why not?' Ben asked.

Martin smiled, and then being the typical joker, he answered with a serious look on his face, 'Because she is in love with the dog old chap, and I am in fear of losing it all to a bloody rotten animal.'

Ben not sure what to think from that, was fearful in asking his nickname, and wondered why he wasn't introduced with one, so asked anyway.

'Do you have a name we call you by?' Ben asked bashfully, in fear of even a bigger rejoinder.

'Yes, Ben I do,' answered Martin.

Ben was waiting for something, not knowing what was next, so remained silent and just glared at him.

'Yes old chap, its bloody Wilson,' Martin said with a smile that stretched his black moustache across his face, while looking about the room apparently waiting for something else to happen. Ben noticed it and paused a little, just in case Martin had something else to say.

'Well old chap,' enquired Martin, 'any more bloody questions?'

Ben just had to ask, why Wilson and what was the comparison. The entire room had almost gone silent when it finally got the better of Ben.

'All right, I don't get it, why Wilson? What's the significance?' Ben asked.

'Well old chap, I hate to admit it, but it's the bloody name of that wretched dog.'

As soon as the word 'dog' came from Martin's lips, the entire group poured the remains of their now warm ale over his head. Martin stood tall, beer dripping off the tips of his moustache and finished with:

'That animal, that god forsaken animal is probably sitting in front of a warm fire eating my bloody caviar and smoking one of my Cuban bloody cigars; well, it looks like it's drinks all round.'

From that, Martin opened his billfold exposing a wad of pound notes, passed a handful of them to the bar tender and finished with, 'A shout for the bar.'

Pints and beers were passed around the room; Ben even noticed one of the nurses before, who was drinking grandma's lemonade, was also sharing in the hospitality from Wilson. Marks downed his pint and took advantage of the shout, the Chief yelled back to Wilson, 'The next one's free.'

Marks walked around the room with Ben over to the jukebox, a group of men were mulling over what to play.

'Ben Walters, meet captain, John Morgan, squadron leader and your flight instructor and good friend of mine before this atrocious war took hold of the world.'

'Hello sir, please to meet you,' Ben said, without realising he had slipped back to his formalities.

'Well, Ben, it's a pleasure to have you on board, hope you are up for it, we get into it tomorrow at 06:00 so don't drink too much,' said John, who usually complained about everything. 'And Ben, just call me the Cap'

'Next to the Cap, we have the Bombardier, sitting here drinking tea of course. Ben Walters, meet Fred Townsend, "Sperry" we call him.'

'Hello Sperry,' responded Ben with a face of confusion as to the bombardier's nickname, and before Ben could ask, Marks explained.

'Nothing to do with the tea he is drinking of course, it's the model of bombsight used, the "Sperry S-1" soon to be obsolete or so they say,' explained Marks, 'they try not to tell us too much.'

The Cap stood up as he looked at Sperry and said, 'Toss out the tea old chap we have a new recruit to welcome, I think it's time for drink and chat. What do you say Ben?'

'Well, Ben, I think that's everyone, unless I have forgotten someone,' Marks explained, now looking just a little inebriated.

In the corner of the room, Ben could see Marshall walking towards him. He still had his formal clothing by way of the suit but with added jacket probably as it was getting a bit chilly outside. He walked up to Ben and went straight into conversation about nothing in particular, just conversation.

'Ben, in two days you will be flying a very important mission, you will of course return, but things will be different.' With that, Marshall turned and walked out the room. He had walked in and out without being noticed, he had purpose, and that was to see Ben, and no one else. This was strange to Ben, and just as he started to question why that just happened, he heard a familiar voice, the words coming out in perfect tone, and in a manner matching the quality of her voice,

'Excuse me General, I have not yet been introduced,' said the voice.

Standing much taller than he had remembered, and out of her nurse's uniform, Ben immediately noticed it was Emily. Her auburn hair neatly tied back in a black "Snood", holding it just off her collar. She had on a grey outfit jacket, with three big round buttons, pleated skirt and an elegant hat to match. Her black velvet gloves matched her heeled shoes in colour and each had a small stitching of a fine silk lace. The open face of the shoe had three buckles that stylishly allowed most of her foot to be exposed. The heel of the shoe had gained her probably and extra three inches in height to that of what Ben could remember, and to complete her well-dressed attire, she had on a cerise coloured lipstick and a gold bracelet being an obvious set to her gold teardrop earrings. Ben's eyes were drawn towards her femininity as she raised her right hand toward him. He reached out instantly holding onto her petite hand; his mind went racing as he felt the warmth of her palm beneath the glove. It instantly sent a temperateness heat through his entire body and his mind raced with improper thoughts. Her hand shape moulded perfectly with his; he would remember this moment keeping it in his consciousness for eternity.

The young man soon regained his thoughts from telling his story. The foggy distance in his mind quickly cleared regaining clarity as he realised he had woken holding onto the palm and forearm of the young woman. How he had achieved this or how she even allowed it was enigmatic to them both, and instantaneously she pulled away her hand from his clutch as he screamed out her name. The moment passed in an instant as they both stood with confusion that needed instant clarity.

'Emily, it's me Ben!' he screamed again this time with intensity in his voice.

She instantly looked at him followed by a, 'How do you know my name? I, I am confused, do you know me, is this a…a, how, what are you saying I…'

Ben, put out both hands trying to calm her down, she looked at him and shook her head from side to side as she sobbed.

'Who are YOU? I don't know YOU,' she cried.

Chapter 2

Norwich England, August 16, 1953, 2 days later:
The young woman had woken in time to see the first glimpse of the morning sun. She had spent the past few days trying to fully understand her recent ordeal with the young man at the parklands surrounding Old Morley Hall. Had it not been for the fact he made her feel very uncomfortable when he just shouted out 'Emily,' she may have still been in contact with him. Had he perhaps introduced himself first or even if she had, maybe things would have ended a little different. Had she made a little too much fuss over him yelling out her name? She didn't know him, she didn't recall his name ever been mentioned from letters she received from her father. He, after all, was involved with their training, and was the commander at Old Buckenham Airfield, *He would have known him, He must have known him*, she thought.

Her annoying uneasy feeling was simply because he had screamed out, 'Emily.' Was that it, just it, or was she uneasy about the fact he confessed to believing he knew her or the detail in what he said? He knew her name without ever meeting her, or was it just because he could not have known her; he looked young, too young. Was he the twenty-two she guessed or older? Alternatively, had he just appeared younger? Either way, it was now starting to get the better of her and strangely enough, she needed to find out more about him. She finally settled on just two things, one, he was or must have been in the war to be able to tell that much detail about the base, as it was undisclosed after all. The second reason was, he must have been a very young looking twenty-two when he joined the 451st if he still appeared youthful looking now. He looked around her age, or somewhat younger, she continued to argue with herself; each and every time she settled on him not truthfully being able to be who he said he was. She wondered why then he would have simply come out with her name and the most distressing thing to her was he did get it right, had she mentioned her name to him, she couldn't remember. Did he know her or was this some sort of obsession or simply a ruse of sorts to play with a woman's emotions, and the likelihood of still being in pain from both the conflict of war and the loss of comrades in battle. Emily, for all accounts, persuaded by the young man's seemingly benevolent disposition, needed some closure, either he was disingenuous, or he was whom he claimed to be – she needed to know for certainty.

'Photos!' she suddenly screamed out the word, 'That is it, photos.'

'How could I have been so innocent and naïve!' she again shouted out, 'and to not think of searching old photos.' *That would be it, an old picture,* she thought to herself. With that, she raced upstairs to pull out the old shoeboxes of photos that had been crammed away out of sight on the top draw of her dresser.

The boxes she hoped would contain many letters and old portraits and prints she had kept, some even before the war. It was inconsistent to that of her normal behaviour that now, after all this time, something; someone had triggered a locked away memory. She removed her pastel grey slippers, placed a purple pillow on the floor and seated herself comfortably. She opened the lid off one of the shoeboxes and the aroma of her father's Aqua Velva after-shave still palpable from within box, wafted about her nose. It irritated her nostrils, forcing her to tighten her lips and wiggle her nose from side to side, instantly stopping the itch. Forgotten memories of her youth unfavourably overwhelmed her mind; they hurt her in the knowledge that up until this very moment, they were lost. She randomly chose a letter, carefully opening it so not destroy 2½D stamp on the face, why, perhaps just as a keep sack of an era tucked away from her past. She opened the snowy white envelope and removed the neatly folded note within, it read.

```
26th July, 43
My Dearest Emily,
     Training for bombing has been mostly tiresome.
We are ███████ and hour days, this will speed up the
crew's readiness and prepare them for a mission
expected to be around ████ so we need to be ready.
     I am forgetting dates here with all the███████
hours, so forgive me if I am out a bit with things,
and we will be back soon, next █████ I would think?
     I have a new recruit coming soon, he is around
21, not sure of his name as they don't tell us much
here but he is a ██████████ I think in we expect the
experiment to be completed, Tomas can be wearisome
sometimes as you know.
     I must sign off now and will write again soon.
     P.S sorry again for all the blank-outs I try to
write and tell you things without the war offices
checks of our Mail, after all we are not supposed to
█████ remember.
     Faithfully Yours, Dad
```

It was nice she thought to read her father's letters after all this time, especially this one as it perhaps opened her mind back to her past, one that she had seemingly forgotten. She needed to focus in finding something in a message and remembered the young man telling of a date of August the 9th. She also thought to herself for the sake of some sanity, she had to assume he had to be the person in his story, so to reduce confusion in her irritated mind; she would now consider him simply as Ben. The second she thought this, she called out deafeningly, 'What am I saying? He just can't be who he says he is, he just has to be someone else?'

With that, she immediately began to cry, and out of frustration, picked up the shoebox and tossed it across the room. Letters and old photos scattered everywhere, she immediately buried her head in both hands and fought back the tears.

'THIS IS NOT RIGHT!' she yelled out, partly crying and laughing at the same time. Her giggling was perhaps a defence mechanism for her inner most emotion against all the anguish which the young man had now stirred.

'I have to stop this,' she said to herself, 'it is not going to get the better of me and I do not believe he knows who I am, and that is that.'

With that said, she stood and decided it was time for a cup of tea. On her way out of the bedroom, she noticed a photo lying face up. She took a deep breath, a breath that fought hard against her increased heart rate providing just enough air to fill her depleted lungs. The light-headedness she felt was from a combination of getting up off the floor too quickly and looking at a photo of a flight crew standing next to a B-24 bomber. She bent down to pick up the photo so she could examine it in more detail. Holding it in both hands, eyes tightly closed, she momentarily pondered over all this fuss she had just caused herself. She sighed then opened her eyes just enough to focus on the crew of ten personnel standing next to a B-24 Liberator. She turned over the photo, which had been dated August 12th; it was the day of the mission that sadly one plane and crew were denounced MIA somewhere over the English Channel. She studied the photo and its occupants; undoubtedly, she was looking at the aircrew, and kneeling adjacent the main landing gear was a young man, a man with a face to that she just met two days earlier. She put on Dover's collar and attached his lead, thinking it was time to go and find who this Ben fellow was?

Buckenham Base 1943, August 10, 05:00 hrs:

The barracks had a conversant quality you would expect from within after a heavy night of drinking. Apart from a leg or arm hanging over the side of a bunk bed that convulsed involuntarily, there was a complete and utter stillness in the room. There were odd shirts or jackets and pants of all types flung over the iron rails of bed heads and other nonessential items of clothing hurled over the open lids of footlockers that were probably intended to be part of the stored contents. It was still a bit gloomy outside having rained most of the night, and marginally ghostly, probably from the low cloud cover and fog. Small amounts of carbon dioxide mist where visible from the breaths of the occupants in the room and the warmth of the room gradually diminished from the potbelly stove losing the last of its amber glow.

The barracks door flung open letting in a haze from the fog surrounding the quarters. Standing in the doorway, was Marks, still looking a bit inebriated, yet he showed a demeanour of authority.

'OK boys let's go, we are being fast tracked on a mission, briefing in an hour, 06:00, Hanger 5.'

Marks enunciated in his finest voice he could put together at five in the morning, having spent most of the night drinking with the crew.

The room immediately went from the calmness of torpor, to an excitement and anticipation of the pending assignment, the crew now stirred in their bunks as Marks completed his short speech. Some men were already sitting up in their beds, others by now wearing their flight jackets and tying laces, one in particular, ensuring the bows again where of equal proportions. Cap looked over at Ben who was having problems securing his hemp bootlaces, looking a little concerned the aglets showed signs of wear.

'Come on son let's go, briefing in an hour then it's some touch and gos,' announced the Cap. That was indeed what Ben wanted to hear; some flying time. After all, that is what he was there for. Ben stood, put on his flight jacket and walked out the barracks with the Cap. With the rain still falling, and just a misty drizzle, Cap and Ben elected to jog with the crew to the mess hall.

The sprinkling of rain reminded Ben of his childhood and the school bus trips he took as a youngster. He remembered how quickly it could storm then settle back into a light shower for days and how lush the fields were after. He recalled many parts of his life, both unforgettable and others just faint impressions and notable retentions he would never forget. It was the rain this very day that had triggered the thought something perhaps imprinted in his mind from his youth. A recollection that was now spurred on from the rain that he didn't quite see at the time when he had first crossed paths with Marshall Hartley, a sensation of perhaps someone he had already seen or something he had already experienced from his past.

The morning of August 10, 1930, 13 years earlier:

Charlotte looked one last time as Ben hiked down the long driveway of their farm. His school bag slung over his back full of books, as if he were on an imaginary expedition and the books where his provisions that filled the entire contents of his leather satchel. Carrying a stick as he always did, he drew lines in the soil as he walked, or waved it in the air perhaps imagining it where a flagpole and he would use it to mark his claim on the make-believe lands he would conquer. It was almost religious what he did, but every time he performed this ritual, it was as if it was his first time for Charlotte. He looked back as he always did, waved and blew her a kiss.

'See you Mum!' Ben yelled out at the completion of the kiss.

'It's Charlie, call me Charlie,' she insisted. 'Charlie,' she whispered one last time knowing he was now too far to hear.

'Yes Mum,' Ben replied teasingly, then turned his head back facing up the driveway, smiled and silently said to himself, 'Yes Charlie… I will.'

The walk usually took 15 minutes to get to the bus stop. Ben always met other kids on the way, and they would kick a stone as if it were a ball or throw a rock or simply tease one of the girls by pulling out a ribbon or undoing a plat in their hair. This morning was no different, apart from it being slightly overcast, perhaps going to rain, for a kid aged eight, that sort of obsession wasn't high on the list of important things, and as long as mud was involved, Ben didn't care.

The school bus arrived as it always did, and it was constantly a fight to see who was first on, you never ever wanted to be beaten by a girl. Ben and the other boys fought their way through the girls, kicking dirt over their white frilly socks, and stamping on their black polished shoes. Once on the bus, if any girls where in the back, it was short lived. Ben and his companions would do the expected and chase them out of the seats.

The bus driver saw the same thing every day without fail; he knew it one scene after the next, as if it were a well-scripted play. He could almost count the seconds, usually ten, then without fail, there was silence. They all stopped their play as if each where part of the mechanisms of a clock that had run out of its perpetual motion needing winding. Each child now well-disciplined once again either reading or doing leftover homework.

It was a further 20-minute drive from where Ben and his group were picked up from before the bus would reach the school. The driver every now and then looking up to his rear vision mirror just to check they were all still there as the silence was sometimes unendurable, and he much preferred the bedlam of the children playing.

The bus would always get the kids to school a few minutes before 9 am. The walk from the bus stop to the school assembly area usually only taking a few minutes; ample time to get themselves into their allotted areas of class grade, the youngest being closest to the headmaster's stage podium. Ben glanced across at the clock tower adjacent to the path from the entry gate as he always did and checked the time.

'Seven minutes to nine,' he said silently to himself, smiled and hustled himself out of the bus and started his fast walk to the assembly area.

Ben and his colleagues continued their swift pace towards the stage when it finally started to rain. Their strides now a reckless run towards any shelter they could locate. In the confusion of finding the best place to make refuge, Ben thought it was quicker to head back to the bus stop, not understanding why his classmates ran in the opposite direction. Ben soon realised it was a mistake having noticed all buses had driven off. He thought at the time it was a dumb idea to head back that way so turned and ran towards the school. As quick as the rain had started, it unexpectedly stopped and in the uncertainty of his situation, he stood there partially disorientated into which direction he was now facing. Looking around, he finally noticed the clock tower's red-tiled roof, regained his orientation, turned and headed towards the school.

Ben stopped briefly and focused at the thought that the rain had suddenly stopped. Confusingly, he looked at his surroundings, soon noticing there was no sign of puddles or wet grass, and it was as if it hadn't rained at all. He continued to walk, almost immediately realising the lack of any people or cars on the street. He glanced across at the school and could not see any of his classmates nor teachers; he assumed they must have gone straight to class due to the downpour. Not thinking any more of his situation, he simply focused on just getting to his lessons.

He had passed by an old man without really noticing him. Should he have, when he was clearly the only person on the street? The old man was not that old, actually only around 40 he guessed, tallish and very smartly dressed; his eyeglasses sat low on his nose, allowing him to just see over the bridge of his spectacles, and faced directly at Ben. Oddly, Ben didn't acknowledge him as if he was not even there, perhaps he had focused on him at the time but simply getting to class had more importance.

He headed inside the building looking at each viewing window in the doors of the classes as he went by and saw students and teachers at their lessons. Ben turned the final corridor to his class and was immediately confronted by a congregation of teachers, and people he didn't recognise. They were standing in the hall outside his room mulling over something and pointing and waving their arms. No one had recognised him just standing there; he was politely waiting for them to move away from the door so he could enter. As he peered through the crowd looking for a way through, one of the teachers noticed him standing there and instantly grabbed his arm. Ben thinking, he was in trouble immediately pulled one of those faces any eight-year-old did just before they cried.

Ben looked up at the teacher, tears in his eyes and nervously spoke, 'I am s-o-r-r-y miss for being late,' extending his sentence perhaps just enough for her to see he was genuinely upset.

By now, everyone who had gathered in the hallway was looking at Ben, all starting to ask him questions at once.

Ben confused, continued to cry not knowing who to answer; people where pushing their way through the crowd to reach him, one in particular had an embrace he knew only too well. Ben desperately tried to wiggle himself free from the clutches of his captor, their eyes welling from tears, her mouth quivering unable to find words. Ben's crying suddenly stopped, his face now portrayed confusion from his surroundings and in particular his mother standing before him. The crowd of people grew, and people were asking similar questions, all of which had made Ben more confused, his mother finally spoke:

'Ben, where have you been? I was so worried, the police have… I, I didn't know what to do, it has been hours… Where have you been?'

Ben looked up with uncertainty, head slightly tilted sideways, he answered with bewilderment:

'Mum, I was just outside finding a place to keep dry when it had started to rain.'

'Ben, what do you mean? Were you hiding? Did you not want to go to school?' asked Charlie.

'No,' replied Ben, 'I came straight in after the rain stopped; it was only a little bit of time I was out there; we all went in different —'

Charlie interrupted him, 'Ben, what do you mean you came in after it rained?'

Ben spoke with sincerity in his voice, 'I know I came in straight away from the bus almost; it rained and stopped just as we got here, then I came inside. Mum I am telling you the truth, I promise.'

Charlie looked at him and spoke now in a lowered happy tone, having found her son, 'We will talk about punishment later,' she whispered.

Ben still confused, looked at Charlie, then at his teacher; he spoke again with total belief in his words.

'I don't know, why I am in trouble?' he asked.

Charlie gazed at Ben's teacher, who now expressed her own opinion.

'Ben, the rain stopped over four hours ago; you have missed all the morning's lessons.'

Ben turned and looked outside the hallway window and to where he was able to make out in the distance the black dial face of the clock tower. His heart was now racing as his eyes tried to focus on the clock face in the distance. He hoped that this was all some sort mistake, perhaps some silly game. He made out the perpetual motion of each clock hand still counting away; Ben's heart pulsed uncontrollably as he unmistakably looked at the clock time, it unquestionability showed eight minutes past 1 o'clock.

******

Charlie, at the principal's request, took Ben straight home and he recommended he would possibly ring the police just as a precaution. Not to be disciplined but it had been known for some time that there had been young children, especially young boys approached by a man, who had even been seen around the school. The thought sent an instant chill through Charlie's body; she didn't want to think this had happened to Ben but knew the police, in hope, could provide a logical answer.

The drive home for Charlie was unsettling. She had for the past four hours, not known if she would ever see her son again. She was unsure why he had done what he did but for now, he was safe. She didn't want to upset him anymore than he already was, so punishment would come much later or at least when she found out the reason for his apparent untruthfulness. The drive home seemed to take forever, and she thought it best just to let him shed any tears he had left, just in case the principal was right. She would leave it to the authorities to deal with any questioning they would have, so as to approach this in the right manner; after all she was a single parent and felt perhaps the questioning would be better from the police. She looked across at Ben whose sobbing had now stopped. He sensed her gaze and as he turned, she exploded into tears.

'Ben,' she cried, 'I was so worried, please tell me everything is all right and no harm has come to you please tell me.'

Ben looked at her sadness and said as he had always said, 'Mum I am telling you the truth, it started to rain and I turned back to the bus, I was only there for —'

'Ben, it just can't be,' she interjected, 'it was four hours you were gone, and I managed to get to school before you.'

'Mum, I went back to the bus; I know I did, I was there only for a little bit, nothing more I promise.'

Charlie's car eventually pulled into their driveway and in the distance she could see a waiting vehicle parked in front of their porch. Two men were standing about the car, one was puffing on a cigar, blooms of smoke encircled his face concealing his complexion as he exhaled his breath, and the other had a folder in his hands and was writing some notes. She pulled up adjacent their car and was immediately helped out of her vehicle by one of the men. Ben looked a little intimidated from one in particular's appearance and remained in the car; he too was soon helped out. Charlie guessed the principal must have ended up ringing the police and would thank him latter.

'Hello Miss Walters I am detective Peterson and this is Vermont, I hope everything is alright now and please, I don't want you both, especially your son to feel like anyone is in trouble; it's just a formality that we need to investigate'.

'Charlie, its Charlie you can call me that if you wish', then looked at them and then at Ben, and said with certainty, 'I know we both have to go through this, but I know my son and somehow I'm not sure but don't think he is lying.' Vermont asked if it was possible, they could all go inside where it was more comfortable, Charlie agreed.

The house was probably mid to late 1800s. A modest farm dwelling, modern for the area but still had the archetypal country appeal. It had white painted casement sash double hung windows, and a stone and red brick façade. The driveway looked very much like crushed granite, which was common to this area. The house had two stories with three chimneys, two in the main house and the other in a sort of observatory room. It had solid timber floors, pretty much worn with scratches and chips out of the boards making it very periodic and fitting to that of a house around a century old. Odd scattered rugs and carpet runners adorned the rooms beneath chairs and tables, and old photos on the walls were neatly fixed between the dado and picture rails making it very homely.

'Can I get you some tea, detective, perhaps a scone and jam, I only baked them yesterday, so they are very fresh? Or a glass of water, milk?' Charlie continued to prattle on focusing on nonsensical chatter.

'I think we should apply ourselves Charlie to the situation at hand and get the questioning over with, so you two can have some time, if that's OK Ms Walters?' he finished with his formal side.

Detective Peterson then looked across at Ben, who had not been focusing on any of the conversation happily playing with his toy plane. The old toy didn't have its wheels and propeller but still could fly through the eyes of a boy and was easily doing loops and wing overs from the confident hand of its young pilot.

'Are you having fun with your plane Ben?' asked the detective.

'Yes sir,' Ben replied politely.

'Are you happy at school and have many friends?' continued detective Peterson.

'Yes sir, apart from Nancy Belrose,' said Ben.

'Oh, why don't you like her?' asked the detective.

'She has red hair and freckles,' said Ben.

For a while the detective continued talking, unbeknown to Ben it was a line of questioning he would use to make a minor feel more comfortable, less intimidated from the interrogation process, and a way he could develop a story as to what may have transpired. He could simply chat away and slowly develop his train of thought in and around Ben's responses.

'So, when it rained, Ben, did you get wet or take shelter?' the detective tested Bens reply with a more direct path to where his whereabouts may have been.

'I went back to the bus to get out of the rain and they had left, so I came back to school, and everyone was gone and only saw an old man at the gate.'

Ben had just given a bit of a lead to detective Peterson, a lead he needed.

'Do you know him Ben?' inquired the detective.

Ben nodded, and answered with a long drawn out 'Yeeesss, he is my father.'

Peterson continued with questions, most seemingly based around Ben's father and nothing about where Ben was during the four hours, questioning that really didn't seem logical or apparent to the situation. It was as if Peterson had taken a special interest in this man, that of Ben's apparent father. It seemed that Peterson had disregarded a stranger talking to a boy, in fact it was as if he would have allowed it.

Peterson and Vermont soon finished and asked Charlie if they could continue and talk with her alone outside.

From his viewpoint at the window, Ben could see Charlie and detective Peterson chatting near his vehicle? He saw his mother holding her arms up against her chest, she was fidgeting with her palms, then clutched each elbow for a short moment, then finally burying her head into her hands.

Detective Peterson eventually asked, 'Ms Walters, if you are getting upset and there is some problem with the boy's father and he is harassing both you and your son, perhaps we can ask him kindly to keep his distance, if you understand my point, can you tell me where I might find him?'

'Detective, I am very sorry but that is not it, you see Ben, well, came to me a little younger than he is now, he is sort of adopted, well more to the point he just landed at my door, I mean I found him just wandering about so I took him in. I am not sure where he came from, please don't tell him or take him from me, he is all I have.'

'Ms Walters, I am still not seeing or understanding Ben suggesting he saw his father?'

'Detective, Ben believes he sees him or a man anyway, he just calls him his father. I thought it was just his dreams but after a few months he was very much descriptive and rather unconventional in what he described about things to come. I was afraid he would be seen as needing medical help and taken from me; please, I myself am unsure if he is lying about this man now and am still unsure where he was in those four hours he went missing. Can we please just say it as if he was absent or came home or something?'

'Ms Walters, I will need to file a report and could be very selective on my wordings, if you do something for me and tell me what things, what was unconventional?'

'Detective, I feel a bit silly in telling you, but he well talks of a war, a great world war with a horrific ending. He speaks about a bomb that will be dropped from an aircraft ending an entire city in seconds; thousands of lives will be lost.' There is one more thing detective, when he tells me this in detail and if asked about it the next day, he has little or no recollection of it, that recollection well fades, but every now and then something I guess reawakens that memory.'

'Ms Walters, I will keep this report nice and simple so can we keep this to ourselves and ask you not to speak of this to anyone.'

As the detective's car drove off, it had left Charlie questioning herself about what she had just spoken about, and thinking if it was the right thing to do? Or had she told the inspector something about her son that had left him defenceless to doctors. It was silly she thought, stupid in fact as there was no way a child could know of a future event, and with such a detailed observation. Was it highly unlikely? Or just doubtful? How could he even dream something like this up, it was uncertain he could, totally improbable, she turned and walked back to the house.

The squad car came to a stop on a long stretch of road about a mile from town. Peterson looked at Vermont, who had tightened his lips and squinted his deep-set recessed eyes. They both got out of the car, transiently paused, and chatted a little, Vermont dwelling over the strange anomaly, probed Peterson on his beliefs over Ben's vivid stories.

'So, Peterson, what do you think of the lad's tales to his mother?' questioned Vermont.

'I would say the boy reads too many comic books, when he should be doing his lessons. He is just a kid with an anomalous imagination,' alleged Peterson. 'I would say very typical of a boy his age, very typical, and if he were mine, I would take the strap to him, give him a good long whipping just like my father did when I told lies.'

Peterson said no more of it on their way back to the station. It played on Vermont's mind, how a boy of eight could dream up such an account of things to come. And how someone can be so articulate, with such an imagination at his age.

Vermont, over the next month wrote notes, and watched the boy to the point he became obsessed with it, just to see if the man, Ben's father would return, and make contact.

It was a few months on and there were now more disappearances of boys similar in age. Vermont took on the case, and over the next few months, six boys in total had gone missing, and were later found, in shallow graves.

It was decided at the time Vermont was to be the prime suspect for their disappearances. Peterson had handed in Vermont's notes on Ben and the other boys, of which the prosecutor found Vermont guilty of manslaughter and seemed like a simple open and shut case. Vermont spent two months in custody until there was another boy who went missing. During the investigation, Peterson's wife ironically had left him after she found he had molested their own son. Peterson later admitted to all seven deaths and was subsequently sentenced to life in prison for their murders.

Vermont had by this time, pleaded his story of Ben and became so obsessed with finding the truth that he had been placed in a psychiatric ward during the trial of Peterson. He was eventually hospitalised and kept under 24-hour care, after he freely admitted the truth behind Ben. The charges were dropped against Vermont, but he was to remain under care for the next 13 years. Banham Police Department abandoned the case study of Ben as there was no further evidence of how he went missing. Nor of the person or persons who had apparently misappropriated him. As there was no sign off any injury to Ben, nor any indication of the possible abuse from Peterson, the Banham Police Department had informed Charlie that they were of the belief the boy had just fabricated his story to her, and the case was subsequently closed.

******

Buckenham Base 1943, Hanger 5, August 10, 06:00 hrs:

Hanger 5 was built to some extent independent from the others. Hangers 1 to 4 shared the same roof covering and concrete apron slab. Each had four individual sliding doors; the centre two could slide back providing one big opening, spanning over 160 feet. Apart from some load-bearing steel columns between the building walls, the entire area was more or less an open floorplan and could house up to six B-24s at any one time. Generally, hangers 1 and 4 were for over-all maintenance and body panel repairs, leaving an outsized open area in the centre for more of the un-programmed tasks or improvements. Hanger 5 didn't have the rectangular shape as did the others; it had more of an elliptical shape similar to the main building's facility. Its barn doors where smaller in width and almost the same distance across the façade, allowing the doors to slide back a full 119 feet. The width and depth just big enough to fit in a single B-24 nose in, with the twin vertical stabilisers just outside the doors opening. Internally at the end of the hanger, was a freestanding chalkboard and around 40 or so timber chairs, much like a school classroom and was where the squadron's pilots, bombardiers and navigators, would mull around for their briefings.

Ben and the Cap wandered together across to the tarmac from the mess hall. It was still raining but had slowed down to just an annoying drizzle. Hanger 5 was only a short walk so they both didn't see the need to hurry. The maintenance entry doors were shut to the hangers except for two middle side entry doors which were slightly ajar making it somewhat a difficult task to squeeze through. Had it not been for boxes of plane parts and oil cans blocking the doors, they would have gone that way. Ben and Marks eventually made their way to the front of the hanger doors and looked up at the enormous numeral "5", now in need of a repaint with visible signs of wear from the blistering greying white tint. The

"5" had black edging giving the number some perspective, its paint too was also in need of repair. Inside the hanger it was clear to Ben why he had chosen this path in life. There were probably other influencing factors, but he knew only too well he wanted to be a pilot.

He stood between the two hanger doors looking up at the gigantic twin perpendicular rudders hinged off their vertical stabilisers. The big fat body of the aircraft in front of him looked like an engorged humpback whale with outstretched pectoral fins, gun turrets sticking out like the nodule barnacles on its bulky body; he was looking at one of the newest of the squadrons B-24J Liberator Bombers. The fresh-looking silvery skin looked almost hoary in colour and the only painted surface was the tail section both having a white circle with black outer edge and black 'J' in the middle of circle. The 'J' was not because of the model, it was an insignia that would be used for the 451st squadron. No other markings where visible on the aircraft, which he thought rather odd. Ben continued through the doors looking back up at the horizontal stabiliser as he passed the rear of the great fish and towards the main undercarriage. The remaining crew had finally gathered into the hanger, all of which had now formed a bit of a circle under the port wing about the main landing gear. The men were all examining in different directions looked intently at the bomber as it stood silent and new. You could only imagine if the aircraft were alive, you would here its prodigious heartbeat of the enormous gigantic aircraft wanting to become airborne and fly deep into battle.

Halverson and Marks were preparing some notes on the chalkboard, while Ben, the Cap and Chips were standing adjacent the nose of the massive awkward looking plane.

'Sort of looks like a box with a couple of wings strapped to it, doesn't it Cap?' described Ben.

'You know if we get shot down in one of these things, we would definitely not need a casket, they most certainly look like a flying coffin,' he finished as both Ben and Chips gave a look of abomination, yet still could see the amusing side.

'Ok men, gather round,' yelled out Marks. 'We will have time to look her over soon but just want to give you all a bit of a brief on us, and what this squadron will be doing.'

The group hustled their way over to Marks, who was in front of the chalkboard with Halverson. The notes appeared to be finished with almost the entire surface covered apart from a small area in the middle; Ben guessed that was set aside for off the cuff paraphernalia.

'Ok, let's start,' said Marks in his most important sounding voice.

'As you all are now all aware, we are a group of, well, unknowns to put it mildly and are not supposed to exist. The squadron, the 451st will be for the better part, covert. We will run this fleet out of the base until the administration tells us otherwise, and it will increase in number by around December of this year and be completely operational by January '44. I know you don't really want to hear that this war will run that long so that's why we are here. Halverson runs our radar division, and Ben you may remember I lightly touched on that with your walk around yesterday.

Ben, nodded in acknowledgment, leaned across to the Cap and disclosed to him that he hoped the radar would make a big change to the war.

Marks continued, 'We now have our full complement of aircraft-25, this being the latest.'

Ben remembered, as he walked across the field, all the arriving bombers coming from all different directions. His count was 24, the 24 he initially saw were painted in varying colourings, what he assumed were bought here from differing squadrons. He vaguely remembered a polished hull Liberator that flew over, independent to the 24 coloured planes, his guess was this one.

'This is our 'J' model, and I will give the stats in a minute Marks went on to say. She is big, fat and looks like she will not fly but let me assure you, she can, and carry, she has a belly big enough to fill and drop a shit load of shells onto the enemy, which we intend to cripple.' His voice escalating in both strength and tone as he finished off his sentence.

'She will at 30,000 feet, have a max speed of 300 mph, with approximately 61,500 pounds all-up weight. We will be specifying 25,000 feet, which will give you a speed of 278-mph and a 7.3-hour endurance. Our payload will be 5,000 pounds of bombs, which will give 10 at 500 pounds each or 5 at 1,000 pounds, depending on the bombing run. You have 1,200-hp in each engine at take-off, at 2,700 rpm with a military rating of 31,800 feet should you need it. The 2,364 gallons of fuel will give you around 1,700 miles, so she is a good strong plane so don't listen to boys in the B-17s.'

Marks finished with a resonance of total zest, while Halverson looked a little more anxious. Before the gathering could pick up on Halverson's apprehensive, Marks provided him with a little gusto, and leaned across and spoke at a level high enough for him to just get the joust of his prompting.

'Tell them about the radar that will give them a little purpose,' he said.

Marks hadn't intended for Halverson to think of the crew as depressed and look at the pending mission as a failure before it happened. He just wanted to keep up the momentum and provide them all with a little hope the war would be short, given the new aircraft, radar and the classification of the new surreptitious defence system – Marks intended all of these things to come somewhat together and show the men all of this effort was not in vain.

Halverson swallowed then began: 'OK, right, radar as it is now called, is for want of a better term, Range and Detection Finding or simply RDF. What this simply means is if an enemy aircraft is approaching, we will see it, hence the "detection", the range bit we are almost there but in short, a haze on a screen tells us their coming and approximately how long? We are advancing in this technology each and every day so just to reiterate, we can see a virtual display of approaching aircraft or ships and will show up as a cloud type haze on the screen. This would indicate a squadron flying in formation or on the water as an armada of ships. As we are still refining it, this cloud haze is almost giving us individual dots, still as a cloud but the dots represent actual plane or ship numbers, one dot, one plane and so on.'

Marks looked around the room to get an indication if anyone was not understanding so far. He went on to discuss the new B-24J models reasoning of the 'J' on the tail section, and in short was only representing the model, and how the administration would use this unit [451 st] as a sort of a learning curve for future squadrons of the Liberator.

'This squadron has 25 of the best planes, pilots and crew and although we are covert, and fly missions from an undisclosed base, we are just as important'.

He reminded them that by December '43, a new squadron, the 453rd, would be formed and join the 451st but not clandestine, but more to the point, known to the enemy.

Marks looked across at the Cap and gave him the nod, as he could see Ben looking back at the nose of the Liberator, thinking he was biting at the bit to get airborne.

'So, Ben, what do you say, you want to get some flying done?' asked the Cap in a somewhat excited tone himself.

Ben looked at him, and back at Marks and nodded in approval followed by a, 'YES SIR.'

Marks, with the aid of Ben, pulled the hanger doors back exposing the sheer size of the new Liberator. The Mule was an old farming tractor that had been modified to push or pull aircraft about the base, it puffed a bluey charcoal coloured smoke from its exhaust stack as it was steered into position at the nose of the bomber. Ground crew hooked up a 4-inch round steel arm around eight or so foot in length and connected it to the nose wheel of the bomber, the other end attached firmly to the Mule. A grey smoke haze bloomed out of its exhaust stack, filling the hanger as the Mule raucously pushed the bomber out onto the tarmac.

Ben could now get a much clearer picture of the aircraft as it stood majestically in front of Hanger 5. The last wheel chock was placed under the main gear allowing the Mule to be unhooked. Ben walked around the aircraft, the Cap and Chips followed him, watching his reverence to an aircraft he was soon to be a part of it reminded them both of the first time they too stood in awe of the Liberator. Walking along the side of the fuselage, Ben ran his hand feeling every bump of rivet and shape change in the side of the 24's body. It was bus like in form and looked clumsy as if it wouldn't fly, but Ben didn't care, he was happy to have been chosen to be part of this squadron. As he approached the nose of the great beast, he stopped and turned towards the Cap and Chips who were standing just in front of the port inner propeller, both running their hands up and down the leading edge, checking for dints and chips that could distract the clean airflow over its surface.

The ground crew had arrived in their tanker truck, which towed a small single axel trailer also with an additional fuel drum attached. The tanker parked in nose first, facing the inner port engine, men busily arranging a ladder and running out the fuel hoses. One man stood on the wing while another walked up the ladder which leaned against the leading edge of the wing. He passed up the fuel hose, the pressure pump attached to the truck soon coming to life allowing fuel to flow into the massive fuel cells of the bomber. Ben continued his walk around the plane when he saw in the distance a jeep driving towards him, the passenger, even from the distance the jeep was, was one he had recognised in an instant. The vehicle soon stopped allowing its passenger to delicately climb out. The fuel crew, Cap and Chips turned toward the jeep, all now motionless in their actions, as the figure of a slender woman climbed out and walked towards the bomber. She made her way towards Chips and the Cap, giving them both a small wave of acknowledgement to their presence as she passed them by. She was focussed and manoeuvring toward her seemingly oblivious catch. Ben looked at her as she strolled towards him, he momentarily looked behind, thinking she was here for someone else. Her Helena Rubenstein's notorious "Regimental Red" lipstick glistened even though the slight drizzle of rain had turned it almost a lustreless matt colour. Holding her bag over her headscarf so as to not get it wet, she stopped under the wing of the Liberator and stood looking in Ben's direction.

'Hello, Flying Officer Benjamin Walters, I hope there is room for me on this flight,' she said with the very smallest of grins so as to not look too ardent.

Ben, looked at the Cap for approval, he gave him a gentle nod, Ben then turned back at woman who was now standing soberly diffident and confident, he went to speak but nothing came out of his mouth. All he could peace together was a single word, and he virtually shouted it at that, 'EMILY,' remaining silent for what seemed an eternity then finished with a whispered, 'are you,' was all that came from his mouth.

She, took control and assertively said, 'Of course.'

The ground crew packed up their equipment and the old door-less fuel truck drove off toward the maintenance hangar, the morning rain still falling, perhaps getting just that little bit heavier. A couple of ducks had wandered over from the grass apron and were wading through some deepening puddles that had formed on the tarmac. Ben, the Cap, Chips and Emily had clambered through the rear hatch and made their way up towards the cockpit.

Marks and Halverson watched as the hatch shut behind them. He looked at Halverson and just before he spoke, Halverson commented.

'Well, Harold what can we say, he must have impressed her in some way, looks like we know what nose art will going on this plane.'

Marks seemed happy Ben had impressed his daughter, and as he was a kind and considerate young man, Marks had welcomed it.

******

The afternoon of August 10, 1930:

Charlie had just sat down at the dining table sipping on a cup of tea, still thinking about Detective Peterson and Vermont when there was a knock at the door. Thinking they had both returned, she walked back to the front door and opened it without giving it a thought. Standing there to her surprise was a man in his 40s, smartly dressed wearing a black suit, and a bombin hat. He smiled at her and before she could speak, he removed his hat with courtesy, perhaps easing her concern of who he was.

'Hello, Ms Walters may I speak with you for a moment?'
'I'm sorry, can I please ask who you are?' she inquired.
'May I come in and I will explain,' continued the man.

'Yes of course,' said Charlie, not even contemplating the gravity of who he was or could be? She unwillingly felt comfortable with him and strangely saw this as something that was needed. Why exactly all these things crossed her mind, or why she allowed herself to think otherwise was that she perhaps was seeking some sort of veracity in all of the past few hours' events. They both walked into the dining room and sat in two Gainsborough Leather library chairs, the man allowing Charlie to sit first.

'I am sorry to impose on you, Ms Walters, but needed to talk to you about your son.'

'Are you associated with Detective Peterson?' she asked.

'No, Ms Walters, I am not, and this will sound very strange and only have limited time here so please may I continue?'

Charlie was very confused and could only come out with, 'I am sorry, please continue.'

'Ms Walters, there were two men just here and soon they will be back looking for me. They will ask you if you have seen me or where to find me, and you must tell them you don't know what they are talking about, sound confused as to what they are asking, it is very important that you do this, and it —'

Charlie interrupted him then quickly stood, 'Please sir, tell me why you are here and at least your name.'

'Ms Walters I can't involve you too much with knowledge of who I am or why exactly I am here, there is already a fissure and I need to correct it.'

'A fissure, correct it… what, what are you saying I don't understand any of this, please sir, tell me who you are.'

They both looked instantaneously at the figure of Ben standing off to one side. His eyes where focussed on the man, he looked at Charlie then back at the man.

'Mum, it's him,' said Ben in a quiet tone.
'Who?' inquired Charlie.
In a resolute tone, Ben replied, 'The man I see sometimes.'

Charlie momentarily remembered Ben mentioning of a man, always similar in his appearance, age around 40 and with glasses just happening upon him at the most anomalous of times. He would be there, then as quick as he was, simply gone.

'Ms Walters, Charlotte…Charlie, this is going to sound very confusing for you and I can't tell you who I am but please believe me when I say you can't tell both Peterson and Vermont I was here. Ben's visions are very real, he will only remember portions of this tomorrow as will you, and I need to let you know that each and every time we meet will be as if it's your first. I don't have much time as the men are now on their way back, don't let them take Ben, they will threaten you that they will tell the authorities about Ben's being orphaned and left at your door as a boy, and need to take him to an institute. The more I tell you, the more I need to fix and shouldn't be here any longer, so please tell them both you haven't seen me, and I will make this right.'

The man stood and walked to the door...

'Please tell me what this is about and how did you know me as Charlie, and if you don't want me to tell them I saw you, then why did you come, please tell me what is going on, and why did Ben says you are his farther and how does he remember you? I can't understand that I haven't met you yet, you are taking as if I had or have or will, I am confused, please sir, what is going on, who are you? Please tell me what is happening.'

The man handed her a sealed envelope and asked her to keep it safe until the men that will return, leave. He told her that tomorrow she would almost forget he came and so would Ben, and eventually it would be just a passing memory to them both and may or may not have even happened. He said that when Peterson and Vermont return it may be as if they will portray it was their first time...

'They will if they knew I were here, alter their line of questioning', he went onto say.

He explained to her that a thought is something that could be both imaginary and simply a deep recollection of a true past event even if it were fictional. It was like if you knew there was going to be in a car crash caused from a tyre blowing you wouldn't drive that day, but how could you ever stop it from blowing on another day and still not have that accident if you didn't know it were going to happen?

'Charlie, when they return to talk to you, they may also now ask about me specifically and perhaps a relationship as Ben's father, thereby you already would have known them, then you can keep safe this envelope until its needed.'

'Needed?' asked Charlie, 'When will it be needed?'

'Only you will know that Charlie, and this envelope and its contents simply put, is your tyre blowout if you want to think of in that way. One more thing, when they arrive they may test you, simply pretend you haven't seen them before and they will most certainly ask about me, if you know them and pretend you don't then they won't know I have been here, then they will go and I have done my part.'

The man turned and simply walked out the door.

She went out after him still holding the envelope in her hand, the man was not there, it was as if he simply vanished. She stood motionless and soon focused on a car parked in the driveway. Peterson and Vermont climbed out the car, they stood still, both looking at her for a reaction. She was almost immobilised from not understanding where the man now was and just as confused as to how he knew Peterson and Vermont would be back. They both waited for what Charlie preserved as to be eternity, and without thinking she held her ground, she played the part of playacting as something in her told her she needed to. Peterson and Vermont looked at each other providing a small nod gesture noticeable only to them. They waked up to Charlie, and Peterson with an outstretched hand introduced himself.

'Hello Ms Walters, I am detective Peterson, and this is Vermont; we have been sent by the school to investigate your son's disappearance.'

Charlie's role-playing continued without fault replying in, 'Pleased to meet you Inspector. Would you like a cup of tea?'

As she walked inside, her body shook uncontrollably, and she carefully placed the envelope in her handbag then oddly instantly disremembered about it. It would though be another 13 years almost to the day before it would be found and read. She swayed their attention away from the bag by igniting the gas on the stovetop, making some sort of reference as to it sometimes being hard to light. She filled the jug with water, placed it on the flaming burner and casually turned towards her probing visitors.

Chapter 3

Norwich England 1953, August 14:
'Who are YOU? I don't know YOU,' she cried, the words still in the thoughts of Ben as he sat back into his timber bench seat. Emily could still be seen hurrying away across the field, she had attracted some onlookers who were concerned and where asking if she was OK. Her son was looking back at Ben, who again appeared nonchalant to his surroundings, almost back into his torpor state. Ben focused on his words he had voiced to them both, was he starting to doubt his entire story. Was this some sort of deception by the war office into his now being here? He didn't understand what was going on, was it a faded memory or some sort of trickery. Ben was only days ago bombing a set target, a fuel refinery plant in enemy territory and now he was sitting on a park bench in Norwich as if the mission, and the war never even happened. Waiting for what, when all of this was not possible, was he to believe he was where he was, was even true?

He remembered comic books of superheroes he read as an eight-year-old; his favourite was *Armageddon 2419 AD,* by Philp Francis Nowlan. It told the story of a man, Anthony Rodgers, who worked for a radioactive gas corporation; they had sent him into an abandoned coalmine, to investigate some unusual activities. While he was there, the cave collapsed releasing a radioactive gas; Rogers fell asleep in a state of suspended animation for what he thought was hours but woke 492 years later. The story at the time was so real, now he was faced with the fact he had somehow ended up in 1953, when to him only days ago he was in 1943. He was not a child anymore and didn't believe in fairy-tale stories, if he was to believe what he now knew as fact, his best chance of any respite was with Emily? Ben stood from his seat and contemplated what he needed to do to find her. The past few days had been confusing, flying into enemy lines to drop bombs, to crashing his plane in an abandoned airfield, to waking up in hospital, now sitting at a bench in a park, not knowing where or what his next move would be.

The "silhouette" of a man that the woman had noticed during Ben's account of his life's story, walked slowly toward Ben. He had not yet been noticed by Ben who was still re-counting his next move with waving hand and head movements, thinking precisely what he needed to do. He playacted the gentle hand movements as if rehearsing every step that he would now take in finding Emily, when he was suddenly interrupted by a voice he knew only too well.

'Hello Ben,' said the man.

Ben immediately turned to the figure of a person now standing directly in front of him. It was somebody only he would know if he was to believe his life up to now. The voice was comforting and allowed Ben to instantly feel relief. His stance matched that of Ben's, his height was Ben's height, his features matched in almost every way reinforcing to Ben; he knew him. The man then spoke again.

'Ben, it's time for you to come with me.'

Ben's heart raced almost palpitating as he stood there staring at Marshall Hartley, who only days ago was also in 1943.

******

Ben knew it as Old Morley Hall, Marshall termed it, "The Sector". He hadn't up to now been that garrulous with Ben as all of Ben's questions would be answered in due time. Marshall gave nominal responses to his analytical questioning as they walked up to the hall's grandiose entrance. Two large iron gates that had weathered over time were showing signs of rust, possibly still working as they were hinged back onto two reddish coloured large brick piers each side of the bridge, on which they were now standing. Each brick column had capitals of perfectly rounded stone balls. A small buttress curved slightly from the top of each pier to the walkway of the bridge, blending in and forming into a small edge running the length of the overpass, possibly as wheel stops for the early horse drawn carriages. The Manor was enclosed by an Anglo-Saxon moat, originally dug to acquire the stones, probably later used as part of the construction of the 16-century mansion. Its brick facade was neatly set out with two building extensions identical in size and shape, three stories high, each with a loft. Joining the two outer wing extensions was a centrally built structure similar in shape and looks but perpendicular to each wing and thus forming a "H" pattern for the building footprint. The entrance door was offset to the right, seemingly odd when all other parts of the house where very much symmetrical. It fitted in nicely with the surroundings having a whitish brown coloured crushed granite driveway contrasting precisely with the deciduous trees on the property. Marshall liked it here, but more for the fact it was not portentous looking, in fact the building looked rather unimportant and for the locals, was, and had been here for centuries.

Marshall had waited for days not interfering in Ben's process as if he knew every step, every action, every thought. He had patiently waited, and he knew that Ben would eventually reach a milestone. A significant point that he would need to get to before he would come to Ben, a point in which Marshall knew exactly. Had Ben through influence, not reached today, not reached the point where he had sat back down into his timber bench seat, not seen Emily impulsively run off in wonder, Marshall would have not come to Ben. There was more to do, and much more to explain and Marshall expounded to Ben as they continued through the manner into the bowels of building's endless rooms and corridors. They finally walked down a flight of steps that had been carved from the stone foundation material similar to that of the building exterior. They arrived in a cellar, walls covered in "moss like" growth, and a musty aroma filled the room. Bottles of wines stacked on their side, lined the walls in neat rows all resting on a solid timber purpose-built frame, and leaning slightly forward so as to seal the cork. They were covered in dust and years of debris, blending into the cobwebs as if they were a cocoon with embryonic creatures within, waiting to divulge their inner secrets and giving birth to hundreds of cave dwelling arachnids. Ben looked about the room and wondered why they had ended up down here when Marshall stopped and reached into his pocket and pulled out what Ben perceived to be an inconsequential looking type of key.

Marshall inserted the small round gilded device into a slot adjacent the door inside the cellar area, turned it sideways then removed it. The door opened sideward and slid inside a cavity of the stone foundation wall. Another set of steps spiralled down to a single chamber room; the room was small in size comparative to that of the rest of the house. The room's only differences as with the steps where the clean lines of the walls, floors and ceiling not period to the home. The room was free from refuse, any sharp corners and unwanted clutter as if it had just been built; each transition of surface be it the floor or walls or ceiling or steps had a small concave section as if the entire room, and entry had been moulded in one piece. There was no visible lighting or switches, yet the opaque polished surfaces omitted a faint glow enough to provide adequate illumination for its occupants. Marshall understood the room and its contents others would find it hard to comprehend even if it had been explained. He placed the device into a second slot adjacent the opening they had just walked thorough, turned it then removed the key. A panel opened and a neatly fitting door slid silently with no mechanical sound out of the cavity and now tightly filled the opening as it made a silent 'ssssh' noise telling the occupants in the room it was now sealed. Marshall walked over to a centrally located pod. It appeared to be part of the floor but plainly separate. Its round moulded pallid white sides similar to a cupped hand blended in nicely with its surroundings.

'Well, Ben, I know you have many questions and can guess from the look of passiveness you are giving me, either you are taken aback from the room, or you don't know what to ask me first, I would say it's both.'

Ben looked about the room, and tried to comprehend its structure, there was nothing much to it apart from the pod like device in the middle of the room. To one corner was a cobalt blue type of futon, he guessed as silly as it sounded was a type of settee, or daybed of sorts He thought of himself as someone with a bit of logic; well, pilots needed that element of rationality. He moved his hands over the surface of the walls frustratingly unable to evaluate its construction, and the material in which it was fabricated, the reasoning behind it, and ending in it had no lucidity or sense about it, and came up with it was just a room. Ben again logically evaluated his situation and the room and even evaluated Marshall, he momentarily took his mind back to when things started to become well, "impossible to be". Was he dreaming? Was he going mad? Nothing made any sense to him. He let his mind drift back just to see if he could piece things together, very well knowing nothing about then or now, had any veracity to it. It was unlikely he was in 1953, totally impossible in fact. He briefly thought about the date and year and how ironic it was to be almost exactly 10 years plus the 7 hours of duty time from the bombing run that is was since he left that day. He went back to his comic hero, Anthony Rodgers, who woke hundreds of years later, and thought to himself, was that imaginable? As an 8-year-old yes, as a 21-year-old no, but still he was here. Was it thinkable…was it plausible…or was it likely? No, it was highly unlikely, it was without a doubt totally improbable.

******

10 years, 4 days earlier, August 10, 06:49, 1943:

The cockpit of the B-24 provided its crew with good visibility. The instrument cluster, central throttle quadrant, trim wheel, gear and flap controls all at an arm's length to the pilots. The large control wheel was robust and ugly, but effective and provided good aileron control. As far as pitch control for the pilots, they would need to bring the wheel hard back almost into their chests to complete the flare and subsequent stall onto the tarmac at landing. Two large rudder pedals for each pilot completed the package giving this plane a tick of approval.

Ben had fastened his harness and quickly looked back at Chips who was standing directly behind him. Emily was seated in the navigator's chair and could just see Ben; she smiled and pouted her lips in a silly gesture. Chips looked at the instruments awaiting engine start.

'OK Ben my boy, the start sequence is pretty simple, No.3 inner right, 4 your inner left followed by 2 my outer right and last No.1 your outer port – nice and simple,' instructed the Cap. 'I, in this case, am doing this as I am acting co-pilot and captain, Chips will be behind watching engine start, then having a look out through the top hatch for any unwanted smoke. 'You will feel how heavy the yoke is as it is cable driven and there is a lot of movement needed by you so remember this plane was not designed for comfort, OK so far?'

Ben just nodded probably still taking it all in.

'All pretty much what you expect, we have prop pitch, throttles, then mixture-left to right in that order. We recommend taxing with controls locked; steering seems a little easier as you have less to concentrate on. We also only have breaks to turn so no nose wheel for turning so it just free spins. Just down there [the Cap pointed to a small viewing opening just below the centre console] is a window used to ensure our nose gear is true and straight before throttle up on take-off.'

Ben looked down at the small window around six or so inches across which had a hinged flap to shut it off, as to why it had a flap, he didn't ask as he didn't want to sound like it was a meaningless question.

'We have hydraulics for this bird that run gear, flaps and breaks on my right is this leaver [the Cap again pointing this time to a red bar, hinged at the floor], which when pumped gives us backup hydraulics if we lose pressure from a leaking line or hull breach from enemy fire.'

Ben, this time managed a few words, 'I sort of noticed the wing as we came through the bomb bay, it was, well, exposed and with all the electrics and bombs, I'm sure I saw and smelt fuel; is that something I should worry about?'

'That's brilliant,' said the Cap, 'and now I know why you were sent to me, most miss that. The Liberator has an auxiliary hydraulic pump located aft of the bomb bay. Its electric motor could and has on occasion arced causing explosions, we leave the bomb doors slightly open at start-up to allow cross through ventilation – this is only to minimise the risk so pre-fight, we check for leaks; in-flight, we check for leaks and especially before landing, we check for leaks.'

Ben now thinking his question about the flap over the viewing window for the nose gear might not have been that injudicious of a question but would leave it for another day.

The rain outside was now a constant. It appeared to be set in with a minimal wind of 10 or so knots and was north-easterly in direction. They taxied up to the holding point of Runway zero seven and waited for clearance.

'451st J Two Five, you are cleared for take-off,' came a voice from the tower over the radios.

'Yes, I know Ben we are a little informal but we are the only ones flying today, so what do you think, thought of a name for "nose art" yet, OR are we sticking with your plane number 25 in the squadron?' asked the Cap.

'Well, I did think of something but wasn't sure.'

Emily's heart raced thinking was he going to choose her, well he was sweet on her and did kind of show that at the bar last night when they did, after all, dance for hours.

'Come on son what's it going to be, your pet dog a sweetheart perhaps?' the Cap probed.

'Well is it a problem if I have two?'

'Two!' shouted the Cap, 'Son, are you greedy and not happy with just one love, you need two, boy you are good.'

'Well, I thought if I was allowed to put two impressions of artwork, I wouldn't be judged; well, I mean I would really like to put "Charlotte" as my main oeuvre, but on the starboard side, leaving my side for well another name, one I, well, would need to ask if, well I just need to ask that's all.'

'Charlotte, she has bought you up with a good heart son, I think I am going to like you,' finished the Cap.

Emily sat back in her chair and looked up at the top turret, the rain was hitting it like small bullets. She wondered what it must be like in battle at night, away from the crews' loved ones. She was happy Ben had taken the time to think of his mother and have her impression painted on the side of his plane, even though she would probably be drawn not quite as you would expect, but none the less, tasteful. She smiled to herself hoping she would be with him on the left side, her portrait overseeing the flight, a painted seraph, one to ensure the crew would fly home safely.

'Throttle up nice and slow son, I will call it, then back on No. 3 and 2, use breaks and No.1 to pull us around; those are big engines out there so don't worry about No.4, she will jerk round.

The B-24 pulled around and lined up on the runway, and a quick check of the compass was done – its lag from the turn taking a while to settle, eventually falling around onto an easterly heading. Ben tilting his head to look through the view window on the floor to just check if the nose wheel was straight.

'All good, Cap, I'm good to go.'

'Tower, 451st J Two Five is rolling, Runway zero seven, thanks and see you soon,' the Cap sort of sounding like a true captain. Ben quickly looked back at Emily as she sat up then smiled, her glossy lipstick shimmered from the small amount of dull light coming through the turret dome.

'Cowls are 1/3 open, flaps at 10, mixture rich, trim at two degrees nose up, rudder three and to the right, ailerons are neutral and two thousand seven hundred rpm on the engines, go for son,' instructed the Cap.

The Liberator careered down the runway, droplets of the rain on the windscreen now dispersing off as the plane increased its speed.

'As she gets about a third down the runway, she will pull to the left so just a bit of right rudder. That's 80 indicated Ben, in 10 rotate. Just hold that nose attitude…aaaand rotate… hold it just there, that's good,' said the Cap.

The Cap had called it at 90 mph. Ben just held the pressure off the nose with the yoke, lightening the weight on the nose wheel as the B-24 lifted gently off the runway. 'Gear up,' called the Cap, 'that's one two five approaching one three zero indicated Ben, you're doing well. Reduce power to two five five zero rpm, and flaps up, that's one four five indicated, Ben no more than one fifty, that's 150-mph indicated with flaps down, just hold that attitude, and she should settle at one five five IAS [indicated air speed].'

Ben's focus was now on his instruments. Flying in cloud was demanding, with a constant rotational check of attitude, indicated air speed, attitude, rate of climb, attitude, altimeter and so on. The artificial horizon allowed the pilot to get a three-dimensional view of where his plane was while in cloud. An attitude indication constantly checked with cross checks against rate of climb, altimeter and so on. It was around eight or so minutes and 7000 feet when they broke free of the rain and cloud, the cloud base was probably 800 feet with a good four or so mile visibility in rain. Ben eventually turned left onto a heading of three four zero degrees for a further 10 minutes, then onto a heading of two five zero degrees giving him a very long base leg of around 12 minutes. Ben would do a left descending turn back onto zero seven, which should give them a four or five-mile final approach in cloud. The instrument approach was officially not really that exact with only a directional beacon which they would pick up on the base leg then intercept.

On "base", which was Bens left descending turn the Cap would show various aspects of the planes handling, reduced engine power settings, stall characteristics, flap speeds and so on. During the next seven or so circuits, Ben did an approach on three engines, flap failure, gear failure procedures and what to do in total hydraulic failure. On their final circuit and full stop, the Cap announced Ben as their newest captain.

They taxied back to the hard stand in front of Hanger 5, as they taxied, Emily had found a spot standing just behind Ben's seat, her hand rested on his shoulder.

'We done…well done,' she said, 'I feel safe with you on our side, Flying Officer, Benjamin Walters.'

******

The cloud eventually lifted, and it cleared to a mostly sunny day. The Cap, Ben and Chips had to meet the rest of the crew back in Hanger 5 to go over procedural requirements of the B-24. Some fuel load checks which included: bomb inventory, rate of climb over distance travelled, and endurance in hours. It was all meaningless to Emily, so she left, and apart from some rounds that needed to be done in the ward, had a free day. Marks had joined the crew with the news that in two days they had a mission. He would not speak of it yet, and the crew had that time to get their aircraft combat ready. He had arranged for the artwork on Ben's bomber to be started later that day and asked Ben to jot down some notes about his mother, some personal things and pictures. There was a rumble outside which was not the onset of more rain, it was the sound of the 24 other Liberators firing up their engines. Six were off to do some low-level formation flying, and from those six, the remaining aircraft in the fleet would mimic. Not all pilots in 451st were trained in, formation flying, and even instrument training was kept to a minimum to those that needed it, it was war after all and sometimes there were cost cuts.

The crew finished around midday with their weight and balance calculations. Chips who headed the ammunition crew, was responsible to ensure the total rounds issued to each quota where done. He had himself, Spot and Murph as the forward section, the two waist gunners, Sparky and Micky in the mid-section; and spot on his own in the aft or commonly known as "tail". On all accounts, he needed to ensure they had ammunition, its known storage location and contingencies. The bombs even though where loaded by a separate crew, Sperry took charge of that once inside the plane. The weights of everything, inclusive of fuel then fell onto the shoulders of the flight crew. Sometimes the war office would push the boundaries, but thankfully in the 451st's case, that was overruled.

The crew headed off to the mess hall for some lunch. It was supposed to be grannies pot roast but ended in some sort of a stew, mash and peas with carrots, and a thick russet coloured gravy. The peas, of course, ended up almost mashed like the potatoes, as they always did, but nonetheless it tasted good.

Marks and Ben had met one of the crew from another B-24, whose job it was to draw on the sophisticated nose art graffiti. Rembrandt, as he was known, used any materials available to him so he could paint up a likeness from pictures or sketches given. He added in a clowning effect to the artwork making it fun yet with a "suggestive" theme, a bit risqué well to the point of being still tasteful.

Ben had asked for the word "Charlotte" but incorporate "Charlie". Rembrandt assured Ben it would be a portrait of beauty.

It was crazy weather; just a few hours ago it was a bleak day, unwelcoming and depressing with limited visibility, low-level cloud and rain. Now the sun was heating the remainder of the day without any contest from a cooling season. Ben headed back to the mess hall, hoping some of the stew would still be there, when in the distance he could see a figure approaching on foot. They were aside a bicycle, with both hands firmly clutching the handlebars and strolling toward him. Ben somewhat lagged in noticing it was Emily as she had since changed from this morning's flight, and that would be Ben's excuse for not instantly recognising her. She wore a red waist height skirt fitting tightly just under her breast line. A loose white buttoned top with collar and short sleeves. Her shoes were what Ben thought was a type of canvas, pied in colour, with string straps tied around her ankles. They were what he remembered as a type of wedge or cork as his mother had once explained. Her auburn hair was pulled back from her face into a long ponytail that showed her natural curls, and it flowed over one side of her shoulders. She had a large bow on top of her head which perfectly matched her shirt in both colour and fabric.

'Hello, Flying Officer Benjamin Walters, I was wondering if you had some spare time to come for a picnic, I have a satchel of lemonade and roasted chicken.'

Ben looked around her and noticed a rattan hamper attached to the saddle of her bike.

'I, well, probably need to just check with —'

Before he could finish, she jumped in,

'It's OK, I have checked with Father, he has approved me taking you for a few hours. Anyway, he has insisted we all have today to enjoy as he said it will get a little intense in the next 12 hours or so. So please come, say that you will.'

Ben looked at her almost doll-like face as if it was moulded in porcelain. Without blemish, her skin was seamless, her eyes were one with the pale pink blush and stiff curling lashes. He remembered the first time he saw her and the intensity of the moment, and how he had no control over his seemingly obvious flirtatious behaviour. She was in control, she kept him at bay and remained professional throughout his medical examination. He could still feel the bite from the needle in his buttock and was sure it went all the way to the bone, and was still sore and bruised, especially when he sat.

'Well, if I have been instructed by your father, I best not let him down then,' he smiled.

She playfully hit him, and responded, 'Tell me you would go anyway, don't tease me,'

For the first time since meeting her, he now felt like he was the one in control. Without noticing it he had now managed words and a sentence, and she had now become timid and bashful.

'OK Miss Marks, lead the way.'

With her arm now firmly clutched around his, Ben took control of the bike. They walked and chatted in unison eventually leaving the confines of the base. They headed towards a large clean grass section at the end of the lane in which Ben first arrived a few days ago. Large enough to be perhaps a park and was probably set aside this way from one of the farmers. A perfect place to relax with full view of the airfield yet far enough away to be anywhere in the world. The bases crew would be here soon, and she wanted this time alone before they all arrived.

'So Flying Officer, you grew up around here you said.'

'Yes, not that far from here at a place called Banham, and I lived just outside the parish in an old farmhouse, around an hour's walk. There was an old grass strip nearby at a farm, where we would watch old bi-planes being used.'

'Banham is part of the Parish of Guiltcross, Norfolk. It was close enough to Buckenham in a way that Charlie would take me on weekends to carnivals that were at Old Morley Hall's grounds. The planes in the carnival would fly either back to the base here for fuel or to Banham strip or straight onto the next town, after an aerial display.'

'So, your father, is there a story there and did he fly in WW1?'

'I never knew what happened to my father, Charlie would never speak of him, and I never really asked. I had on occasion tried to bring it up but felt she didn't want to discuss it as she always changed the conversation onto something, generally flying as she knew I had a love for it.'

'So tell me, Flying Officer Benjamin Walters, how did you get this love for flying?'

'It was I think around '35 or '36, no it was 1936, I had just turned fifteen and it was August, we were going into town to see a flying display and I was as usual…'

Banham England, August 1936:

Charlie had yelled out to Ben this one last time.

'If we are going, we are going now, please leave that until we get back,' she suggested.

Charlie was, of course, referring to Ben reading one of his all-time favourite books; well, comic book more aptly as it did have pictures, it was, of course, *Armageddon 2419 A.D.*

He ran out the house almost forgetting to shut the door, Charlie just needed to stand there and give him one of those looks and he knew. The drive to Old Morley Hall was just under eleven miles and Old Buckenham was only around 3.7 miles; the airfield itself another half a mile further from Abby road. They had stopped to chat with a local farmer, and friend in town, William [Bill] Butterfield, or as he preferred Old Man Bill. Ben had seen an old bi-plane flying low over his fields, and asked Charlie if it was OK to call in and see him.

'Hello William, how are you keeping and is Elizabeth over her chest infection?' enquired Charlie.

'She's doing well, and my back is a little bit sore but both of us are still fit. How are you keeping, Charlotte? And Ben, you have grown; what are you now, 16?'

'No sir, I have just turned 15,' Ben said as he tugged on Charlie's jacket tail, promptly reminding her why they were here.

'Ben was inquiring as to a plane he saw over your property, and if you knew about it,' asked Charlie.

'Oh yes, we had read an article or heard a news broadcast on the wireless about some fields in Dayton, Ohio, whereby the fields were sprayed from a plane as they were infected with some moths. A few pilots had modified a Jenny or something —'

Ben excused himself and expertly said, 'Curtis, it was a Curtis Jenny.'

'Well done boy, I see your love for flying is immeasurable. Anyway, we had sent a telegraph to the farm owners and got a reply and information about the "dusters", as they are known, and thought we would give it a go. Perhaps Ben, you could come over some time and talk to the pilot, he is as keen as you, a bit heroic at times but he does what he does for the love of it.'

'And the designer of the plane was Benjamin Thomas,' said Ben proudly.

'That's so unexpected,' said Bill, 'You must come and see the plane now. It is unescapable as if it were a message from God Himself.' Old Man Bill had a devout persona for mass on Sundays even to the point that he volunteered on some weekends to help maintain the St. Mary the Virgin Church as it was known. Built in the fourteenth century from natural flint stone found in the area; Old Man Bill gave back to the church with the much-needed help in maintaining the structure, and the church provided back to him and Elizabeth the faith they both sought.

'Charlie, can we please visit, can we?' Ben's passion of planes showed in his rejoinder to Bill's suggestion.

The day out for Charlie and Ben at the fete was faultless. The stands had their normal produce on show, with homemade jams, and a mixture of crops. Drinks stands of lemonade and iced tea, scones and cakes. Some trinkets and old wares and a showing of prized animals, all judged by the winner from last year. It was a good system, fair, and remained unbiased that way as the winner from the previous year could not enter the following and so on, giving everyone a reasonable chance at taking the prize. The highlight of the day for Ben was when the aerial display of old bi-planes was on. The group was called The British Empire Air Display. The display, as it was advertised, was to be more exciting than the last [if possible]. The show would boast the flying "Chain Gang", "Leap Year Parachute Race" and the smallest plane in the world, the "Flying Flee", it was also the cheapest aeroplane on the market at the time. The show needed to be in Yarmouth both the 3rd and 4th of August, but this year, it would do some minor stunts and formation flying for the town. They would on their way through give a display which someone had organised as was done through someone, who knew someone and they knew someone else. Charlie suggested it was too far to go the Yarmouth, and even further to go to Ipswich thereafter, Ben was still happy as he got to see the planes.

Ben eventually got to see his Jenny and meet the duster pilots. Old Man Bill ultimately offering Ben some odd jobs about the farm allowing him more time to see the Jenny. He would watch the duster pilots fill the makeshift chemical barrels, refuel and fly to adjoining farms. Bill had set up a chemical storage facility on his land, which was a central place for all farms needing spraying. Over time, Ben eventually got to fly as passenger in the Jenny and in due course, got some "stick" time. Probably not kosher but nonetheless seen as probable sense with a pending war looming, and any "stick" time was good time.

It would only be around another three years when Germany would invade Poland, 1st September of 1939, some would say it would be the official start of the Second World War. Others argued it was July 7, 1937, from the prolonged war between Japan and China. Officially as Britain and France declared war on Hitler's Nazi Germany, Pilots were desperately needed in England. Courses where shortened, and instructors were few and those with potential, were snapped up.

The United Kingdom needed help from its allies in training its pilots, so subsequently, air-training agreements were then made with Canada, India and United States. These international arrangements were of course vital in helping with the schooling of the massive numbers of pilots needed at the time. Ben was given the opportunity but would have to leave almost straight away. He was given an exception by two weeks so as to help finalise with his mother some much-needed tasks on the farm; he would need to leave almost immediately.

4 years later, Banham England May 1940:

'Charlie, I won't be gone long, not quite a year with the preliminary training. They are saying 34 weeks, then I will be sent to an Operational Training Unit [OTU]. That will take around eight to fourteen weeks, depending on how I go.'

'Ben, it's not that I don't want you to go, it just that this war scares me. We are now bombing Germany and I fear you will have the need to go when your training is completed, as I don't think this war will end soon.'

'Charlie, don't think anything bad will happen, I may be staying here as a coastal patrol recognisance pilot; they are saying this is also needed. I am now 18, I want to volunteer Charlie, this is me; it's what I have longed for all my life?'

Ben of course lied to Charlie, he knew at the completion of his training, he could be sent anywhere and most probably would; for him, as long as it was flying, he didn't care.

Well, I have packed you some things just so you don't forget home, and among them is your favourite book, *Armageddon*; read it now and then and don't forget who you are, I love you my boy and please take care.'

Those parting words that day, were words of someone who sounded as if it was the last time they would see each other. Ben would remember them but now he needed to focus on his flight instruction.

******

Ben's training would be completed by December of 1940, taking only 28 weeks and was seen at the academy as a quick learner. It was his previous teachings on the Jenny that had provided him a head start on the other would-be pilots. He advanced quickly, and methodically, relearning things even though he knew them, he chose that they would be his first, providing him the advantage over his class. He eventually had returned into turmoil, finding that Britain was being bombed by Germany. It had started by September 7 and would last eight months. 16 cities where bombed for 267 days, London attacked 71 times. For 57 nights straight, the heart of London was attached by the Luftwaffe. More than a million homes where either damaged or destroyed. 40,000 people lost their lives, half were from London. At the midst of the bombing, one particular house was destroyed. All the occupants killed except one. A woman had survived for six nights under the rubble of brick and stone. She was rescued on day seven, a day that most of the fires had been extinguished allowing rescuers to find survivors. The woman had developed pneumonia from the constant dampness of her surroundings under the rubble. She had been unable to call out as a large piece of roof rafter was pinned against her chest restricting her lung capacity. She was taken to a makeshift hospital, but developed complications shortly after. On day nine of her ordeal at 11:31 am, on the 14th day of December, 1940, she was pronounced dead. She perhaps gave up living that day as she knew her son would be arriving safely back in England; Charlotte Walters, Charlie, was just another tragedy of war.

Barham August 10, 1943, 14:34 hrs:

The memories of Ben's life strangely enthralled Emily in a way she had no control. She too managed to take his words and picture them in detail of him as a youngster and growing up. His stories of his youth and farm life were something she now treasured. Ben's mind floated and promenaded around his youth of tails and his upbringing. He dredged up from the resonant fading recollections of his childhood, fading only perhaps from disinclination to retain from the hurt they caused in keeping. He perhaps felt somewhat relieved in telling the hurt he had to someone else, and Emily for him, gave, what was painful in telling, some much needed respite.

Ben now ultimately relaxed, searched his painful past, giving Emily insight into his indignant self-interest he had in the guilt and subsequent cause to his mother's death. If he had only stayed just that little bit longer without enlisting, perhaps she would still be alive. She had needed to go to London and check on family because of the raids and wanted to persuade her mother to come and live in Banham, away from the bombing. Charlotte was convinced she could encourage her mother to return but tragically she was unable to, and Ben would carry that burden forever.

Old Morley Hall 1953, August 14:

It was as if Ben had lost all concentration of the moment. Marshall was patiently waiting for Ben to regain his equanimity having been triggered into recalling a memory, from perhaps something in the room. Ben realising, he had drifted off with the thoughts of his youth and war and how was it possible to be 1953, he then refocused back onto the room.

'Marshall, this all doesn't make any sense. Every part of my life up to now; well, a few days ago did. Its war, and I accept that, what I don't except is here, now, you, me, this room, why and what is going on?'

Every time Marshall had spoken up to now, was always brief. It never seemed to make that much sense to anyone else and was as if Ben was the only one who ever seemed to understand what he was saying. Sense, to the point Ben remembered the crew's nebulousness expressions, or ostracism towards Marshall's briefings. He recalled the unclear faces of his crew when Marshall had gone over the plans of "Operation Night Owl". Or when he was in Hanger 5, as if only Ben was meant to understand Marshall's apparent focus on him alone. It was almost as if it had never meant anything at the time to the crew, nor was it important. Strangely, it was as if Marshall was never there to anyone except Ben and Ben had perhaps just visualised the thought that he was.

'So Ben, why are you here now? The room is simply a mystery to me, you, and would be nothing to anyone else. It's just a room, a room that is unquestionably individual, well individually different to anything you have ever seen up to now, yet very much significant to something,' said Marshall.

Ben looked about the room again trying to fathom its purpose. *What is the room and why is there a chair in the chamber*? he thought. He asked Marshall how he found the room in the first place, but Marshall went on to describe the room actually avoiding the question. When Ben evaluated what just happened, and seeing Marshall evade the query, he could not put words together to ask the same thing again. It was as if he were encoded only to question that what was to be answered. It simply didn't make sense, was it a concept, idea or something thought up in his own mind and portrayed to him by Marshall. Marshall unprincipled in his answers to Ben's interrogations, discernibly asked a question with a question, the two unnoticeably knowing perhaps what an answer will be, from a question they both knew in the first place would happen?

'I need to sleep,' sighed Ben, 'These past few days have taken their toll on me. I am tired, very much exhausted and need to rest. My body aches, everything is confusing, you won't tell me why I am here or how I even got here. Emily doesn't know me and it's as if she never did. Emily!' he yelled it out, 'What about Emily, she would have known you, she would have seen you at the base, she spoke to you, didn't she? Help me explain that I am me, I mean she is who I knew. I don't know any more what is real or who I am, I am just so exhausted.'

Marshall moved over to the pod, looking across at Ben and told him his week had been long and he needed some respite too.

'Have a rest here, I will go upstairs and take relief there, we will try and work through this together in a few hours,' Marshall suggested.

Ben didn't argue and could only focus on the weight he now felt in his body, and just needed to sit. Looking across at the blue settee, he could almost feel it drawing him in. He sauntered his way over to the pod instead and lightly touched its top curved section feeling its rounded clean lines, then ever so gently, glided into it. He laid back, its shape contoured unerringly to his own body. He could feel himself and consciousness drained away from his current thoughts. What was now left of his awareness, he noticed a colour change within the room. The pallid white turning to a lavender, blackening out the outer walls bar one. The wall facing the bed appeared to open with his mind not quite processing the event. The wall soon exposing a series of glass windows, which inclined back partly melding into the ceiling contour. The room continued to darken, the purple colour turning rich and ornate, mixing in with the still slightly glowing walls of bleached white. The room's simulated light levels began to recede, eventually fading to almost nothing. Ben continued to fall deeper into a state of almost unconsciousness. He had still managed to process the rooms eventual change, noting it was distantly dissimilar to what it was. In front of the glass windows, a very faint glow was underway, with a blur of mixed colours. The distortion changing into what appeared to be an image of hazy, almost out of focus, yet detailed pixels of colouring and shadow, virtually dimensional. Ben's awareness had momentarily stopped, slowly declining him towards sleep but still able to focus on the image, making out a shoreline of waves rolling up onto a beach. There were two planets proportional in size and in close juxtaposition to each other off to one side of the image. The slightly larger planet had a smaller moon orbit about its axis; to him this image was fictional. The pod made a swish noise and two independent segments of Perspex folded together closing the bed off. The Perspex that enclosed the bed was almost completely translucent, and for Ben, just added to the confusion, in fact it was not material manufactured in Perspex at all, and likened to the two planets, something that could possibly only be imagined.

The pod now archetypal to a silky case, spun by a larvae and Ben could be likened to the pupae now secured in this machine-driven cocoon. Ben's eyes were drifting shut, with just a hint of the sound of waves coming from outside the pod. Eyes now tightly closed, the room darkened to a black, the wave sound eventually stopped; and he had fallen into a deep unremitting sleep.

Chapter 4

Barham August 10, 1943, 15:33 hrs:

Ben was enjoying his time away from the base, even though he had only been there less than 48 hours. It was the ongoing war, and unknown missions he was now involved with; that gave him the apprehension he felt. Marks had been through the foundation of the "four fifty first" squadron, and how it was surreptitious to the enemy. Twenty-five aircraft, two hundred and fifty flight crew, and a further one hundred and seven ground personnel. Marks had advised that in the latter part of 43, ten DH.98 Mosquito aircraft would also join the base as a night bomber, inclusive of the additional 453rd squadron, its 25 aircraft, extra ground crew, cooks, mechanics, nurses and doctors, the base would have close to 900 personnel by the beginning of 1944.

He enjoyed the furlough even more from the fact Emily had gone to so much trouble in preparing the picnic hamper of such a perfect lunch. She understood Ben's life up to now and amenably felt his discomposure from his mother's death as he did. Emily although saddened by the apparent weight he carried from his belief that he was the sole cause of his mother's death, could see his burden somewhat lifting as he opened up to her.

They both where quickly distracted by a small dog as it ran by, chasing birds, not achieving anything other than its impaired discoordination from, perhaps, being just a puppy. Her uneasiness in finding out his mother had passed away was soon preoccupied from the dog's puerile actions. Her absolute despondency of Ben's story of the hopefulness he dealt with, was soon forgotten by both the puppy's actions and her encouraging laughter from the puppy tumbling over itself from what they both assumed had to be its own shadow.

Marks had insisted all individuals were to meet at the park around 16:00, as the mission would soon be announced and their unrestricted time now, would soon progress into their own responsibilities of war.

The final stragglers from the base had all arrived at the park by 15:50 hrs, and Marks had been mingling and enjoying the relaxation and, of course, the food prepared from the base's cooks. He did sneak a little chicken from Emily's hamper trying not to be noticed by her; she would, he thought, most certainly have scolded him had she seen. Marks could never allow that so he was very careful in his objective of taking the chicken. Emily, of course, as always, had caught him, and as always, pretended not to see.

The gathering had eventually assembled into small groups. With only ten nurses at the base, competition for them was high. Most of the officers and enlisted men had wives or girlfriends, and same for most of the operational ground staff. If you wanted to get technical about it, which often happened with pilots and crew, there were a total of seven men to one nurse and the competition for one of them was now just down to single person, Ben.

There was a chill in the air as the sun finally fell low over the distant horizon. Some of the groups of people had dispersed back to the base, others concreted to form bigger groups finally ending in just one mass of around 20 or so. Much of the attention was around the puppy who had decided to himself he preferred a throw rug and a warm knee in which to settle, than to continually chase his shadow. Emily was caressing the puppy's one white foot as it stretched out over her entire thigh. It would have been the perfect portrait to paint, almost a *Jupitar et Antiope*, the "Nymph and Satyr", by French artist, Antoine Watteau, had Rembrandt bought along canvas and paint.

'He is just adorable; can we take him back to the base?' sniffled Emily. A clear indication she was just on the cusp of desperation. 'He would be no trouble and we can all share him, a mascot, he can be a base mascot, Father will approve.'

Ben looked at her and saw one of the faces he used to pull as a child, just to get his own way. He conceded and suggested as they walked back to base, they would perhaps choose a name. It had to be significant and one that only they both knew as to its origin.

It had been decided that the remainder of the group would go back to the base bar for some dancing and poker; well, perhaps a few more drinks too. Ben could see the Cap leading the way with the remainder of the crew close by. A few of the nurses had arms clasped with some of Ben's crew, who were telling those heart felt stories of none returning after a mission, it would go as:

'This will be my last night on earth with a woman,' or something like that.

They were stories the nurses knew off by heart and believed it their duty to provide underlying wishes of romance this one last time to men who may never see past this war. Of course, you always got the real stories of love at first sight, or the stories of nervousness from a young man, who had in his mind that he genuinely would not return and didn't want to burden a woman of a love lost from war. Those stories were the ones the girls just emotionally broke down to and just wanted that man even more.

They all slowly meandered their way back to the base taking the easiest track, which was to approach the airfield from the south west end, then walk up the entire length of runway "zero seven". A faint glow from the overhead moon was just enough to illuminate the runway markings, the white cracking paint of the "seven" blending into the concrete runway as if were liquescent snow. The moonlight was almost eerie, the puppy intensifying the moment every now and then by just stopping and ogling across at the fields, perhaps at a rabbit or a distant cow. Its black body shape melding into the shadows and was only be visible from its solitary white paw.

'So, Ben, tell me what it's like to fly, and just be up there? I so wish for this war to be over and you can take me flying, just the two of us,' Emily announced. She held on tightly to Ben's hand, her palm now radiating heat as the two strolled down the runway, palm to palm. He would every now and then rub her pointer finger with his, perhaps just to gauge her response.

'At night is when you become one with the plane. Landing is only a challenge when there are wisps of cloud and one minute you have a horizon the next you are flying on instruments. Towns are typically blackened out or have limited lighting and when you fly overhead the runway using the ADF [Automatic Direction Finding] and see the pointer fall back 180 degrees it's your sign that you made it. Your approach is assessed as you get a glimpse of the airfield lights and windsock for the very first time. You fly left as you descend from 2,000 feet, pulling back the power to two thousand four hundred RPM, keeping an eye out your side so as to gauge the start of the threshold or for aircraft out of formation. Your downwind leg is no time to relax, and runway lights are seen for the first time putting the runway length into perspective, your flight is by no means over, there is still much to do. One six zero knots and passing through one thousand five hundred feet on decent to 1,000 feet and reduce to one fifty knots. The crew is stirring and taking about their first drink after landing or writing in a diary about the mission or planes lost or targets hit or a letter to a loved one. Your plane challenges gravity as it remains aloft even if you have lost an engine as it twists and vibrates and smells of burning aviation fuel that stings your eyes or swells your lips from the constant licking you do. The flaps are now lowered just ten degrees to tell the plane that you are back in control; the nose slightly lowers perhaps bowing in submission. You're now abeam with the threshold, so you continue the heading for another three miles. Quickly you are at 1,000 feet above ground level, you turn onto a base leg and let your speed wash off just that little bit more, pull back on the yoke and the speed drops. As you turn onto final for the first time, the lights show you a perception of a shape, long and pencil like, the surroundings are shadowy and sort of looks like a sole warship in the ocean, nothing else for miles. Set 20 degrees of flap, and move the props to high pitch, adjust yourself in your seat, check your harness and gear down. Now you are feeling the intensity of the flight is coming to an end. Your flaps are now full, and you are dropping at 500 feet per minute, your airspeed is set at one two five knots as you decent down to 150 feet. At night, you need to judge this just right, look outside, over the nose, and how fast the runway lights are moving past. You flare now, and at one zero five knots, your wheels kiss the runway, you hold…hold…hold the nose as long as possible, and the final part of the plane, it's nose wheel touches down, your mission is a success.'

Ben's account of a landing at night told Emily how dedicated he was as a pilot and for the war effort. She soon realised they had walked the entire length of the runway and had reached the apron area of the hangers. In front of Hanger 5, the ground crew were finishing off some maintenance to Bens Liberator. It's "J" insignia illuminated from some light stands positioned about the aircraft, lighting its fuselage like the clock face in the tower near Ben's school. They continued to walk up to the plane; its twin vertical stabilisers, tall and lanky, were facing the hanger so they approached on the starboard side.

'We are going in for a card game; are you two coming?' said the Cap, Roger and Chips, both arms around each other's shoulders staggering and just being able to walk, turned and simultaneously called out to Ben.

'Are you…Come on then…Ben my boy…Miss Marks…cards, we can play cards…' was all that came from Roger and Chips, nothing at all made any sense.

'We will be there in a minute, just going to look over the plane,' Ben answered, not really directing it to Roger or Chips it was more for the Cap; he was still slightly coherent having had less to drink, but none the less probably had his fill.

The Liberator stood majestic against the night sky. Its silvery hull caught the light from floodlights surrounding the plane, brightening its motionless image, perhaps bringing it somewhat to life. Ben was watching four men about the plane; one was sitting on the spinner of the propeller looking in against the cylinder heads. Another one was holding the blade tip in a neutral position, perhaps to stop it from moving. There was one was on a six-foot ladder with both hands behind the engine cowl; he had spanners and wrenches as he tinkered with engine components. While the fourth was just sitting in a jeep, no one knew what he was doing, perhaps just to watch. A bicycle was standing sideways on its stand just forward of the noise wheel, a man was packing up his equipment of paint tins and brushes of varying sizes. He turned toward them at the same time Ben noticed it was Rembrandt.

'Hello Rembrandt, you are out late,' suggested Ben.

'Well, not really late for me, had stringent instructions from Marks to have this finished today, so late from that account, I guess you're right.'

Ben looked up at the side of the fuselage and made out a painted shadowy image on the hull. The light stand that was close by was facing back toward the starboard inner leading edge of the wing, Rembrandt had finished with it so it was turned back onto the Liberator, enhancing its lustre of the silvery hull

'Can we please turn the light Rembrandt? I would dearly love to see Charlotte's image,' pleaded Emily.

Rembrandt had in fact finished off the portrait of Charlie. He had spent the afternoon on it after Ben's flight earlier that morning. The image done at Ben's request was on the starboard side as he was keeping the port side for additional painting. Ben helped Rembrandt turn the portable light and faced it up toward the image on the nose of the B-24. The outline of the painted shape was no longer shrouded in mystery. The image from the light had given it an inner glow of its own, bringing the portrait alive. The woman's likeness was painted as if she herself were disobeying gravity and flying. Both arms were spread out to the sides, one hand holding the cape attached to the rose-pink swimsuit she was wearing. The other hand was holding a bomb with a Nazi Luftwaffe emblem. The words "Special Delivery", written above her, and Charlotte painted as if embroidered in gold lace, was on the cape. On the bomb was worded, "Adolf, my gift to you from Charlie". It matched Charlie's persona he thought, and Emily could see Ben was content.

'Rembrandt, thank you so much; my mother would have been proud,' acknowledged Ben.

'You are welcome,' replied Rembrandt, and well, I have ummm also…

A figure could be seen mooching toward them. The shape turned into two men arm in arm, both trying to put the lyrics together of a song but the words were slurped, and totally out of harmony….

[singing]

'There'll be blue-ooo… birds… over-aaarhh… the white… cliffs… of Dover. Tomorrow… just you…'

The song, of course, was nothing like Vera Lynn's version, but for two men that had had their fill of alcohol today, it sounded just great.

'Hello darling, my little girl,' whispered Marks in Emily's ear.

'Dad, Father, stop it please, you are being silly, please, Ben is here and I…'

The Cap, who was Marks fellow vocalist, looked up at the portrait of Charlotte.

'Well, Rembrandt, that is beautiful now we…we just… have to see the other side,' slurred the Cap.

Marks was wobbling on his legs even though the Cap was partially holding him up. Marks bought his index finger up to his lips and let out a "shishhhhhhhh" sound followed by a slurred, 'they… don't …know yet.'

'What are you talking about, Father? Is there something…'

'Perhaps I can clear this up,' said Rembrandt and insisted Ben help him move the flood light this time around to the port side of the bomber.

They positioned the light facing up at the silvery hull. Marks and the Cap followed them in a bit of an erratic style almost missing the moment of elation as both Emily and Ben stood fast, looking up at the portrait. Painted in a sitting position, the woman was wearing a much-shortened version of a khaki coloured dress, perhaps WAAF? She sat both arms stretched back, the skirt was high about the buttocks and just showed a hint of a dusky coloured lace underwear. A black stiletto and silk stockings shaped the legs with definition. The darkened black lace top of the stocking held hard against the leg with matching black straps disappearing behind the skirt. Her auburn hair and corresponding rubicund colour lipstick was an image of beauty and finished with the words, "Emily" followed by, "Red Headed Woman", painted in bold yellow lettering.

Emily looked at Ben, and all she could get out was, 'It's beautiful, it's just beautiful.'

Ben, looked across at Marks and the Cap, and simultaneously they both gained enough coordination and silently did the "shishhhhhhhh" sound while shaking their heads back and forth. This was Ben's indication not to say anything and take full credit for the artwork of Emily.

Emily looked at Ben, the Cap and her father, then cried.

'Thank you so much,' she said, 'I will, sorry, I am proud to be on this plane thank you again.' She leaned forward and held onto Ben. Her arms clasped his body as if tentacles of a cephalopod, her chest thrust into his and he instantaneously felt the shape of her plump breasts. The cold night air stiffing her nipples as she pushed her womanly shape into his. She whispered a few words in his ear…

'Ben, it's time we left this party,' and she embraced his hand once more as they did when walking on the runway.

'Um, I think we are going,' said Ben, addressing his words to the trio, who by now had plans to head back to the bar.

'Before you go Ben, for my album, can I get a quick snap of you two next to the plane, port side with Emily's portrait, if that's alright?' asked Rembrandt.

'Yes of course you can; Emily, is that alright with you?' and with that Emily walked over and held on tight to Ben as Rembrandt took his photo.

Rembrandt set up his camera and shot his picture, then went about cleaning up his paints and brushes, then called out, 'Time for that well-earned beer…'

'The puppy, where is the puppy?' cried Emily.

The dog had curled up on a small drop sheet that Rembrandt had, sat his paint tins on. The puppy had brushed up against the side of one tin that had a surfeit amount of white paint around the rim. Emily clapped to the dog to waken it, and did not notice down one side was a smear of bleached white paint. The puppy was none the wiser and just jumped on his hind legs and tried to bark, only achieving a whimpering yelp. Marks and the Cap were followed closely by Rembrandt, as they headed back to the base's bar. Emily had regained her equanimity having thought the puppy was gone, and they too walked off towards the bar. The puppy's white painted side illuminating in the moonlight giving off a gentle glow, glimmering against its darkened body. Emily looked down at the dog's silhouette noticing the white paint was almost down the entire length of his torso.

'Ben!' she screamed, 'the song Father was singing with the Cap; it's the perfect name.'

'What, call him white cliffs, that's a bit…?'

'No silly, Dover, let's call him Dover.'

The name fitted perfectly. Mimicking the cliffs, it was an instance in time, only they knew, it was a moment that meant something significant and would be remembered for life. The puppy in a short time had become very attached to them both. That night would be that last time for another ten long years until the puppy would once again here Ben's voice.

Norwich England, August 16, 1953, 10:03:

Emily always seemed to have to pull back on Dover's lead, to slow him down. She would constantly yank it back just enough so he would slow his fast-unpredictable pace. Dover would then cough a little, lick his muzzle, shack, then off he would go again. Emily was thinking of what Ben had told her and saw it as something made up in his mind yet with impeccable detail. She had wondered why, and had gone over every scenario in her mind, and she could not come up with any logical reason as to why he would say who he was. Where would she look for him, would he be back at the park or near Old Morley Hall, or would she just consequently stumble across him without trying? She approached the same bench she and her son first met him two days ago, hoping he would simply be there again. He was not, nor did she have an indication in her mind on what to do next. She spoke aloud to herself, hoping it would give her some direction, but nothing.

Her son was visiting a school friend so it was just Dover and her who would work things out. Dover was getting over a broken leg having spent the past week at the animal clinic in Attleborough. He had got it caught in a cattle grid at Old Man, Bill's farm entrance and nearly had to have his forelimb amputated due to the amount of cracks in the bone, six in total and one very splintered break. Emily suddenly yelled out, and all thankful to the dog's hospitalisation and from the near-death experience he had.

'The cemetery!' she cried out, 'That is the answer, Earlham Road Cemetery,' she said with confidence. She turned, Dover close by, and the two headed out of the park and towards Norwich.

******

The cemetery at Earlham Road just outside Norwich had been laid out, in 1856. A good portion of it had been dedicated to the causalities of warfare as far back as the South African War, in 1899. Emily had walked up and down the varying paths of the headstones, looking intently for something she actually had no idea of what. She was looking for any indication of a name or something that may help her cause. She had been here before many times but then she may have passed something of significance that now would make sense. She eventually came across a row dedicated to the victims of Old Buckenham, and the 451st. She hadn't recognised this row before nor did she notice a large memorial stone next to a plaque of the 451st insignia, also in stone. She didn't remember it, or perhaps see it, but it read the following:

We commemorate the fighting courage or all our causalities of war. In particular, the brave men of the 451st Squadron, at Old Buckenham Base. Whom of which sacrificed so greatly their lives' this day, and will be remembered with honour and the bravery they showed.
The valiant men, of 451st J Two Five, who did not return this day were not at rest, and we give their families some hope, by letting them know that they are now at rest, and will forever be at peace from this day thereafter
To the 10-man crew of J 25,
WE HONOUR YOU
Co-Pilot – John Morgan-The Cap
Navigator – Martin Hensley-Wilson
Bombardier – Fred Townsand-Sperry
Top Turret Gunner and Engineer – Anthony Marks-Chips
Nose Gunner – Alexander Dunstan-Spot
Tail Gunner – Henry R Wilson-Roger

Ball Turret Gunner – Peter Murphy-Murph
Left Waist Gunner – Samuel McClain-Sparky
Right Waist Gunner – Michael McClain-Micky
We would also like to acknowledge our Captain
who bravely flew this as his first and last miss ion, as he was the youngest
pilot to succeed as Captain, Ben Walters [Benjamin] of which also was
pronounced MIA, this day, the

12 day of August, in the year of our lord, 1943
AMEN

Emily's sombre sentiment from reading the headstone had left her with the clear fact that Ben was not who he said he was, nor was it right that he both played her emotions and was deceitfully imagining to be a hero of war, perhaps he needed help or was rationally insecure for a differing reason. Being who she was and what her father had instilled in her was to be the best she could be in any situation, and if she could perhaps help this young man in some way she would.

Old Buckenham August 10, 1943, 23: 49 hrs:

Ben, Emily and Dover had been walking for what seemed hours. They had walked along the runways entire length again, and more stories were told of flying, Emily becoming a nurse, and they compared their training. Ben had picked up on a slight apprehension a vagueness perhaps, something about her past she seemed to without being aware of it, simply just skip over it, he let that thought go. They eventually had found their way back to Ben's Liberator, the floodlights still shinning on the nose, an eerie aura shone over the artwork. The ground crew had all gone perhaps joining Rembrandt and the others at the bar. They could hear the music playing and every now and then had become inaudible from the boisterous laughter, the Cap was still rehearsing his words to Vera Lynn's song. The underbelly hatch of the B-24 was open and Ben thought it only protocol to shut it, including unplugging the power to the floodlights.

'Ben, perhaps I should take Dover back to my barracks and let him rest; he looks awfully exhausted,' suggested Emily.

'Well, will you come back or would you like to, I mean…?'

'I will come back and meet you here, Flying Officer Benjamin Walters, perhaps we should also enjoy the night, maybe get us a cheap bottle of champagne or something from the bar, even some lemonade, I am a bit thirsty,' said Emily.

The bar was alive with flight personnel. Empty bottles of all four beers available, were strewn over the bar top. People were throwing beer mats at the mirror background perhaps trying to hit the Chief in some way. Some of the red and green bar lights were not working possibly from the throwing of the mats, and as always, Chips was trying to fix them: typical of a fight engineer. His having too much to drink was the only thing stopping him from achieving this, apart from his lost coordination, and at every second attempt had another slurp of his drink, spilling most of it. Some of Grandma's homemade lemonade was still on the bar, almost untouched but the small amount spirits left on the shelf and empty beer bottles to a bystander indicated a large amount of alcohol, had in fact been drunk. Marks was sitting at the bar rigid in form, his swaying from his earlier rendition of a song had been replaced to an inflexible posture. He was just ogling at the bar, and had a mug of half-filled black tea in front of him. He was holding a hand written note in his free hand, the other just resting on the handle of the mug. He looked over at Ben who stood confused trying to make sense of Marks grave appearance.

'Hello, my boy, it is time,' announced Marks.

'Time?' inquired Ben, 'you mean —' and before he finished, Marks interjected.

'I have just received the orders via the radiophone, and we go in less than two days. Go and enjoy my boy, make tonight, this night count, tomorrow, we prepare for this mission and I'm afraid it is going to be a bad one.'

Marks pointed to the dusty old bottle of Moet on the shelf, and instructed the Chief to put it on his tab.

'Give the boy an ice bucket and a couple of glasses,' he asked the Chief, then turned and faced Ben, 'Now go and enjoy it with my daughter.'

Ben made his way back to the Liberator with the bottle of Moet, hoping Emily would approve. He didn't want to mention the words he just had with Marks as he didn't want to make bad a situation from the otherwise wonderful evening they both were having so far.

In the distance, obscured by the shadows was an approaching figure. They had darkish clothing on and what appeared to be all one colour. The figure ambled out of the shadows and into the light surrounding the aircraft. It was Emily, she had changed into her base WAAF uniform. Being khaki, it matched that of the image Rembrandt had painted on the Liberator. Although it was at a length more appropriate than the image, it was still very much similar.

'Take me into your plane, Flying Officer Benjamin Walters and let's make believe we are free from all of this, and up there flying without a care in the world.'

The two climbed up through the underbelly hatch and made their way up to the navigation station. The area was just forward of the main wing spar and bomb bay, providing the navigator and engineer ample room to complete their tasks. The Moet had chilled in the bucket enough for Ben to break open the cork and toast to a wonderful evening. Emily sat and sipped her glass with a smile that was imperceptible from the glass she kept close to her mouth. Ben could sense something was afoot, for one she had changed, and two she from the inside, was undeniably smiling.

'Why are you grinning?' asked Ben, having now admitted he had seen it all along.

'Ben do you think I am as pretty as the girl in the painting?'

'Emily, it is you and was portrayed from a picture as was Charlie.'

'Well, I mean as interesting as men would see in the painting, well not all men just you, do you see me as exciting? Does that picture excite you, do I excite you now?'

'Emily, you do, and my words don't always come out right when I am around you. I need to be a gentleman and show you respect. Your father is my biggest fear besides you and now, Dover.'

'You,' questioned Emily, as she playacted in hitting him, 'Ben, how do you see me now.'

Emily stood and carefully placed her glass on the navigation station workbench. The top turret allowed in enough light to fill the space, giving it a slight glow. Ben was just able to make out her womanly shape as she stood in an almost ethereal level of light. It provided the space with an air of ambience now veiled in mystery from this shape, who now stood before him. The slight chill to the air made their breath noticeable from the puffs, filling the room with elfin like clouds of miasma. Ben's inhaling was unpredictable, and he was gulping in twice to one exhale. He had lost all his coordination in breathing and the situation now becoming worse as Emily with both tiny hands, loosened her jacket top button. The collar fell apart as if it were animated or by some mechanical means. She loosened the second button, her face now unified and blended temptingly with the low levels of light, which in itself were desirable. Her rubicund lipstick was lustrous against the glow and she lifted her head slightly exposing her neckline, her cleavage now unprotected from the low-cut top garment. Her mind told her she was now defenceless, vulnerable to him, her body told her to continue. As she turned slightly to the side, Ben's eyes were drawn toward the flank of her enviable breast line, well rounded and secure in a darkish black undergarment, possibly onyx in colour. The pale skin colour of her breast could be seen as she turned even further, now with her back to him. She lowered her head and removed the white bow then gave her head a shake from side to side allowing it to be full bodied and disentangled. She shook her head once more by flicking her head fully forward, her long amber hair falling over her face exposing the nape of her neck. She lifted her head back up, the hair now fell down in its place, falling half the length of her back. She stood motionless for what seemed an eternity, perhaps to question her motive or was it the expectation he would walk up to her at this very moment. She closed her eyes hoping he would and for what seemed a lifetime, was probably only seconds. Suddenly, she felt her heart stop, the continuous beating palpitated, and she felt the warmth of his breath against the side of her neck. He stood there motionless, close to her without touch, emotive and impassioned. Her hands were at her side, palms were sweaty and swollen. They tingled and were numb, she had no feeling or sensation in any part of her body; she wanted him to touch, just so she knew she was still alive. Ben unable to calculate his next move also closed his eyes, soon becoming one with her. He could feel the heat from her palms as his hands ephemerally touched hers. His fingers flickering gently as if on the keys of a piano and he was Sergei Vasilievich Racmananioff, composing a Sonata, and this moment was his first oeuvre. Their hands clasped, the dampness of perspiration could be felt. She guided his hands toward the belt buckle around her waist. He loosened it out of its clasp and unravelled the belt from her skirt. A clang noise could be heard as the clasp hit the aluminium floor panel of the plane, dinting it slightly. The skirt fell away from her hips and onto the floor, the chill in the air now touching every part of exposed skin. The jacket just long enough to provide her a small amount of dignity, but still uncovering and exposing her feminine figure. She immediately felt the shape change in his body, his trousers becoming firm and he quickly pulled back from her, embarrassed from his uncontrollable actions. She turned and took one-step back, now revealing herself to him.

'Am I like your portrait now?' she asked.

Ben able to get an indication of what she was now wearing from the limited light in the cabin. Her jacket exposed, breasts plump and risen, augmented and voluptuous in a black undergarment with tiny specials of a white silky lace. She had on black nylon stockings and matching black stiletto heels. Her thighs were visible exposing the skin, only hidden by two straps down each leg. The tops of the stockings fastened back to the suspender belt indubitably about her slim waste. Her underwear was also dark and visible below the jacket. She could feel the dampness from within and her underclothing becoming moist as he stood there looking at her. She watched as he loosened his belt, he momentarily stopped, her heart raced then subsided to a continuous thump, thump, thump when she realised he changed his actions to remove his shoes. His belt, like hers, made a clang as it hit the deck of the plane it too dented the floor panel, and trousers soon followed. In the silhouette, she could make out his form as she walked towards him and felt his warmth, their bodies meeting in agreement. His heart was beating through his chest, as their bodies finally met. Emily felt a rush of adrenaline in her body as they melded together, her underclothing now saturated as his firm hardened shape pushed between her now parted legs. He held her close as he kissed the side of her neckline, and both his hands ran down her dampened perspiring back. He could feel the sweat off her body fall down to the now dampening waste line of her silk underwear. They kissed, eyes tightly closed and their minds racing with adulterated thoughts. Ben's hands slipped down to her buttocks, the firmness was felt from his caressing fingers. She bought her hands around her waist to his jacket front, undoing each button in swift succession. She pulled his shirt off his shoulders and it too fell on the floor. She unclasped her one remaining button off her jacket, exposing the full shape of her undergarments. Her underwear had lace inserts of little rose shape patterns, and thin silk straps tied in perfect bows at each hip. She unfastened her brassiere, exposing her breasts, nipples hardened and shapely, the areola swollen and pink against her pale skin. Ben's hands touched each breast feeling and memorising their shape, moving his fingers over the nipple as each became more stiffened as his sweating hands caressed them. She moved her palms over his chest and down to his now totally enlarged form. She felt his organ pulsating in her fingers as each tip slid up and down its shape. She pulled his underwear away from the tip of his masculine profile exposing its full length. He reciprocated with his hands and slid them down the front of her petite undergarment, his hand instantly feeling the saturated gusset. He unhurriedly slipped his hand towards her form; the warmth of her inner body lathering around each finger as he inserted the tips gently inside her. Her uncontrollable moaning now audible exciting her pace into complete submission.

'Take me Ben,' she pleaded, 'I want you inside me, I want to feel your shape and warmth.'

Ben could not find the words, all he could do was continue to caress and kiss his way through this. He gradually fell onto to his knees and leaned toward her, his lips just touching her inner thighs. Her legs uncontrollably opening and she felt a warm gush of watery fluids run from within and down each side of her inner thigh. His mouth kissed, and tasted her juices, from her inner leg, then slowly moved his tongue up eventually finding his way to her moistened opening. His mouth running up through her passage stopping at a point which made her tremble out of control. She pulled him up towards her, their shapes colliding this time with total control. He felt the wetness of her opening as his manly structure penetrated her for the first time. His hardened appendage feeling her pulsating opening as it tightly grasped him, his strokes were deep within her. Her screaming could not be controlled from his irregular momentum, as she moaned and pinned her body against his. Her nails cut deep into his skin, and he too moaned in acceptance. The rhythm and pace hastened, their movement without contention, they were in total harmony, he thrust deep into her, her moaning intensified, she yelled out,

'Ben…take me…please I…I can't wait any longer…please have me now…'

Immediately the two let out a yell and Emily felt a throb she had never experienced. Her body became floppy almost lifeless, Bens head felt instant vertigo from the draining of his fluid into her. The sweat from their bodies became tacky as they slowly cooled. She felt her shape about his organ as it pulsed and ejaculated. A thick gluggy liquid fell from within her and down her legs; he stayed there just to feel the same.

'Emily,' he said, heart still racing, 'I am, I mean I was —'

'Shishhhhhhhh,' she said, 'and whatever you are thinking, I am too. Ben that was wonderful, and please you be safe when you go on the mission, I want you back just as you are.'

******

Old Buckenham August 11, 1943, 20 hours before operation "Night Owl":

It was showery, damp and cold. The gloomy day that the base had woken too, didn't appear to be going to stop any time soon. The base was already a hive of activity, with most personnel now actively carrying out their day-to-day invariable routine tasks. Aircraft were being fuelled, oils topped up, hydraulics checked, every hatch door and opening was either unlocked or released. Planes were lined up on the hardstand diagonally in a row of 12 each side of Hanger 5, and a solitary Liberator in the middle; Ben's. Flight operations personal were progressively going through their check lists, in and out of hatches, ladders were below engines and cowling covers off, mechanics testing and altering components over and over again. Engineers tweaking gears and instruments and tyre pressures. If there was any doubt or something not working just right, it was changed.

The crew chief of each B-24 had set individual tasks for all personnel, Sperry took that role on Ben's Liberator. Halverson was making his way from plane to plane ensuring the sequence of checks was in an organised fashion. Halverson made the announcement as he passed each aircraft: Briefing for pilots, navigators and engineers was at 14:00 hours in Hanger 5. Marks would conduct that, leaving Halverson to provide his briefing for the remainder of the crew, in Hanger 4. The cloud base was around 700 feet AGL [above ground level] and visibility still the length of the runway, this was good, good enough for the mission to go ahead. The briefing would look at the flight and expected weather so as it was at the moment, still a go.

Ben was going to meet Emily for breakfast in the mess hall at 06:12, having left the plane only 50 minutes earlier. Surprisingly, he was not fatigued nor was he repentant over their intimacy. They had truly bonded in the early hours, and Emily's parting words to him before she headed off to the showers was simply, '*merci*'.

A shower was surprisingly a worthy remedy for any nonexistence of sleep. It would give the body a convincing energy as did a thermos of black coffee on a night bombing run. How would Ben act when he saw her again, what was he supposed to say? Perhaps he should just say nothing and let her say something first, for the first time he now started to question his actions; well, their actions.

The aroma of powdered eggs, burning bread and a hint of caffeine could be almost savoured as he approached the mess hall. There were only a few spots left to sit, and most that had finished were just chatting about the mission, of which the entire base now knew of. Marks and Halverson were in deep conversation near a window looking outside at the depressing conditions. Ben could only guess that they both were assessing the cloud base, or how many bombers would return, or hoping they had every possible scenario covered. The war was fast approaching at an accelerated level of intensity. Both sides were conducting extreme relentless bombing runs. Ground troops would hold a position for a day, retreat, then regain the same position the next day. For the men on the ground, there was seemingly no gain, nor achievement, it was nonsensical and inexorable for the otiose loss of life and would last for another two long years.

'Good morning son, did you have a pleasant evening?' inquired Marks.

'Yes sir I did, well I mean I didn't have much…I…went to the…' Ben all tongue-tied, tried his best to answer Marks with something that didn't imply in any way he was with Emily, nor did he want to give the impression he had the perfect intimate night with his daughter.

'It's OK son, we are all adults here,' said Marks.

Ben instantly felt the weight lifted off his shoulders, replied with a, 'Thank you sir.'

'Just so long as you were not with my daughter,' smiled Marks contemptuously but in a good way.

Emily made her way in through the door to the mess hall at exactly 06:12 dressed ready for work. She had on her full nurse's uniform, tunic pulled tightly about her slim waist. Her headdress pulled somewhat back blanketing her auburn hair. She had a clipboard held tightly to her side as if the papers attached to it were safeguarded for a reason. She walked straight past Marks and up to Ben.

'Good morning, Flying Officer Benjamin Walters, did you sleep well?' she asked.

'Well I did but don't think… well, perhaps a little more sleep would be better?' he replied.

'I hope you haven't eaten yet', she asked, 'if not, perhaps we should now and I would feel better if you had a little more sleep before the mission.'

It wasn't long before the hustle of the morning's food service was over. It was only a three-hour turn around until the entire base would be back for lunch break, so clean up, and preparation was almost an incessant undertaking for the cooks and kitchen hands. Emily had headed to the base's hospital to complete rounds, and check on inventory, catalogue any shortfall of medical supplies of which she would re-stock as necessary. She knew her provisions were sufficient but it was needed in her own mind just to satisfy herself. Ben had around three hours before briefing and he needed to clear his mind of all of the events of the past 24 hours, not for the fact he wanted to forget them, he just wanted to enter the mission focused.

There was a small section of soft dead grass at the rear of Hanger 5, mostly used for the storage of items that didn't really have a home. It wasn't the most pleasant of places, old drums of oil refuse or unused parts of damaged aircraft components usually found their way there. The grass was mostly dead or dying from the aroma of petroleum or having had been used as some sort of cleaning area of engine workings that were washed down with a crude spirit or contaminated fuel waste. It wasn't a satisfying place to be but somehow Ben found it calming, soothing to the point that it was almost away from everything that had come before him in the past 24 hours. He, for the first time, had come to realise this was all real and in a few hours his briefing for a mission and the possibility of not returning home. He lay down on the spoiled grassland, his clothing melding with the surrounding odour of discoloured and browning grasses. The intensity of noises about him diminished to a nothingness, his mind focused and the noiseless sounds now about him allowing his eyes to slowly close, Ben had without contest to his racing thoughts, now fallen into a deep sleep.

******

'Ben, Ben, wake up,' Marshall said in a characteristic not common to him. It was more of a hurried tone, perhaps disorderly and astonished.

Ben opened his eyes and saw Marshall looking down at him. Ben's outer surrounds were blurry and confusing, he could only focus on what was directly in front of him.

'Time to get up Ben, you have had more than enough sleep; do you feel refreshed?'

Ben now looked around and was able to focus on his surroundings. He was able to centre in on the lavender colouring about him. The two segments of Perspex that had folded down closing the bed off were opened and the walls turned from the unembellished sullying colours, back to its placid white. The glass windows in front of him revealing again the two planets with the smaller moon still in orbit about the larger one's axis. The walls had irradiated from the dark purple colour to the silvery white, the shape of the planets slowly diminishing in the increasing snowy light levels. Ben sat up looking about the room and processed immediately that he had slept perhaps for hours. Marshall stood over him as he climbed out of the pod, the room had now returned to its former self.

'Marshall, what is going on, how did I get here?' enquired Ben?

'What do mean, how did you get here? You came with me four hours ago, we both needed to rest so I slept upstairs, you fell asleep here in the pod.'

'Marshall, I fell asleep at the airfield, perhaps a few hours ago behind Hanger 5. How did I get here, what is happening, what's going on?'

'Ben, nothing is going on you have been here all along, you met me in the park and we came here together.'

'Marshall, what is happening to me, why am I here, and who, um I don't understand, why is, how, tell me what's going on, what year is it, tell me? Marshall tell me the day; what day is it?'

It's the 14th, yeah it is, it's the 14th, August the 14th, 1953, is there something wrong?'

Chapter 5

August 11, 1943

Operation Night Owl briefing 14:00 hrs:

'Welcome everyone, as you all know I have received our orders for the mission, and from here on in, it will be known as Operation Night Owl. We will be wheels up at 02:00 so those a little slow from last night's few to many drinks; that is 12 hours from now,' Marks announced.

He looked about the hanger for any sign of misunderstanding, hoping clarity of the events to come had all of their absolute understanding as this was to be an essential mission. He suddenly became aware that all were not in attendance, and waved to the Cap with a gesture, the Cap understanding his body language worked out Marks was implying of Ben's whereabouts. The Cap shook his head side to side in response, he obviously also didn't know.

From the back of the hanger, a small rear door that led out to the refuse dumping ground suddenly opened and Ben raced into the briefing. He had confusion in his face and appeared lethargic, his cloths mud-covered and soiled, and had an aged appearance about them and were redolent of gasoline and oil. Ben found a suitable spot amongst the bomber crew but strangely stood reticent to his companions. Marks momentarily contemplated Ben's remiss attentiveness to protocol, overlooked the late arrival, then continued:

'At 01:45, all crew is to be at their stations and be waiting for my indication for the overhead flare to go. On my signal and confirmation, and all bombs are locked and loaded, the thumbs up will be given by each captain, then it's a go for engine start.' Marks continued to look about the room for any sign of uncertainty, stopping at Ben who was looking around the hanger as if he had oddly never been here before. The crew stood uneasy waiting for the next words to come from Marks.

'OK, so where are we going?' announced Marks.

A bed sheet was pulled away from a large table that was positioned in the centre of the gathering. There was a scaled map sitting on the bench around six-foot square, showing England, Norway and Germany. There were three white cords stretched out forming a large triangle, from Buckenham to Esbjerg, then to Peenemünde and finally back to the base in England. Marks went on to give the men a brief of why Peenemünde. He spoke about the mission's importance, then what they may encounter and the possibility of sneak attacks over the English Channel on their return. He also spoke about how in May of '42, a lone spitfire piloted by Flight Lieutenant D.W. Steventon who managed to get some pictures of the Peenemünde Airfield that has provided evidence of construction activity with some circular emplacements, and how interrupters think they are rocket tubes. It was later confirmed a V-2 was launched in October of the same year. He went on to describe this mission, although covert, was and will be part of Operation Hydra, and is designed as a flow in effect to disrupt the German secret weapon development as best they could.

Marks finished by telling the crew to take a good look at the map, 'Know the area, know it well, it is enemy territory,' and he also suggested that all may not return. His instructions were, 'Rest well, and be at the mess hall in six hours.' Marks was finally done as quick as he started and gestured to Halverson to bring Ben to his office ASAP.

Ben followed Halverson but rather than talk, he just looked about everywhere. Halverson noticed this and found it odd as Ben was normally the talker.

'So Ben,' probed Halverson, 'it's not like you to be late for a briefing, did you forget?'

Ben continued to just look around as if trying to understand both question, and his confusing surroundings.

'What year is it?' Ben asked, in what appeared to be a very confused state of mind.

'What do mean what year? That's ridiculous and for you to ask that and if Marks has any inkling that you are not up to this mission, you will be grounded.'

'Halverson, I have done it, I have flown this mission I know what happens.'

'Ben, if you don't stop this, I will have you grounded myself.'

'I get shot down off the coast and, I, we don't make it, the crew is gone; I don't see Emily, she doesn't know me, it's, it's, I have seen…'

******

Ben and Halverson arrived outside Marks' office with Ben adversely continuing in his confused state, not helping Halverson make sense of the situation. Marks opened the door, finding Ben still frenzied and equivocal with both words and actions.

'What is all this nonsense you two? In my office, now!' Yelled Marks in a tone not known to Halverson, and clearly even Ben in his state, saw it as anything out of the ordinary.

'Ben, what the hell is going on? Explain yourself and why you were late for the briefing?' asked Marks in somewhat of a resolute tone.

'Sir, I have flown this mission, I know what is going to happen,' debated Ben.

'Why the sir, Ben, and what is this drivel you are going on with?' commanded Marks.

'Sir we don't make it to Peenemünde, it's a ruse sir; we are just flying it so the war office confuses the enemy so when they truly bomb it in six days sir, it is called Operation Hydra please we are an experiment by the Government.'

'In six days?' asked Marks.

'Yes sir, Operation Hydra is part of the overall offensive and in 6 days Operation Crossbow with 596 heavy bombers of the Royal Air force will bomb Peenemünde as part of the first raid sir, we are expendable, an experiment sir, I am expendable and I don't return.'

'How do you know this Ben?'

'Sir, I don't know, I mean you just have to believe me, I don't know what is going on and just a few minutes before I came to the briefing I was with Marshall in 1953.'

'Ben, stop just there, you are delusional, you're talking nonsense and 1953, are you mad and who in the hell is Marshall?'

'Marshall Hartley,' announced Ben with the utmost conviction, 'you know the civilian who was in the lab when I was being shown around the base.' I lose an engine and have to fly low over the channel back to England, and I don't return. The US Government is conducting an experiment south of the channel, in a warship at the same time and somehow because my aircraft flies —'

'Ben, stop this now, I am sending you off to medical for a check-up, you will not be flying if you don't pass,' bellowed Marks.

******

Ben awkwardly followed behind Marks as the two made their way to the hospital ward. A few beds were in use, but most of the ward's nurses were preparing for the possibility of causalities on the missions return home. Emily noticed Ben and Marks who were chatting in the furthermost empty bed in the ward, well away from staff. Marks had given Ben strict instructions on keeping to himself what he had just told him, and let Emily make an unbiased judgement and clear him for flight, Marks needed all personnel on this mission, and flight ready in a little under 12 hours. Marks stood on watch as Emily approached the duo. Marks looked at Emily and explained Ben just needed a quick once over as he may been overcome by the fumes and spilt oils at the rear of the hanger where he had dozed off. Emily without saying a word or presuming something was wrong, conducted Bens check-up, while Marks oversaw. Emily knew from her father's stance that it wasn't a good time to comment or ask what was going on. She was conscious of Ben who was by some means, and for good reason, in need of a physical. It was possibly needed from her interruption in the early hours of this morning that had caused his sudden outrage, he was perhaps developing anxiety or the onset of depression. Emily had overheard him with Marks, but being the good daughter had pretended not to notice. Marks looked at Emily and instructed her to let Ben rest for a few hours, and was in need of some of those drugs you give when someone is somewhat restless. Emily administered a mild paracetamol powder in warm water and Ben gulped it down instantly. His eyes looked through Emily as if she was not there, he seemed afraid to speak or tell her what he had just said to Marks, it was if he had no idea why he was even here.

Ben drifted off to sleep, his inaudible words confused Emily to the point that she either did not understand or was not recognising anything he was saying. He called out her name, and that of a Marshall Hartley, and in short sentences of broken English, he mentioned a coffin or a room with one in it, confusing her even more. It worried Emily and she didn't like to see him like this, so she focused on her other patients to divert her mind away from his confused state.

In the isolated part of the ward near Ben, was a civilian man. He was found few days ago at the base's entry point, wandering about, so had been arrested and placed under house care, whilst the bases security investigated his origin. He hadn't provided much information about himself, and initial investigations found, he needed previous physiatrist care, but what was more concerning was his interest in Ben. He refused to provide any more information about himself so Marks had him examined for cerebral observation by the base's doctors. He would be held and remain under guard surveillance at least until the conclusion of the Operation Night Owl.

August 12, 1943
Operation Night Owl, flight preparation 00:30 hrs:

Ben held his head under the shower's burning water just that little bit longer than needed. His face looked almost sullen, from the blistering heat, whilst continuing to lather his facial features with the last of his rationed soap stinging his eyes in the process. The room quickly filled with steam but soon disbursed from the drafts through the slight openings of the surrounding casement sash windows.

Bens last few hours back in 1953 were soon becoming a fading memory, whereby he was now convinced it was just a dream. Strangely, he still had the voice of Marshall vivid in his mind and his words of, 'August the 14th 1953.' Why? And what was the reason Marshall just happened to be there. Now Marks is even denying Marshall exists and why that was even happening, he had no explanation. Ben continued to dry off then started to dress in his flight gear. He started with bib-front trousers and bolero style jacket, just part of his F-3 heated uniform. Part of his kit was of course the A-3 parachute, F-2/3 gloves and booties all finished off with his B-8 goggles, and A-14 O2 [oxygen] mask. The yellow A-3 parachute harness seemed to hold it all together or so it looked, when they were dressed up in their flight gear. He lent forward to close the lid of his footlocker for what could be the last time and paused at the sight of his book, *Armageddon*. He picked the comic book up and briefly flicked through the pages, thinking back to when he was eight, doing the very same thing. His attention on the book was short lived when he noticed a small envelop fall out from between the pages and onto the floor. Ben picked it up and noticed it was rather old in its appearance. The back was still sealed and on the front was a handwritten note, it read:

Ben, I was given this letter when you were eight, I know nothing of its contents, nor of its provider.

Love as always, Charlie.

Ben didn't have time to open it then, and without thinking tucked it neatly into the pocket of his bib-front trousers.

The rain began to fall as the crew were ferried out to their individual waiting aircraft. Floodlights had been placed around the Tarmac by "The Mule", each light shining onto something important. Ladders were still up against engines, the last of the bombs and ammunition was being loaded as well as petroleum fuels. The last hour seemed to have taken no time to tick by. Ben and crew were just mulling about the main gear of their bomber as the 15-minute flare was fired. Red blooms sparkled and flickered about the night sky providing a kaleidoscope of colours amid the rain drizzle turning it dreamlike and unworldly. The crew's eyes were drawn up into the heavens perhaps to make peace with God or pray to a love one, as the flames and burning embers of the flare fell back down to earth promptly being smothered from the precipitation before hitting the ground.

No words were spoken from the crew as they turned and clambered themselves into the aircraft. One stood alone, looking about as if it were his last time they would see this place. A lone figure walked toward Ben from the behind the B-24's huge tail fins out from the open doors of Hanger 5. The figure, a man in his 40s ambled up to Ben, as if time had little or no importance. Ben wiped clear the driblets of rain from his eyes, blinked to focus at the man now standing before him.

'Hello Ben, are you ready for your flight?'

Ben hadn't responded, his voice was numbed, insensitive to the words he wanted to say, or ask when he noticed the rain had abruptly stopped. The night sky was now a pale purple colour almost amethyst, and the now visible stars were like the runway markers he would focus on during a night landing. As he looked about the tarmac, he could not make out any of rain puddles, in reality it appeared as if it hadn't rained in days. He had this very strange occurrence when he was eight at the school bus and recalled a bizarre man at the time, a man who now stood before him. That moment 13 years earlier, marked the start of some unusual events in his life and it was now becoming a little clearer. That man, this man, and the same man who had at the most arcane and unknowable of times in his showing, now stood before Ben.

'Hadn't you better get into your plane and fly this mission Ben?' implied Marshall, without any emotion or sentiment in his voice.

Ben went to speak and respond with all his years of searching for answers. Nothing would come out, his voice still silent and numbed. ·

'Well, get on board and fly…oh don't forget to read the letter,' whispered Marshall.

Bens, mind drifted back to the day when the strange man, this man came to his mother's house. He recalled all the bizarre events of that day, the two men who arrived in the police car, then that of Marshall Hartley. Marshall turned and headed back toward the rear of the aircraft, Ben as if in sync with Marshall headed toward the underbelly hatch of his Liberator. He hadn't realised that the rain was once again falling, and the night sky was no longer a pale purple colour, and completely indistinguishable to that of the ground. It was ominous, it was wintry, it would by definition place any experienced pilot into total control of his situation and that of his flight conditions. The underbelly hatch was latched and Ben climbed up to the flight deck of his B-24, J Two Five...

******

The squadron of the 451st, taxied away from Hanger 5. The searchlights were dimmed, allowing the pilots own night vision to adjust to the diffused lighting of the red glow of instrumentation inside each cockpit. The tires of each 24 looked almost flat under the sheer weight they had to carry. Wing flaps were at 10 degrees and cowl flaps opened one quarter for take-off. The ground crew were silent as they watched the 25 aircraft taxi toward the runway threshold. Marks held on to Emily trying to comfort her and tell her not to worry and that they would all return, as would Ben.

Marks called out to Halverson, 'Note the time, at 01:58, let's head back to flight operations and watch over our boys as they cross the channel.'

Marks turned and observed the last navigation light of the squadrons final aircraft disappear into the murky night cloud and precipitation. The roar of the 1,200hp engines soon diminished as each plane was swallowed up in the low-level cloud, then there was silence. The ground crew turned and headed back to the base, with little or no words spoken.

******

English Channel, Isle of Wight, August 12, 1943 03:56 hrs:

The south-westerly movement of the channel waters had swung the USS Trilogy with its bow facing in the direction she would be heading, due east. All the crew as well as its commander were station ready. They had been given instructions to be anchor up and underway at 04:00 hrs. They were to start their slow run from the eastern side of the Isle of Wight just south of Portsmouth and head due east past the tip of Selsey to Eastbourne hugging the coast of Birling Gap, then up through to the Strait of Dover and into the North Sea. Once they were abeam Calais and Dover, they were to start the experiment. It was to be part of Operation Hydra due to start in six days, and overall part of the entire offensive know as Operation Crossbow. All that the crew had ever been told was it was supposed to render them invisible to the enemy. The ship had left New Jersey around three weeks ago, where it was fitted out with the specialised equipment manufactured in Philadelphia. An experiment founded there by scientists who were hoping the metallic steel hull in this instance would or could be invisible to the enemy. They claimed to the war department that if a series of opposing in rotation electric motors were placed at exact intervals about a metal object, that object could be in simple terms almost become demagnetised. This simply meant the ships reflection to radar would in fact not be bounced back, it was as if the ship then was invisible.

This divergence in the voltage of each motor had an effect on the molecular structure of steel or any material with its base compound as a metal for that matter. It at experiment stage, monetarily demagnetised the steel; they had to prove this, so each piece of steel was set in a cylindrical manner and had small magnets attached to each of them. The experiment ran for 60 to 70 seconds at which time all 25 magnets attached to the five equal in weight pieces of steel, simply fell on the ground. At the same time, a small portable radar unit in the room lost the green blip of the five individual steel components, including the magnets. It was a success in the eyes of the war department. It was to be fast-tracked and fitted into the hull bilge of a chosen ship at specific intervals and equally spaced. The USS Trilogy was chosen and modified during its build to suite the motors, and she needed to be ready by August of '43. The war was ramping up and the allies needed an edge, they [war department] were hoping this was it. The Germans had technologies too, and this [USS Trilogy] was to be the Allies' answer and end the war.

The Trilogy was almost 700 feet in length, she boasted a beam of just under 82 feet. Her 25,200 tons was pushed through the water at an incredible speed of 32 knots from her four Parsons geared steam turbine engines. 2,209 officers and men were strangely still protected with 60lb decks and four-inch thick bulkheads. Her armament ranged from 38 to 75mm calibre guns, Bofors guns and 20mm Oerlikon cannons, all seemingly strange if the ship was supposed to be invisible, the war department saw it as a "contingency".

The Trilogy's turbines were at 39% as she headed in her east direction toward Selsey, the crew could just make out the lights of Portsmouth as they slowly disappeared in the foggy rain that fell.

August 12, 1943 Operation Night Owl, 04:00 hrs:

There was not a lot of conversation on the flight deck, nor were the crew listening to local wireless stations over the in-flight radios. The squadron had been flying for just on two hours and had flown through some thick cumulus cloud with heavy precipitation. Ben and the Cap concentrated on tracking out on the NDB [non-directional beacon] then onto dead reckoning which was up to Wilson for the next point of their track. They remained in cloud for around 35 to 40 minutes and now were on top at just over 25,000 feet. The odd cumulonimbus cloud would still tower over them possibly reaching 40,000 feet in places.

The stars had illuminated the skies above the cloud, and the squadron had a peaceful noneventful flight so far. The smooth flight conditions allowed for some relaxation and a well-deserved flask of hot tomato soup. Emily had packed some cooked chicken pieces, which they put between some crusty stale bread, left over from lunch. The tomato soup was still hot in the thermos and the mug in which they drunk out of helped keep their hands warm in the cool conditions. Small amounts of frost from their breath could still be seen even though it was actually slightly warming in the cabin.

They had almost flown the entire mission up to the PNR [point of no return], above the cloud tops, made up of varying types of clouds. The north-easterly direction took them out over the North Sea and toward Esbjerg; Wilson had managed a position fix 20 minutes out, he called it in to Ben.

'Ben, I managed a few fixes from Amsterdam and Bremen, so I'm happy for you to fly this track for another six minutes at this speed, then turn right onto a track of 115 degrees that's one one five, and that should take us directly somewhere toward Peenemünde. I can get a fix off Demark and keep us clear through the Femer Belt, over the water.'

'Will do,' announced Ben.

Sir, Micky here, I have just received a cryptogram from base, telling us to avoid Peenemünde, and head down to Hamburg; there have been heavy casualties in Poland, and we have received word they are aware we are coming.'

Marks had word from the war office that there was also some bombing taking place about Poland, which was a manoeuvre to take focus off Operation Night Owl.

'Micky, what are they saying about the bombs? Are we dropping them, what are we doing?' asked Ben.

The silence within the cabin was soon broken and explosions of the surrounding flak could both be heard and felt.

'Squadron leader to all aircraft: Set climb power and let's get above this,' ordered Ben.

'Micky here again, Ben, just heard from base we are to drop them on Denmark, sir, all 25 aircraft.'

'Denmark, denounced Ben, Operation Gomorrah was finished why again Denmark', he questioned

The flak increased as the B-24s climbed. The Pratt and Whitney engines noisily complaining as the oversized radial engines fought hard to increase the aircraft's height to a safer altitude. At just over 30,000 feet, the air cooled considerably but a small price to pay as the flak could no longer reach them. It was short lived though, as over the radio came…

'Enemy at our six o'clock, looks like ME109s sir,' announced Roger, from his restricted habitat in the tail gun.

'Sir the bombs are armed!' yelled Murph as he prepared to enter his aberrant environment of the ball turret. Sparky, who after locking the turret hatch, raced back to his port waste gun.

The gunfire started, and the formation of bombers shook and vibrated. They could not outrun the 109, their best defence was to stay in formation and attempt to outgun their opponent.

Sperry's voice was heard over the radio, 'Bombs good to go sir, let's drop them, that's Denmark below.'

The bomb doors of the 24s opened simultaneously as all ten 500-pound bombs from each aircraft fell towards Denmark. Their screaming sound would soon be heard from the ground and the full force of the 250 bombs would be felt as retribution for Germany's attacks on England. The aircraft would each experience the instance loss of the 5,000-pound weight through the control column, forcing Ben and his fellow captains to momentarily push forward on the controls, stopping the pitch-up moment of the bombers.

20mm bullets fired from the nose cannons of the 109 piercing the hull of the Liberators, ripping holes in the bellies of the bombers, destroying the strengthening ribs of the structure in their wake. Fragments of shell, aluminium and wiring were flying about the cabin in any direction. The shrapnel piercing the body parts of the crew, and the blood-stained floors and clothing of the men, now a distinctive consequence of war. The 109s Daimler-Benz, liquid-cooled V-12 engines shrieked, and squealed, the sound pierced and resonated about the cabins of each bomber. The 109s fired their cannons relentlessly as one would fly past onto its next victim, another came in for the kill.

Reaching the coastline just south of Esbjerg, the 109s suddenly turned, heading back to toward Hamburg, without a single kill.

'RADIO CHECK RADIO CHECK!' yelled Ben, 'Do a count, on causalities and ammo, we have a way to go and we are not out of trouble yet,' he instructed.

The squadron headed directly towards Norwich, hoping they had seen the last of the 109s. Each captain had checked and radioed in their causalities, damage and ammunition count. Considering the attack lasted eight minutes, the damage to the aircraft was minimal, with only seven causalities, all able to continue with their responsibilities. Ben's aircraft suffered the most damage being the plane out front, and singled out by one of the 109s. He had noticed slightly low oil pressure in the starboard inner engine. A small contrail of smoke was trailing from the exhaust outlet, and partial flame could be seen, possibly from the oils igniting against the blistering heat of the exhaust.

'What do you say Cap? We wait till we see the coast before we shut it down,' suggested Ben.

The Cap agreed, and instructed Wilson to give him a time count.

'We should be 20 miles out very soon sir, so that by my count, at 08:50 or close to it.'

Ben decided to put over an announcement giving the squadron Wilson's latest estimate on time.

'This is Squadron Leader, we appear to have seen the worst of it, and we should be seeing the coast very soon. I am nursing home on three good engines, so we may drop back very soon. All aircraft are to continue at cruise speed, and I… we will all see you back at the bar for a drink – Ben out.'

The coast of England was almost now visible. Still at slow decent, they approached 25,000 feet and passed through it at rate of around 100 feet per minute. Thinking home and safety was less than 30 minutes away they suddenly became aware of a recognisable whirr sound. Over the nose of Ben's plane and turning sharply to the left was the familiar underbelly of the ME109. The squadron went to evasive action as the plane turned and headed back straight at Ben's bomber. Its nose 20mm cannon and two wings mounted 13mm machine guns spat bullets straight at the cockpit of the Liberator. The widescreen glass cracking instantly and a large section of fuselage showed signs of a split in the hull. The 109s starboard wing gun was in a direct line of sight to Ben's one crippled engine, the 13mm bullets hitting directly at the engine cowl. The cracked section of fuselage suddenly ripped off the starboard side of the cockpit pulling its occupant, and that of the Cap with it. He was instantly sucked from the aircraft and drawn into the spinning blades of the inner engine. It burst into flame, the propeller slowed instantly. Ben quickly feathered the prop blades as the 109 turned rapidly to avoid hitting the bomber behind Ben. The squadron fought back, at the lone 109; all planes directing their firepower onto it. The 109 reticently turned and again evaded a hit from the opposing fire of bullets. Chips had followed the rouge pilots relentless attack from his top turret position, spinning his gun sight almost a full turn. He figured he didn't have a good line of sight, but shot anyway at the 109. Then the German pilot gently rested his finger on the gun trigger as he lined up the cockpit and its unsuspecting pilot that of Ben for the very last time. His finger depressed the trigger without thought, just as Chips had pressed his, the 109s cockpit glass was instantly shattered forcing the aircraft to bank sharply. The explosion took the 109 directly into the outer wing edge of Ben's Liberator tearing off a small tip and partially jamming the aileron. Ben fought relentlessly at his controls, trying to keep it the Liberator straight and level. The 109 fell towards the sea and out of sight, Ben and the squadron somehow regained their formation protocol.

'RADIO CHECK, RADIO CHECK, give it to me!' Ben yelled without any formality or to regulation.

Each pilot came back in turn with a total head count of two dead which included the Cap. 16 in total injured severely and may not survive, and with a flight time of less than 30 minutes, things were not good.

'Squadron Leader here, I am worse off than I thought,' and as he spoke, his plane fell out of formation descending at rate of 300 feet per minute, causing him to pull even harder back on the controls.

Ben gave his last radio message before falling out of range to the remaining aircraft.

'I will descend low as I try to tidy this plane up. Our track has been pushed further south from our attack and we are only around 15 or so miles to Dover so first beer is on me, Ben out.'

'Wilson, log the time at zero eight five five,' instructed Ben.

******

Liberator J-Two Five, under the hands of its skilled pilot made its journey towards England. The rigid movement of the aileron meant Ben would be flying a partial left turn. He corrected this with his one good engine and rudder control for straight-line direction. He still had pitch control without the rate of climb which was to be expected. Sperry had made his way up to the cockpit helping with throttle for pitch movements. Ben just flew his course keeping his control as best he could.

'Well, it's now or never Sperry, let's turn towards base, see anything that looks like you might know where we are.'

Sperry looked up and could see the formation of bombers, which he figured, was the squadron, at their 2 o'clock and around 3,000 feet above them. Ben radioed in:

'Squadron Leader radio check.'

A crackle came over Ben's radio, and he could just make out...

'...Ben...Harper...here...descending...to...can...base 12 miles...passing through 6000...'

'Well Sperry, let's try a turn,' pleaded Ben.

Sperry increased throttle on the good port engine and decreased starboard. Ben applied a little right rudder and as much pitch as he thought. The bomber started its slow right turn but still descended through one thousand eight hundred feet at 50 feet per minute rate of descent. The plane kept descending and the White Cliffs of Dover were now a welcome sight. They put their position somewhere between Calais and the point of Margate.

A lone Mark 2 Spitfire, on a surveillance run flew over a warship, which its pilot had seen in the distance. It circled and turned about the cruiser flying low at times, then would pitch up and perform a barrel roll over the bow of the vessel. Ben's flight path would take him directly over the warship just before reaching the coast of Dover, and safely back onto home soil.

******

The USS Trilogy had now sped up to 12 knots and was approaching the point at which the experiment would take place. The chief engineer was ready to fire up the series of motors in sequence of order. They were to be odd first, then evens at that set and precise sequence, all 12 electric motors would take less than 70 seconds to be at full revolution speed being 12,000 revolutions per minute.

The odd motors starting at 'one' began their clockwise rotation, the motion began sluggish at first as if constrained. The torque of the motor whirred and shrieked as the armatures rotated past the stators. The copper windings about the odd motors conducted the flow of electricity in a "positive" charge, negative coming from the even numbers. The firing series was timed exactly as one motor reached 1,000 rpm the second would start. The motors could be heard through the engine room, and as number three, then five started the sound of the massive steam turbines driving the Trilogy were barely audible. The even numbered electric motors now turned counter clockwise as the time approached 09:00, at a point where the ship was almost abeam Calais. From within the ship's bilges', a trembling could be felt through the thick steel hull, it was as if the Intrepid had thumped against enormous seas peaking and shuttering over the mountainous waves. The ship's "bleep" was being tracked from a radar unit near Norwich, England, and the commander of the Trilogy called the base.

'This is USS Trilogy, USS Trilogy, Operation Crossbow experimental water craft is in position, at my mark do the count we are good to go in 5…4…3…'

The countdown could be head at the base and Marks and Halverson were watching the green screen and the clockwise rotation of the sweep arm about the face of the radar. At each turn, a mass of white was showing his bombers on their return, and the ships image over the Strait of Dover could also be seen. Marks looked at the clock and noted the time at 08:59.

The crew of the Trilogy tried to adjust their understanding of the differing sounds that could now be heard about the ship. The vibration was still felt but seemed to be less intensive.

'…2…1…initiate.'

The final sequence of the experiment had stated, at precisely 09:00, on August the 12, 1943. It was to be for a maximum of 70 seconds, and the chief aboard the Trilogy did the count, '10, 11, 12…' being heard over the intercom speakers at the base.

Marks and Halverson were witnessing something strange, the shadow of the ship for all intensive purpose was no longer on the screen.

'39, 40, 41…'

…yet the count was still being heard. Marks put a call though to the ship, there was no answer, however the voice over the intercom was still there

'59, 60…'

Marks looked again at his screen to ensure it was still operating. He could see a white mass heading toward the base, as Halverson went to contact Ben. He had return communication from one the squadron's bombers telling him Ben's plane was crippled and out of formation, he had sustained some damage but still flying. Emily had heard this and held onto to her father's hand as she listened to the call. Ben's squadron were just 17 or so minutes from landing and had descended through one thousand five hundred feet then levelled out. The field was ahead and just visible, where they would fly over at 600 feet turn left onto a base leg and short final to land. Halverson again contacted the squadron, they advised Ben was out over the Strait of Dover heading toward the cliffs. Over the radio came the final count…

'69, 70 cut power the motors.'

The engineer hit the stop button, cutting the electricity flow to the copper windings instantly, the humming sound became less audible, the engines then began slowing. The motors again became sluggish and reduced in rotation speed, and they seemed to decelerate more rapidly than they had begun, then simply stopped.

Marks and Halverson heard the count, Halverson again tried to call the USS Trilogy:

'USS Trilogy, this is Buckenham base, advise on your status of Operation Crossbow.'

'… shsssssssssssssssssssssss,' came over the radio.

'USS Trilogy, USS Trilogy this is Buckenham base, I say again this is Buckenham base, advise on your status of Operation Crossbow, is Crossbow now completely ceased. I say again have you completed, is Operation Crossbow finished?'

Halverson continued to call the ship for a further 11 minutes with no response. The noise of the bombers could be heard approaching the field, and all personnel hurried outside carrying field glasses.

'The count please Halverson, if you will,' demanded Marks.

'9, 10, 11…18, 19 and that's 20 that's two zero,' finished Halverson.

Some stragglers could be seen approaching low over the fields. Their engines smoking and grinding with loss of oil pressures, the farmers below looking up as they flew over praying for their safe return.

'21, 22 and 23,' continued Halverson.

Emily and Marks both scanning the skies for the last 2 bombers, Ben's and that of Harper's. It was now almost 17 minutes since the experiment had started, and all 23 Bombers had arrived safely back at the field. Ben's and Harper's planes were possibly crippled and had probably landed at an alternative aerodrome suggested Marks, to ease the burden on Emily's concerns. A radio operator ran out of flight operations and down to Marks. He had the news that they were again in contact with the Trilogy.

The last of the bombers had taxied up to the hard stand, and chocks were placed under the wheels. Ground crew were putting out smouldering plane parts, and nursing staff were seeing to the injured placing them in stretchers. Number 24, was seen arriving low, and slow out towards St Peter, Emily was instructed from her father to head out toward the tarmac with some medical staff and a few ground crew and prepare for the worse, Marks knew this would take her mind off Ben in the short term.

Marks had arrived back at fight operations and called the Trilogy.

'USS Trilogy, this is Buckenham base, we lost you for a bit. Is all OK?' announced Marks.

'Marks, is that you, its Thomas here, how are things out there?'

'Goooood Thomas, I need to find one of my planes, did you happen to see it, pass by?'

'Yes, sure did,' responded Thomas in a less formal tone than usual, 'One flew over top of us at around "O" nine hundred, he should be with you in around 20, he was flying a little slow but nonetheless still up there, is all good there, how is Emily?'

'You say arrive at 09:20 we haven't seen him yet, we are still missing one, and all others are accounted for. Oh and she's good, a bit anxious but good. Thomas, you did say 20 past the hour, that's well past that time now.' Marks looked at the timer on the wall and it showed 09:27, just to ensure he was seeing it correctly.

'Marks your clock is a bit out old son; I have us at 09:04 we finished just a few minutes ago.'

'I don't know what's happened then, anyway thanks for your help, I'll send out a surveillance aircraft to look for him – Marks out.' That would be the last time Marks and Thomas would ever speak.

The Trilogy continued its voyage out through the strait and into the North Sea. Not known to the captain that day nor to Marks was that the ship's clock had one way or another, lost around 17 minutes, being a direct effect of the experiment. Unbeknown to the scientists the testing somehow immobilised the boat into an indeterminate state for the duration of the research. At exactly 09:19 the overhead B-24's from Ben's squadron arrived safely back at the base, this being at the precise and detailed moment the experiment had finished. The countdown aboard the Trilogy lasted its predetermined 70 seconds, at which time Ben's aircraft had flown thorough the magnetic field.

The Trilogy remained out of contact for the duration of this time, that time and to this day has never been resolved, nor has the ships whereabouts ever been discovered. She sailed out past the Strait of Dover and was never seen of or located again. The war department had lost contact shortly after Marks and Thomas had their final words. They had determined at the end of the war that the Trilogy was either sunk or captured, all her crew was neither found nor heard of again. To this day, it has been denied that the ship ever even existed, and all 2,209 officers and men on board were never given a post war funeral, nor their families any reasonable explanation of the loss of their loved ones. It was to be determined by those in power at the time that the USS Trilogy experiment never even occurred.

Marks had ordered a surveillance aircraft to head out over the Cliffs of Dover and look for Ben and his crews' missing bomber. He was now one-hour overdue, and Marks and Halverson made contact with all other bases in the area and even called homeland security personnel and local farms to ask if anyone had seen the missing aircraft fly over. Marks would have to let Emily know the news that Ben's aircraft was to pronounced MIA and assumed it had gone down somewhere in the Strait of Dover. A MK2 Spitfire had flown over the coast for over two hours, at the same last known position fix to that of the USS Trilogy.

******

Emily had had the need to set up an improvised operating theatre in one of the 24s that had landed off the runway due to brake failure from its low hydraulic oil pressure. The belly turret had jammed during the air battle with the 109 causing its operator to be entombed facing instant death on landing. The bomber's pilot struggled at the control column holding the aircraft in flight for as long as possible in ground effect, until its sheer weight caused the port main gear to collapse, crushing the turret into the ground as the aircraft came to a stop. Ground debris and fragments of the plane's body panels had pierced the belly turret, its operator had suffered extensive injuries in the process. Ground crew had the need to remain at the aircraft putting out spot fires during the doctor's efforts to safe him. A small section of smouldering engine cylinder not extinguished continued to intensify in heat throughout the medical staff's determinations to free him from the tangled wreckage. Fuel lines and oils still exposed to the heat generated from the engines, slowly built up in temperature.

Nearing flash point, the officer from the turret was finally freed and placed on a waiting stretcher. Emily held onto the saline drip as he was carried away from the wreckage. Marks had looked up from flight operations in time to see him pulled from the wreckage and watch medical staff carry him off to safety. A final drip of oil hit the now cooling cylinder head but the smouldering mass turned to flame. Emily had her back to the aircraft, as the oil ignited and erupted in fire, causing a mild detonation. Marks, who was occupied in talks with homeland security at the time, had noticed the flash, and tried desperately to yell out for them to take cover. The burning oil tracked back to a fuel line, the vapours from the ruptured pipe quickly ignited. Marks dropped the radio phone and stood helplessly as the entire port fuel tank shattered, sending burning fuels, aluminium fragments and burning oils in all directions. The ground crew and hospital doctors, had managed to see the build-up of smoke instantly recognising its pending rupture and immediately prepared for the detonation.

 As the smoke cleared, it was noticed a section on wing flap lay on top of one of the nurses. A metal hinge gusset off the flap had pierced her body and her white uniform was now red and blood covered. She lay still, her unmoving, limp body was twisted and broken, she lay lifeless as doctors tried to free her from the wreckage. Her head had signs of trauma, possible from a blunt hit, and her face had been pushed into the mud breaking her cheekbone. Marks had arrived at the scene and observed a nurse's lifeless body, lying amongst the wreckage being turned over and placed onto a stretcher. Had it not been for the lilac flower she always wore as her lapel pin, she was totally unrecognisable. Marks supported her motionless body as his daughter was carried away.

Chapter 6

Norwich England, August 16, 1953, that afternoon:
Emily arrived home from having been to Earlham Road Cemetery, considerably now more confused than she was a few days ago. She had met a young man who had told specifics of a war and that of the covert base at Buckenham. The base was not supposed to have even existed, and the detail in which the young man told of it, he would have had to actually been there to know this. She had now witnessed a gravestone with the young man's name and crew of 451st J Two Five. She had found an old photo of the B-24's crew and him standing there with them, and he ostensibly was identical to the one she had just met in the park. Who was he, and why now, almost 10 years after the photo was taken and that of the war, did he just happen upon her in a park? She nestled back into her brown Cognac Leather Chesterfield Sofa, with a freshly made cup of English breakfast tea. She looked at the china cup, a waft of steam gently rose from around its rim, and although it had a wedge of lemon in it, its aroma was non-existent. It was as confusing as who the young man was, and she hadn't any craving to even drink it. Her father had an identical sofa to hers and she could never really remember how she came across this one. She, with her meeting of the young man Ben, even tried to contemplate from the war to now, and how fast that time seemed to go by. She had difficulty even understanding her time after the war, it was as if it was just a waning recollection of past times. A memory of what she then thought, she couldn't quite ruminate on something, anything, from then to now, in fact the more she tried, the stranger the thought of it became. What was happening to her? Was it because of this she didn't know the young man and perhaps she was the one, who, for some unfamiliar reason, had misplaced this memory? Was it because of the cold and heartless times of war, or had something happened then that she could no longer recall now?

She focussed in on the battle; cast her mind back, just to see if she had that ability to reminisce and evoke on any memory wondrous or hurtful. She needed to know if it was her to blame for this confusion that she now disputed on herself, or his ability to convince he was someone he was not. The sofa providing a more relaxed atmosphere than she expected, she, unpredictably, felt she needed a well deserving nap.

Emily reached over to her china cup, thinking she may get a hit of the aroma of the lemon and tea, and as the liquid swirled about the cup, she once again didn't have the desire to drink; then simply placed it back onto the small teak desk next to the lounge. She laid back on the sofa, a lilac pillow she used as a headrest didn't quite match the colour of the settee, but something about its shade made it just impossible to throw away. Emily relaxed, closed her eyes, and took her mind back to then. She just wanted some lucidity into the past few days, providing logic to who and why this young man was now in her life. She rested, head settling into her purple pillow, her hands clasped together as the light levels outside, darkened. The room intensified in silence and the darkening night mixed with the room's cerulean light, becoming almost obscure and opaque. The blackening night sky was being slowly overwritten by an innumerable amount of more pleasant tints of dark blues and mauves. Emily, with her mind now rested from her past few days, relaxed her awareness to recollections more vivid. Would it be something she could, without any doubt, build an image of in her mind, and that of a war to which she felt she had now had no memory of. To Ben, this young man, his memory, was something to him that was real, to her; it was if he had never existed.

August 12, 1943 – 1 day after Operation Night owl:

Marks, like all personnel on the base during the past 24 or so hours, had little or no sleep; whereas, Halverson and the ground crew had a responsibility to ready the base for the next mission. They could not dwell over the past operation, nor could they mourn, this was war and they had to focus. The war department had contacted Marks to tell him of another pending operation due to happen on the night of 17/18th of August. He was unaware of the detailing but all he knew was he and his remaining squadron would be involved with it. Marks wondered if Ben with his assumed confusion was telling the truth about Operation Hydra but now, he just needed to be who he was and how he needed to be seen by the base, and that was to lead.

Marks couldn't fathom the loss of any of the individuals but he had to endure it. He also tried not to let this element alone be an encumbrance on his duty and obligation as Commander and Chief. 23 from 25 aircraft were still operational, and although there were heavy losses on both sides, his 451st had suffered personally to him. He had become a father figure to practically all of his staff, from flight crew to nurses to cooks. Marks never segregated them into rank, too him one man was just as important as the next. The one thing that was abundantly puzzling was Ben and the crew's complete disappearance. It now started to play on his mind at the possibility of capture by the enemy and perhaps one sole person on board was in fact a spy, and under duress diverted back to Germany.

The runway was still evident of war, debris and plane parts still scattered over taxiways, and landing aprons, with ground operations busily running around like eusocial insects, highly organised and uniting, with team like abilities. Marks once again focused on his immediate assignment and although his loss in the past 24 hours was unfathomable, he needed to get this base on the ready for the next mission. He had by all accounts sent out a recognisance pilot; in search for the missing bomber to its last known point that was off the coast of Dover. The MK2 Spitfire had been back to the base twice to refuel, giving Marks the news each time there were no signs of oil spills or wreckage, it was as if J25 had never existed.

Marks sat by his daughter in the recovery ward, her extensive injuries were not severe enough that it would give her any long-term disability and she would only suffer the hurt, that being the loss to that of Ben, now pronounced MIA, and for all accounts, deceased.

******

Ben woke, and after focusing, he repudiated to accept his surroundings. Had it not been for his fight gear, he may even had not recognised who he was. He looked around at the unimportant things that made some sense, one being his A-14 O2 mask limply dangling about his neck. The moulded face cover had coagulating blood over the mouthpiece, promptly doubting what injuries he may have had when he didn't understand any pain. A smoke haze from damaged flight instruments soon took away his concentration in trying to understand his situation, allowing him now to focus on the silence that filled the flight deck. There was no moaning or cries of pain to which Ben would have assumed would be evident as he slowly made more sense of his situation. It was now apparent his Liberator was motionless.

Its twisted and bent frame and cracked cockpit windshield glass obscured his outer surroundings, had meant he had somehow reached land, and Ben could only assume from his last memory, back on English soil. He could not recall his last moments apart from the encounter of the USS Trilogy, which he then supposed was just moments ago. He was still fastened into his seat, but on an angle and looking out his port side window. The main wing of the B-24 had separated from the fuselage, leaning out flat over the ground. He guessed the wing spar had sheared off as the main hull tilted to port, yet the wing looked level. He unfastened his buckle and forced his way out through an opening in the hull and onto the ground. The ground appeared solid as if on he was on a road, yet grasses were apparent as if in a field and most noticeable was what appeared to be spear thistle, a wild prickly weed known to grow almost anywhere in England. The more he focused, the more his surroundings became familiar, yet vastly different to any of his past memory. What was strange though, was that there was no noise or sound, yet his surroundings looked very much like something he knew, and that was it did look like the base.

He continued to look about restoring things together with resolution into being something he now accepted as familiar. He wasn't focussing on anything, nor was he understating what was happening as he assessed his body for signs of trauma, any blood or pain. Apart from the mouthpiece of his oxygen mask all bloody, he felt fine. Did he crash? He just could not focus on truly anything nor did his mind ask if there were any survivors? *Was this not strange?* he thought as he just seemed to want to focus on where he was more than his crew.

He again looked about, slowly putting into perspective what he confirmed was the Buckenham field. How he concluded this was something he could not work out just like the need not to look for any survivors. It soon became apparent the entire area was noiseless, it was familiar to something he knew, yet unnatural and dreamlike. He unremittingly had no need to or desire to be anywhere, was it the shock of having just crashed, or did his mind simply disavow the facts? Perhaps this was one's body and minds process into deceitfully masking the superficial trauma he must have and being just part of the healing process. He didn't truthfully know this as he had never encountered it before. He had seen death, he had been involved in the killing of innocent lives, so why was this so different?

Ben momentarily stopped at some familiar looking markings, the ones a pilot would use that were painted on the runway to know the direction on which he would land after having identified a wind direction.

During flight training, a pilot would do countless take offs and landings, getting the perspective of an approach threshold and apron. This was needed to judge speed, approach angle, distance to touch down, but most importantly, wind direction. The tower would either verify a runway in use or a pilot would look at the windsock to determine wind direction and assumed speed. The sock would either be stretched outright like a pointing finger or hanging limp and oppressed as would the head of child when in trouble. At Ben's feet, he could make out a white painted marking of the runway direction, a two and very much faded almost hoary bleached greying coloured five.

Looking back at the twisted shape of his Liberator, he could see it lined up with him and to the runway numerals; although the numbers were fading, he had to believe he was in fact at the base. But why were there no other aircraft or personnel, or emergency vehicles in attendance.

He remembered back to his first encounter of the airfield and how the surrounding vegetation made it look as if had been simply placed there. He recalled his first impression of the base and that was one could easily have missed it had they not known it was even there. Now that impression was just that much more real, the runway was almost unrecognisable, the hangers were no longer there, and out-buildings were seemingly different. Their appearance still very much comparable to what he recalled, but paints were faded, iron roof sheeting corroding and mossy, to the now much taller height of the surrounding silver birch trees.

He walked amongst the buildings not knowing why and seemed to just stroll somewhat peacefully without determined direction or thought. Where was everyone, Marks, Halverson, where was Emily? She crossed his mind and instantly he felt drained, sensitive to her whereabouts yet seemed to equally remain phlegmatic. Was this a feeling or emotion of shock having been the only survivor of his bomber's twisted and fiery wreckage? He strolled to where he had now pieced together the whereabouts of the main facilities entrance, how he determined this he would never recall and his only satisfaction in doing so was the fact it was not there. He looked about, up at the sun then out to fencing now taking the place of Hanger 5, and the red poll cows consuming the lavish grasses. The grasses were as if man made and nurtured and green, almost emerald, nothing like the remote areas he remembered when he first walked these pastures. Something within told him it was still doubtful he was at the base yet the runway direction markings of "two five" was evident it was Buckenham, and it was in fact runway two five zero.

Was he at a similar base not known to him, and the more he tried to evaluate his surroundings, the more it really didn't seem to be the most important thing on his mind. Amongst the plane wreckage and twisted parts, Ben could only think of Emily. He must go back to the aircraft and look for survivors and perhaps the emergency crew would now be there.

He turned away from where the fence now took the place of Hanger 5 and headed back to the aircraft. He felt completed to what he had just done and it was now time to dispose of his oxygen mask. As he reached for it, it was no longer there and he could never remember even taking if off. Was he in shock of his ordeal and all he could come up with was total serenity and his entire wellbeing felt composed. As he headed back to the aircraft, he didn't really understand why or even what he was doing. He stopped at the runway markings this time of 'zero seven' then simply looked around without reason. He thought it rather strange why he was even doing this and when he noticed the Liberator was no longer there and had seemingly been replaced with farm machinery and workmen busily occupied and loading up carts and baskets of produce, it oddly didn't discourage him.

He walked amongst them not even understanding why and attempted to find the words to ask them how they got there, but nothing entered his thoughts on how to word it. As he walked further on, he became aware they were more interested in doing their tasks than even acknowledging him. He walked not knowing how long, nor direction and without knowing it the base was now far behind him and if he had turned, it would certainly be out of view.

He had strolled beyond the perimeter of runway zero seven and through the village of Black Carr, and then towards the village of Spooner Row. He could see the parish of Morley St Peter ahead and was somehow being drawn there, as if it were a lure and he was the unsuspecting limbless cold-blooded finned vertebrate ready to strike its prey. He abruptly stopped, without any reason or known motive, then looked around one more time watching the people and wondering what was actually happening. His focus was now on a singular building, one that made sense from his past-confused state. He felt somewhat relieved he had actually achieved something, then quickened his walking pace toward the structure. The familiar sight ahead allowed him to unwind both his mind and waning agitated state, now becoming strangely tranquil. He slowed his accelerated walking pace, then stood for a moment, and as he turned and looked up at the setting sun, his body told him to rest here. Ben lowered his head and silently sat back into a contoured oak timber bench seat. He felt instantly comfortable as if it were carefully carved to fit his entire body exactly and as he nestled into it, he serenely looked back towards the building structure that had eased him into this tranquillity, it was the 16th century manor, that of Old Morley Hall.

******

    Emily didn't have any account of how long she may have slept for. She did feel to some degree rested, so that was a good thing. Her days up to now were cluttered with different thoughts of confusion so she concluded she couldn't change anything and surprisingly she didn't feel the need to. It would now be up to her to perhaps conclude a pervious thought and that was to help the young man of his apparent ordeal. She would source him out, befriend him and let him believe who he said he was, then find out why she had no recollection of him or from a time at the base. She thought to herself today was a new day, perhaps a new beginning and so would return to the only place she knew she would possibly find him, and that was at Old Morley Hall.

    Much of the past few days still haunted her, especially when he had so much knowledge of the base and described her as if they had previously met. If this was actually true and she did know him, and had since lost her recollection of him and after the war, then what was the reason? They were certainly two lost souls, he rebuffed to believe she didn't know him, and she denied in believing she did. Emily closed the door behind her and headed out in search of this young man, that of Benjamin Walters.

******

August 12, 1943-21:00 hrs:

    'General Marks, sir you have a call from the war office,' came a voice over the base's intercom. Marks left the mess hall and headed towards the radio room, clutching a stale bread roll. He had a liking for grandma's old-fashioned gravy, which he discreetly dipped the bread into the gastronome tray of the brown slurry as he left. He sponged almost the entire length of the crusty dough into the thick dark onion flavouring; the copious blob provided him a recollection of his wife's own version that gave him a sense of relief from this horrid war. He strolled across the black and white linoleum floor chomping the roll which left more about his face than he actually ate. He, to a passer-by, would have been tarnished as a child, likened perhaps as using his mother's spatula getting every bit of chocolate cake mix out of a bowl, ending with more of his face than in his mouth.

    His walk to flight operations seemed to take forever, thinking perhaps it was a call that Ben's missing bomber had been located, wondering why he wasn't rushing any faster…Marks then slowed his pace and almost came to a complete stop, thinking this news would be something he didn't want to hear; yet something he did need to know. The more he thought about it, the more he tried to blank it out the past 24 hours.

    Marks reached flight operations in time to see Halverson eat the last piece of his crusty roll, it too dipped in grandma's old-fashioned gravy.

    'Great minds,' implied Halverson as he handed the khaki coloured telephone hand piece to Marks.

He placed it next to his ear, and then turned the handle, its usual four or five times in a clockwise rotation. A crackly sound came through the mouthpiece, and a faint but clear voice then came through the ear speaker.

'Marks is that you? Its Billy B, how are things out there? Sorry to hear you have had some losses and got some missing boys. How you coping?'

Commander General William B Dickson [Billy B] as he was known, headed part of the war departments strategy division and oversaw any of the covert operations. Marks had known him since before the war and together they had gone fishing on many occasions, catching crucian carp. They had tried many times to get dace, but it being nicknamed, "the dart", they usually only caught one or two of them, although the common carp was still worthy eating.

Their wives were both part of a social group that prepared quilting, making doilies and laced tea towels and jams that they would sell at the fairgrounds once a month. After the war, they vowed to go fishing once again, and perhaps help with the fates, by making little trinkets or sell homegrown vegetables.

'Billy old boy, what's happening up there? You boys' kind of getting a little chaotic with your missions?' queried Marks.

'Marks, still wearing that silly hat?' probed Billy B.

Bill B was of course referring to his lucky fishing hat, well not really lucky but more so an unpopular gift his wife had somehow made out of leftover quilt off cuts, which he had worn under protest just to keep peace in the house.

'Well I try not to, I have a reputation to be seen as with a little authority sometimes, you know how it is William,' Marks came back with the only retort he knew that Billy B would hate, as pay back for the wanton hat dictum.

'I thought you guys were less formal,' sniggered Billy B.

'Well we are, and now that I am here, I choose not to, well it won't upset Margret, that, that she can't see,' he let out a little chuckle, 'won't upset her.' The hat was Margret's entry in the quilting contest that had her awarded a 1st place prize; she was proud of it and asked Marks to take it with him, as a sort of keepsake of home. He had flung it over a lampshade at his writing desk in his quarters, and as Margret intended, provided him the memories of both her and home.

'So, Billy what is happening?' Marks now knew he wasn't calling about Ben's plane; it would be another mission or news from the outcome of Operation Night Owl.

'Marks, we have decided on another attempt at Peenemünde, in a few days and —'

Marks immediately interrupted, and probed.

'WHEN?' with his voice raised and with the utmost persuasion, then paused, 'WHEN?' Marks asked again this time his voice amplified, 'What mission?' his words travelling down the mouth piercing into the eardrums of Billy B.

'Hey Harold, we are on the same team you know, what's up, why are you being so belligerent, I don't make the call you know, is there a problem?' Billy B now sounding a little confused.

'What will you be calling the mission?' searched Marks, hoping Billy B would give the mission name something differing to that Ben had told him.

Billy B pulled his radio mic closer to his mouth and named the operation. Marks instantly felt an electric chill enter his body and his arms involuntarily developing little bumps, standing the hairs upright as if soldiers at procession.

Marks dropped his radiophone hand piece then repeated the words of Billy B, 'Hydra......Operation Hydra, how in the hell did Ben have the knowledge of this?'

******

Ben walked up the cobbled path of Old Morley Hall and stood between the two rusting iron gates each side of moat bridge. He admired each brick column and the meticulous workmanship of the skilfully laid bricks and uniform mortar joints, and their flawlessly rounded stone balls that capped each pilaster off.

To look around at the familiar surroundings of the park and that of the hall, it provided him with a little peace. It didn't enter his mind of having the need to be anywhere but here. In fact, he wasn't even sure why he was, so just allowed himself to marvel at the building's importance and the remainder of the estate.

Ben elicited memories of how families would come here on weekends and play cricket and feed the water birds. How they walked the pathways and admired the flowers and seasonal trees, and one day would form part of history with their stories. His memories were elated as he stood on the bridge, and he focused in on the people busily drifting around, seemingly without direction or forethought, almost nomadic like. There were mothers with strollers and young children eating ice-cream, and soft balls of pink sugary candyfloss, some had balloons, others carried what looked like their favourite toys.

People were walking in all directions, not paying any attention to anyone or anything, this put Bens mind at ease from his previous thought of them somehow not observing him, and still wondered why when he left the tarmac, the farmers simply ignored him too.

With his now outwardly statue-like presence, a lone figure stood aware to his almost motionless appearance. They stared at him with intent, he wondered if he had then unjustly accused the farmers of their ignorance by not noticing him. His eyes were drawn towards the single person whose staring had now turned into a tiny smile. He smirked back in acknowledgment wondering what he would do or say next, he was thankful that she had returned to see him once again. The two stood at a distance not knowing what the next move would be. Ben knew this would be his last attempt at convincing her he was who he was, but to induce such a belief when she didn't seem to have a memory of him or their short life at the base, was not going to be easy. Ben, thought to himself he would just be himself, so he simply walked up to her as if it was his very first time. He wanted each closing step to last, each moment memorable and something he could recall upon should there again be that missing link from Emily in not knowing him or their time together.

'Hello Emily, I am a little uncertain why you have returned, and I don't want to —'

Ben didn't finish when Emily interrupted him.

'I know I ran off, and don't know why. I think we have much to talk about and I have been very rude to say to you what I did by not knowing you.'

'Emily, it's OK, I won't go back over my past, it's just that I am a little lost with things, since my bombing run, and I am trying to piece —'

Again Emily interrupted him.

'Ben, I will call you by this, and if we just try and piece together some things, it may help me remember a faded memory as you seem to know apparently more about me than I do you?'

'I am so pleased Emily that we can do this, and I too am questioning my memories as to if they are real, or something I may have just fabricated.'

Emily just witnessed a part of Ben what she was hoping, that he would open up to her and in his own time. She hoped he would realise he had probably contrived these memories of her, the war and perhaps this is why she was here, simply to help this young man in his healing process. The two chatted on the bridge about nothing in particular, as they watched children's toy boats in the moat below. They darted and bobbed about in the inundation of water eddies twirling about the rocks and rotting tree trunks, mimicking an actual sea battle in the minds of the boys playing a children's war.

They hadn't noticed the misty rain nor did they feel its dampening effect and wondered why the crowds were picking up their belongings and heading towards the grand door of the main hall. Two guards in period clothing, stood at the base of the marble stairs just outside the door entry to the hall, and the effect of the rain drizzle on them didn't change their posture. They were not there for any reason other than it added to the ambience providing those visiting the experience of the old hall, and its past association with that of Buckenham base.

Emily poked at Ben, something he recalled she did in her playful manner, the day they went on the picnic. She looked just beautiful in her red waist height skirt and petite silvery white buttoned top, he wished he had just told her how beautiful she looked that day. If only he had, would that too be a waning memory and now forgotten?

The two passed by the guards and through the single wooden entrance door into the public gallery space. Its entrance door, although small, was not rectangular in shape, and had a pointed type of arch entrance most likely Gothic, possibly Lancet? It was strange why the door had an arch, yet all the windows were simply a casement type rectangular sash.

Inside the hall, Emily was in awe of the grandiose structure, small to what she would have imagined but the room allowed access to other adjoining smaller rooms guessing it were part of the entire theme of the museum. It was stimulating though at first impression, much like an entrée of crab consommé served before the main course of lobster mornay with a coriander butter.

The rain outside was now a heavy drizzle and most people had congregated inside, walking about the museum and looking at the old wares. Staff were dressed in period clothing from the war and Ben regarded it being of really good authentic quality. The two just wandered around, admiring the artworks and photos and small models of aircraft and buildings and merchandises all in the individual rooms all set to unambiguous themes, to that of adjoining rooms. There was a canteen room, a hospital wardroom, workshop and small oddments of just about everything to do with the base. In the courtyard, there were some automobiles namely service vehicles and one bought a smile to Bens face, it was the "mule". He remembered how it would hook up to the nose wheel of the B-24 and tow them into the hanger or push back on to the tarmac ready for flight. Emily was enthralled at everything, it seemed to give her some new understanding on her forgotten past. As they walked about, they both quickly noticed the building was now devoid of people, and Ben assumed it had stopped raining and most had just returned outside. The thought of it didn't really matter to him, and Emily didn't elaborate on it either, the conversation was just really about nothing in particular, yet they talked as if they had returned to a day in both their lives, where nothing had changed.

Most of the single rooms within the hall had solitary entry doors, one room, a slightly larger one had a pair of French doors, and sidelights. The doors had little yellow and red inlays of ceramics, which harmonised nicely with the hearths of the fireplace in the main hall. They eventually had entered a room that was set up with nurse's equipment and a scene with a ward bed with some very basic mannequins, of nurses and patients that were displayed in one corner of the room. The black and white linoleum floor tiles that did portray the hospital as Ben remembered, and to that of the main corridor of the base. An olive-green painted medicine chest locker with a blackish diagonal webbed frame was set into the door mullions with matching small brass handles as locks and a corresponding eye chart above, it brought back some unpleasant memories for Ben. The cabinet made up of many shelves had tiny quasi-brown bottles filled with some sort of liquid that probably was the only reason for the bottles being that brownie chocolate colour in the first place. Strange looking little white flattened round material representing that of tablets were in shelf below in a clear bottle which almost like the spent chalk pieces his teacher would use as projectiles when it was quite time during classroom study. Finally, a single shelf of hypodermic syringes, and jars full of cotton balls and porcelain bowls and beakers and tumblers and test tubes where all crammed together, nothing like the organised cabinets he remembered in Emily's ward.

The entire scene looked real to Ben; Emily just looked around oblivious to its authenticity, not even making mention of the messy olive-green medicine cabinet. He watched her with a sense of hopelessness thinking this was a part of her life she had a memory lapse of, or did something happen than had caused this to transpire?

'Are you looking as if this doesn't make any sense?' inquired Ben.

'I have a memory of something, and exactly what it is, is the confusing part,' whispered Emily.

'What do you think is puzzling you?' asked Ben.

'Well, when I left you that day at the park, I was confused more so in you saying who you were. And I had just loved your story up to then. I could picture most of it but I guess confused more so you were trying to convince me of something, which was just not possible. I mean you are ageless and if this is the case, then how, or is there is something, you are just not telling me. What has happened and why if we have met then, why can't I remember it, why have you not aged Ben? This is the confusing part.'

'Emily I am not sure what is real anymore. I remember about the mission that was to bomb Peenemünde, and my return and after —'

Emily interrupted, 'Peenemünde, that word, I mean, I think, think I recall something.'

Emily's words to Ben sounded encouraging and he could sense a revolution, possibly her way of forcing a recollection into her vacant remembrance of then.

She went on, 'I can almost see the aircraft and men loading the bombs and yes, I think I can remember the squadron leaving, but after that, there seems to be nothing, I'm sorry Ben, I thought I could remember, I'm sorry.'

'Emily, it is so wonderful just to hear you say you recall something of our past,' whispered Ben, possibly providing her the comfort she now needed to hear.

It had darkened outside, and the blackening sky and the limited lighting inside the museum placed an unnerving numbness, almost undeveloped feeling over their bodies, much as would a child awaking after a nightmare. Ben had, had this feeling when he walked from his plane and only moments later had noticed the plane was gone and the surroundings had changed. This feeling of being alone to him, to an outsider would have seen it as himself had developed a memory loss or in some sort of undetermined state of existence. His face was barren almost empty of thought, it could be seen as his sole was in search of his own being, it was dreamlike it was unreal. Ben hadn't an answer for this thought, yet was now all real, this place, and Emily?

As quick as the thought of "Peenemünde" had entered Emily's mind, it was gone and so was the unworldly feeling the room gave to them both. Their bodies both appeared torpor like, almost non-existent to their own minds, and yet aware of the surroundings. Their saunter around the museum was not orderly or implicit, it was casual and somewhat rewarding to them both. Emily's mind was triggered into remembering something, Ben was understanding his past as possibly factual, yet now was the determining circumstance, that it wasn't.

They both seemed to shun off the fact that all the staff and people were gone, it was late at night and both had little or no idea how they were able to be missed in having been asked to leave at the day's close of trade. Casually, Ben glanced up at a wall clock, it was 7:10. He was eight the last time he had witnessed this noticeable loss of time, when he was on his way to school. That then, as was now had little impact on him, so he quietly just forgot about it.

Adjacent the room that was set up as a ward, was a larger room made up like a hanger. The French doors were held back on little brass hooks, against the iron corrugations of the façade. The lined wall was arched in shape and had a big number "5" made from a rusted type of metal, fixed above the two doors. It very much looked like a scaled down version of the hanger Ben and crew had their briefings in. It was also the hanger which held his beloved silver skinned B-24. He recalled the age-old effect the unpainted polished aluminium fuselage gave, and the white painted circle with a black outer edging and a dark "J" on the tail fins. This gave him his call sign, J-25, the 25 being the twenty-fifth bomber in the squadron.

The French doors had a sort of a cardboard overlay and painted to match that of the original hanger doors, this being a simple way he assumed would not spoil the yellow and red inlays of ceramics set into the doors. The ceiling had what looked like a hessian cloth painted black, that was hung from each corner of the room and in a few spots from within the room. It reminded Ben of the parachutes he had seen during his training that were hung from hangers to dry, or there for repairs. There was a briefing table with map overlaid, old cans of oils, fuel tins, tools, ladders and a bomb trolley the Mule used to tow when loading the aircraft with armaments. Lined along the walls were a selection of photos of some of the Liberators, and a well-built scale model of a B-24, with a six-foot or so wingspan. There were three more but noticeably smaller and one slightly larger than those with a two-foot span. When hung from under the hessian, it gave the appearance they were flying in 'formation' and the differing sizes gave it perfect perspective as if in actual flight. In the middle of the room, was a glass-covered table protecting a wonderful representation of the entire airfield, showing all the buildings, hangers and had only 25 liberators parked on the aprons near the hangers. He could only remember Marks talking about the additional 25 that would join the squadron, and when he thought about some more couldn't recall even seeing them. Ben was admiring the authenticity of the models which bought him back to his youth, at the base. He had not noticed Emily's eyes fixed on him, she was standing adjacent the wall of photographs, frozen, and with a featureless face.

'Emily, are you OK?' inquired Ben.

She continued to stare at him, her expression turned from unimaginative to distinctive. She seemed relieved, optimistic in her appearance, she omitted an aura that beamed sureness and cheerfulness her featureless face was now inspiring and encouraging.

'Emily what's going —'

Before he could finish what he was saying, she spun her entire body as if in slow motion towards the photographs on the wall. She appeared as if she was being orchestrated, perhaps coordinated by an instrumentalist, directing his sonata, yet she gave the impression that she was almost machine-driven and automated. Each move of her body flowed and harmonised with the next; it was artistic, creative and with meticulous choreography. Her body streamed with changing hand movements and gestures that slowed, then became motionless as she pointed to one photo in particular, with fingers of portentous surety. Her entire form was unmoving, she stood eyes fixed to a black and white photo, of a B-24 bomber on the hard stand, Hanger 5 and its arched roofline noticeably towering over the two rear vertical tail stabilisers of the Liberator. At the nose of the great beast of a plane stood two people, a pilot with flight jacket, the other a young woman, it was dated, Circa August 10, 1943.

'Ben it's me, and you, you haven't changed, how is this… it's not possible, I mean I don't remember the photograph being taken, well I should as I… I can see it's me, what has happened with my life that I can't remember, tell me what has happened to me, please Ben, help me.'

'Emily I will with all my power I will, but I think we are both in need of help —' and before he could finish Emily interrupted.

'Ben, why have you not aged, how is this possible, I mean how did we not know each other after, how did I get to here, now what of my past why can't I…'

'What is the last thing you…you saw before you can remember the squadron leaving for Peenemünde?' enquired Ben. 'For me, it was raining, then the rain was gone. This has happened to me before when I was around eight or so, there was rain and a man, who I have seen throughout my life.'

'What man, Ben, what do you mean?'

'It's all mixed up but even when I first came to the base I met Marshall, and again before Operation Night Owl.'

'Marshall, I don't remember him who was he?' enquired Emily

Ben just presumed Emily with her memory loss had not remembered Marshall Hartley, and as far as Marks not knowing that too was very peculiar.

'The more we talk about things Ben, I have those memories coming back to me, but that's it, and can't really remember anything after that up to now,' said Emily with just a little bit of doubt in her words.

'There is something strange happening every time we meet; I mean I think I can only get us both through this if I take it step by step. The first day you came to me in the park, was when I don't really know how I got back to Old Morley Hall, strangely I feel as if my mind wasn't controlling my actions. Do you know why and how you got here today?' asked Ben.

'Well, yes, I came to see you to help you through this; well, I feel like I expected you may have had some memory loss, well unsure why you were saying those things or how you knew of Buckenham or even described a life that I was in. Your story seemed so surreal; it was so believable, but it just couldn't be. And I sort of think back to the day in the park, I was so absorbed by your words, I became spellbound to your story.'

'Emily I don't know how I even got here today and I think about it and I can only best describe today as is with my past ten years, and they both have happened in moments. I can't even evaluate if it were minutes, hours or even days. Strange as it seems to me, it felt like only, well a short time ago I crashed, well I think it was a crash. It almost sounds ridiculous, it's not possible to the point it's just so dam improbable, I must be just dreaming, I don't know.'

'Ben, this may also sound strange, but I can't remember from now to the day you in reality left on the mission… Well, I am now certain you did leave and can see by the photo, that indeed you were there.'

'Emily, I will have to as when we first met in the park go through things in my head and help us both get through this.'

The two agreed and they both felt a sense of surety to that of their ordeal just by talking about it. Ben was glad Emily now accepted him as he was, Emily had some sort of meaning to that of a past she didn't know. There were many questions that needed answers from them both, and Ben was hoping they would work it out together. Ben settled his emotion off its high from the knowledge Emily was almost back to him. He didn't understand the age difference and wanted to learn so much from her and find out about the boy in the park when they first met. He had to establish at what point of his life that turned from reality to this, and how he could inaugurate fact from this apparent fabled existence they were both now in? He looked into her eyes and had forgotten how green and alluring they were. The amatory mien of her features sent his temperament into an impulse of covetousness thinking of his own needs not hers. This was not like him and perhaps just a result of his indeterminate state of mind.

He tried to analyse it as if it was a landing approach. He thought of it as if he was saying descending in a 40-knot crosswind, there was a commitment, a point of no return and the only resolve was a "go round". Then second attempt to land was going to be his commitment, that would be his requisite now to the actual point of where things had changed in their lives, so he focussed on this alone. He searched deep into his thoughts, for something that made some sense, something he could navigate through, something as a pilot he would need to find from as crazy as it sounded, past life to now. He looked for a point he knew from then that may be evident. He thought of Peenemünde, Emily remembered that, then the photo of them both, it was real to her. Peenemünde and the day he went, it rained then stopped. *Marshall*, he then thought to himself. *Marshall was there, why? The note, he gave me a note, that was it, that was real...* he reached into his flight jacket pocket hoping it were there. His fingers searched the depths of the inner linings of the pocket, rummaging and exploring in search of the letter. His heart missed a beat as his exploring digits brushed against a uniform shape, he was hoping was the note. He snatched it from his pocket and without further thought ripped open the envelope and unfolded the note from within...

Chapter 7

Ben wondered why he had never simply opened the letter before now. The envelope had remained sealed, letter hidden, and its contents unknown for over 13 years. He had never thought about it until now, and even thinking back as a child, the need to know anything then was never as important as was reading a comic book. The day of Operation Night Owl, when Marshall had said, 'Don't forget to read the letter', why did it not cross his mind to open it during his flight? Was it because Marshall just unpredictably ambled through the rain and was gone before Ben could make sense of their conversation? There was truly no other place to turn, and for them both, they had little impression of why, or in what manner they were both now here. Ben for all accounts seemed like he was just at war completing a mission and then to his understanding had crashed. Emily's life before now had gone from the war as a nurse to having somewhat of an immaterial recollection of anything in between.

The paper on which the note was handwritten was a type of blotting paper. The wording flowed over the paper, lettering was equally spaced, precisely inked fonts, with immeasurable traditionalism and something his mother had as one of her qualities. It seemed quite odd to Ben the bottom of the "B" had a quirky little tail on it. He knew this as with his own style, something he had done in his own writing and had never anticipated seeing someone else do it let alone be identical to his, it read:

Ben I would predict you are now rather confused? You are probably wondering or better cannot establish between reality and a vision of your past? You are feeling confused, lost, and abandoned from that of your former life. Your world up to now has randomly changed and now that you have met Emily, she has no recognition of her life before now or you. You have discovered with her, a past she now remembers, and you now have a choice, a choice to determine your life from here on, or to live a past you had only just begun? The future, your future is still yet to happen; this choice, your choice is for you, it's yours and yours alone...
Marshall B Hartley

'Ben, what is the matter?' Emily asked with an anxious look and an awkwardness to her voice.

'The note, it makes no sense of anything he, he, Marshall I mean he has said I have a choice, it's me Emily, it's my choice, but how, I don't know what to do, I can't make a choice if I don't know how to approach it? You, you have, I mean does this seem real to you, I was just at the field and my plane crashed, and now I am here – that is not real.'

I don't believe in fairy tale stories, Ben, and nor should you, and we will work through it, perhaps we both have a missing memory and that as a nurse is my rational reasoning as to why we both have forgotten the past, our past.'

'Something, Emily, happened to me on the flight home, I mean with…'

Emily had paused for a second as she interrupted Ben. She had recalled something that at the time was not relevant but now had some connotation to today's events. She paused yet again just to ponder over what had just crossed her mind. Emily was of course thinking of Ben's headstone, which she had thought to herself was totally unreasonable to even think about it let alone believe it could be possible. She passed on that thought, and explained her interruption as something of little significance?

Ben had not seen it that way and pleaded with Emily to tell him the truth.

'Ben, you said something happened to you when you were returning from the mission?' asked Emily.

Ben thought for a moment before he spoke. He questioned himself as to why he would now even believe it. He went back to the flight home and the encounter with the USS Trilogy. What was significant to that moment that perhaps put him here now or even Emily in her situation. She had lapsed what seemed almost 10 years of her life, he the same, and as a logically thinking pilot, he rationalised just this alone, and it was common to them both.

The two stood once again in the main foyer of the hall. The increasing light levels outside told them both it was again daylight. Noticeably, the area was devoid of any public or staff as they cast their eyes over the myriad of static exhibitions and display pieces. Ben drew his eyes from the motionless tedium of inside the hall and focused on the offerings of the new day. The stillness transitorily gave way to the odd birch tree branch gesturing and signalling the morning breeze, reminding Ben of the ground crew marshalling aircraft with their regimented arm and hand movements.

The warming outside of daybreak, with its seemingly motionless wafts of wind puffs unnoticeably evolved the desolate exhibition pieces into living objects. The pieces became alive as the congregations of crowds of people mused over them. Emily and Ben had not noticed the people even arriving, nor did they notice the hall in which they stood was now far from its devoid state. Staff now filled the hall and people were visiting the displays and hurrying about paying attention only to their own goings on. Ben took Emily's hand as he navigated his way through the masses of people grouped about a display or reading the inscriptions and browsing through the books and collectables and knickknacks for sale. There was little or no attention paid to Ben and Emily who to an onlooker had they have noticed, would have appeared anxious or lost, totally out of sorts. The two quickened their pace and trudged past the two guards at the halls grand entrance, and out across the bridge over the moat and towards the park grounds. This place, the hall, the grounds and history with all its glory of a war that these two shared was not a place for them both now. They felt more comfortable in perhaps remaining recluse, solitary and unnoticed, somewhere untouchable to the outside world, a world now unknown to them both. Emily and Ben unquestionably felt uneasy and totally out of place here, and the days and nights made no sense. Emily had partially found a piece of her past, Ben perhaps his future and the two would now have to accept this time as real.

'Emily, I am going to get our photo this is the only thing we now have of our past, stay here it will be quicker if I go on my own.'

Before she could speak, Ben sped off back over the bridge towards the hall. He knew it were only a simple photo, but one they could cherish, one they would remember as a time they both recalled as theirs. Ben arrived back at the entrance to the hall and as usual, the two guards stood unexciting, looking as if they wanted to be somewhere else. They greeted the public as always and Ben did not think it strange they were ignorant to his hurried pace, nor was he concerned they stared at him without conviction or greeting. He ran past the hall kiosk through a crowd a people, his body aggressively pushing past the group without feeling or his concern for their welfare. He felt reprehensible he even done this and without knowing it thinking he had collided with a young child standing alone amongst the crowd. He stopped, looked back to perhaps apologise and could see the young child looking and pointing in Ben's direction as if he were telling his parent, 'that man hit me', but soon realised he was simply pointing at a plane hung from the foyer ceilings structural cross beams.

Ben again turned this time speeding up further his pace back toward Hanger 5's exhibition, his rushing was oblivious to the onlookers he had passed or had aggressively pushed his way through. Ben could sense a slight chill in the air about his face, yet strangely, the cold he could only picture in his mind similarly to that from high altitude bombing runs. The more he tried to create this in his mind and the inattentiveness toward people as he pushed through the crowds, the harder it was to visualise. He did not understand this moment now nor the fact he and Emily were simply unnoticed. He was beginning to think the irresolute world he was in were simply part of his visual understanding of now, perhaps his own reverie, made up from a forgotten past. Focusing on now, was his strong-minded way as was with his training as a young pilot and all that of which, which had been instilled into him.

He ran through the entrance to Hanger 5 and could see the room was full of people mulling about the displays. Ben slowed his pace, not wanting to bring attention to his quest. He gently made his way through a crowd and reached the wall were his picture of the bomber was hung. The group of people were about the photos, one in particular he could see was standing rigid, eyes fixed on his portrait. To take the photo was not possible, the onlooker stood directly in Ben's path, and they seemed unbending and obdurate in their posture. Ben knew it was going to be almost an impossible task but could see it were only a single one person who stood between him and his mission. He gradually walked up behind them as he contemplated his next move, one he would do without thought and with the utmost conviction. Should they protest to his mission, he would simply disrespect them; take it quickly down and run from the building.

They had on a floral knee-high dress and white almost silvery coloured flat house shoe type of footwear. Ben observed the attire, tried to understand it, yet to him seemed almost foreign, something he guessed was a new fashion. A decoration of lavender flowers swirled and spun over the dress in twirling like patterns, it tastefully matched a silvery glossy waste sash, probably used as a kind of belt. Her greying hair attractively held neatly in a bun shape with a knitted woollen black snood holding it together. A teardrop set of earrings matched her clothing and she wore a perfume of a lavender scent. Ben stood closely behind her, drawing in with each breath, the fragrance of her womanly smell, playing out is next move in his mind, detailing each part systematically and precisely to the second.

'It is a beautiful photograph is not?' spoke the woman quietly.

The chill about his face seemed to return and had now moved through his entire body, her tone was comforting, her voice instantly recognised. His body now formed a shape of rigidity, arms at his side unable to move yet his entire body was at the ready to snap the picture off its fixings.

I wondered how long it would be before I saw you again, she spoke in a well versed yet composed tone, as if she had, had years of rehearsal. Each word said with the ability as if he could see it written in an imaginary font only visible to his eyes. The words voiced were so clear, so defined it could not have been any better had it been crooned in an opera. She moved ever so slightly, her frail body responded moments after the thought and with what seemed minutes turned to face Ben. He looked upon her with misperception; the voice he knew, the face was unrecognisable, yet he felt somewhat as ease.

She spoke again,

'Have I changed that much, Ben? Am I not the young woman anymore you remember?'

'Emily, Emily,' he repeated again, 'I…what is happening, how did you, you get here before me, why are you…?'

'Old Ben, why am I old, is that what you want to ask, why?'

'Emily I am sorry, I do not, I mean I am sounding disrespectful…'

'No Ben you are not, it is the truth, look at me I am an old woman, and how old, well let's agree it's old.'

'Emily, I just left you moments ago outside over the bridge, I-I came back to get the…'

'Photo, yes you did, well that is what you wished you wanted to do. Ben, look around and tell me what you see'.

'I do not understand the question, you mean the building, the museum what exactly are you asking?'

'The people Ben, what do you see about the people,' probed Emily.

Ben looked about the room. The groups of visitors were looking at Emily; they were screwing up their faces, shaking their heads and whispering to each other, and gestured with pointing and arm movements, some were laughing.

'Why are they doing this, I do not understand, why?' Ben spoke in a dulcet tone hoping this would take her mind from the disparagement of her bystanders.

'Ben, simply put, you are not here, you are my imagination, and you are a memory of my past that I hold onto,' described Emily.

'That is not true, I know this place its real so how can I understand it if I am not here,' snapped Ben.

'Well you are here as I can see you, look around are they looking at you, can you speak to them, can you touch them, will they reply?' suggested Emily.

Ben thought about this notion for a moment, and as he did he pieced together what he presumed was just the past day, and he could now see the oddities of it all. The time changes in the day that went by so quickly or without knowledge. How the people seemed not to notice him, or was it just their ignorance? Alternatively, how he had no direction or need to do anything other than just wander about. Was this now part of who he was or just her imaginings, her thoughts, her beliefs.

'How do I then see this all from my side and understand it as if it were real when these are my thoughts not yours?' asked Ben.

'How do you know they are your thoughts and not mine, if I put you in my head, then they must be mine and you are not really here, look at the people they are looking at me not you,' whispered Emily.

Ben turned and looked around at the individuals. He walked up to one and stood between them and Emily; they unexpectedly turned and walked away.

'See, they can see me they could see I was in front of them,' rationally suggested Ben.

'No Ben that's not the case, I am known to this room, I come here most days waiting for your return, never knowing how long it will take, some days its only hours, others, its weeks or months, those are the hardest. They laugh, they cry, they try to help me but most of the time I convince them I am just a lonely war widow and they sympathise. I remember when we met, that first time at the hospital, then as is right now, is as exciting as it was then. I do not have many years left in me now Ben, and each day, I value more so when you are in it, something we just do not do when we are so very young. When you came to me the first day in the park, it was almost ten long years since your plane went missing over the channel, and that for me only feels like yesterday?'

'Emily, I remember that day, but you were the one who did not recognise me and I was the one who then remembered you from my story.'

'Yes you did,' said Emily, 'but I was the one who put you in my mind and created this image of you. Ben, I will need to perhaps show you something, something that will be clear to you as to how you are here, be it me who is imagining you, or you me, either way we will go from here.'

Ben did not protest, and Emily lumbered herself into a comfortable working position, slightly bent forward and with the aid of a supporting hand carved chestnut walking stick, then she paced herself with Ben's support out of the building. The two made their way to a parked car; a car Ben presumed fashioned as was with the dress, something foreign, something new perhaps, something yet to be invented? A driver saw her approaching and clambered out of the vehicle, he wore a black suit, white shirt and a reddish tie. His shoes where a glossy black, overall he was smartly dressed. He helped Emily into the car; Ben climbed in and sat beside her. The driver looked back at her through is rear vision mirror, ensuring she was comfortably seated. He could see her clearly in his visor, as she relaxed herself back into the seat. He asked his same old question, the one he done time and time again.

'Is he with you today, Miss Marks?'

She replied with a simple 'Yes.'

He out of respect left it at that then simply asked, 'Where to, Miss Marks?'

Emily in a quite soft tone looked at Ben as she muttered the words, 'Earlham Road Cemetery, please.'

******

The drive to the cemetery this time was more pleasant for Emily with that of Ben at her side. She had had made this trip many times over the years always on her own. She needed to do this for her and for what reason or why, she could only surmise, and that assumption was that he, Ben, was just a fading memory and needed to put him to rest. Since his disappearance over the channel, she had seen out the war, and lived in hope for another five years, he would simply turn up. She had moved into a small but modest flat after the battle with their beloved dog, Dover. She had never married nor had she any relationship with anyone other than Ben. She always saw herself as having a life after the war with him, Dover and perhaps two possibly three wonderful children.

Ben, do you think things would have been different, if you had returned safely, I mean you know with the end of the war, would we have —'

Before she could finish, the car stopped on the service road adjacent the ceremonial area set aside for causalities of the 451st and Old Buckenham base. It was only a short walk to burial site and Ben helped Emily as best he could. The pair stopped short of the headstone.

'Ben, take a good look, have a long look at the headstone, it is your crew, your mission is noted here and as a mark of respect, you by definition, are still missing in action.'

Ben silently read down the list of names bringing back some wonderful memories of the flight crew. He reached the last name on the list of his aircrew then read the remainder aloud.

'We would also like to acknowledge our Captain, who bravely flew this as his first and last mission, as he was the youngest pilot to succeed as Captain, Ben Walters [Benjamin] of which also was pronounced MIA, this day, the 12 day of August, in the year of our lord, 1943.'

Ben was silent for a moment, and didn't have any words to say other than, 'The stone, it says that we are MIA, so we haven't been found then?'

'Ben, think about when you came into my life back in 1953, I created you, you are my vision and that is that.'

'How did I return then from 1953 back to 43, at the briefing of Operation Night Owl, can you explain that when it was my thought not yours?'

'Well, no I can't, other than did you really think it or because of my vision you have; well, I have not really as this is me who has you here, they are my thoughts, my remembrances and my dreams.'

'Emily, I truly can't see it that way when I was at the park on my own before you came. I have trouble remembering how I got there, but do recall, Emily, it was you who then came to me.'

Emily thought about that for just a moment. She contested with herself the notion that Ben had just put forward, and she had a sudden responsiveness race through her body, a feeling she had not had before. This awareness that Ben had claimed placed a new light over things making her wonder if he had had the same thoughts as she did, then could it not be possible he too had her as his own imagination? *Psychiatric doctors would have boundless elation in the challenge of getting into the thoughts of us both*, she imagined, and with that belief, the sensitivity in her body went from an energetic hot feeling to an emotionless stony unsympathetic cold. She felt dizzy at the thought, the idea Ben may also be right in his evaluation of events so far. Was he really with her all those years? Her body felt like it twisted and convulsed with negligible electric jolts that absorbed into her entire now ridged form. Pain shot up her arms and down her legs, yet she felt a pleasing relief, relief that perhaps she had not seen him all those years at all, and she, then, was in-fact in his vision.

Realism for this moment was now certain, and her past although confusing was coming back into her awareness. Emily stood erect, arms outstretched to ease the discomfort in her entire body; her arched back had straightened from its former bowed and rounded shape. She felt fragile, brittle, her mind evolving to her life before now. The vibrant image of Ben standing in front of her was morphing into a shadowy ethereal figure being absorbed from the natural light. His indistinct and inaudible voice becoming more distant almost soundless. The blood continued to race about her veins in uncontrolled spurts starving parts of her brain of the vital fluids it needed. Deficient pressure in her veins left her heart rate wanting blood flow, yet increasing her heart levels with unpredictable beats. Her breath had shortened, the dizziness claiming her equilibrium, her heart slowed even further, and a pulse thumped, sending fluids about her body absent of oxygen.

Ben's image was now gone, and she immediately felt at peace. Had it not been for the appearance of the headstone in front of her, he was now absent from her life. Emily's eyelids quivered with uncontrolled spasms and pupils were bulky and bulbous, her heart was slowing to a thump…thump…t-h-u-m-p. She looked up at the weakening sun; the prodigious orb she thought why she would even see it in that way, and orb she thought again, it's a sun she always knew it as a sun and now she saw it as an orb, something without meaning. It appeared animated from its seemingly stationary enflamed glow, performing a phantasm of moves behind its silhouette as it reached the horizon, becoming swallowed and consumed by the distant landscape.

Her body now felt light and elevated, she sensed peace from the notion; she felt as if she was being drawn upward. Her feet relieved of the weight of her frail body, a feeling not known to her. Emily had virtually stopped breathing, her body lifeless almost comatose. Had it not been for her chauffeur, she practically would have fallen forward onto the memorial.

It took only minutes to strap her into the front seat of the car as he checked her wrist, feeling a small pulsation, a minute beat barely throbbing, yet she lay lifeless. Her head inclined frontward and was held just off her chest from the vehicles seat belt around her shoulder. It took eight long minutes to reach the hospital, the acting surgeon advised if it were nine, Emily would have gone into cardiac arrest. Her immobile body all furrowed and hoary, she lay silent and stagnant and her breath was almost non-existent. The wires and tubes and machines beeping, and morphine dripping through a beaker was the only indication she had life left in her body. Emily had given up. Her years without Ben and just the memory of him now, were almost absent in her mind. She was barely able to lay there and focus on her life's story, and evaluate it in the short time she had left; she closed her eyes and dreamt of nicer times…

******

The past 40 years had gone so quickly from the first time she had experienced Ben in the park that day back in 1953. At the time, she had ponded over it, not understanding her own ability to build his image in her mind to the point she actually was able to make him into a real person. A person that she could communicate with, one she could almost feel the non-existent warmth of his body. As she lay there, her heart monitor slowed its pace; it was time, her time.

She had elected to receive only intravenous pain relief and left alone with the shutters closed and dimmed lighting. She had developed into a recluse yet had to endure the pain of loneliness of almost 51 years without Ben. A tear fell down the side of her check, and she had enough energy to suppose Ben's hand once again holding hers. She opened her eyes but he was no longer there. She felt somewhat comforted by noticing the silhouette of a small gold charm laid out on her hands, a gift, perhaps a token from her image of him that she had perhaps just dreamed up. The emotionlessness taciturnity of her body had now warmed by his imaginary palm that he held softly against her hand once more. She felt her eyes welling and the tears streamed down her cheekbone and wetted the shoulder strap of her lavender negligee-unconventional for hospital attire, but she requested it, and they agreed. Ben used his finger to wipe away the salty teardrop; she smiled at him one last time. Emily was now alone; she had lived a peaceful and solitary life and she would die deprived of truly loving a lifetime, having only experienced that in thought. Her body withering away, isolated and distant from her past she would die abandoned and alone, her strength now weakening, she would die without adoration, she would die and old fragile woman.

The last remaining feeling she now had was the lightness in her body. She felt as if the gurney in which she lay helpless, was being drawn gently away from beneath her. The darkened space gradually regained its light levels, as her entire body little by little was shutting down. The ward appeared to strengthen, fortify, going from a weaker gloomy lightless hospital room to a vibrant and lively unsoiled expanse, with a purple and baroque luminosity of light. The complex patterns of colouring within the space did not make any logic, perhaps it was a way the mind provided ones fading life in their final hours with comfort. With her eyes shut, she felt a cosiness from the imaginary sound of waves on a shore in the distance she had built up in her mind. Her hand slipped from the clutches of Ben's and for the final and last time, at 9:52 on the morning of the 16th of August 1994, aged 71, Emily Marks had peacefully passed away.

Old Morley Hall – "The Coffin Room":

Ben stood in the centre of the sarcophagus, looking down at a frail body nestled comfortably in the purpose-built pod. Its pallid white outer casing of the shape comparable to that of a cupped hand allowed the occupant to be slightly seated upright providing a view through a glass wall directly in line with their vision. The crystal glass walls slightly slanted inwards meeting the ceiling lining also in glass. The room looked out over a white silica sand beach as the gentle waves rolled up to the water's edge pausing slightly only metres from the window, then quietly and effortlessly falling back, as if welcoming the events from within the room. The purple glow from inside the room gave it an air of mystery, a sense of mystique; it both calmed and absorbed its occupants of any unfounded feelings providing them with an unbiased and well-balanced space.

Ben held onto the frail hand of the occupant, who was wearing a lavender negligee, almost see-through and it had a lilac probably closer to a plum coloured waist sash with a small crest fastening it together. Ben not knowing of any words he could have said at that moment that would have made better the situation. He reached into his pocket and pulled out a small white box, petite enough to fit in the palm of your hand. He knelt down and gently kissed the occupant on their brow. Little or no reaction came from within, nor did the occupant smile, a breath was hardly recognisable and small glows of purple reflected in their unemotional bottle green eyes, no movement was evident apart from a single tear now falling down the side of the occupant's face. Ben used the back of his finger to stop the tear falling and spoiling the fragrant lining of the silk bed sheets, not noticing it had dampened the strap of her negligee.

Ben opened the white box, inside an elfin gilded gold-plated chain and locket he had bought as a gift. He tucked the chain and locket under the clasped hands of the occupant letting it gently fall off to one side, the occupant almost innocent of the change. Ben now standing, looked out over the water, the waves motionless, to the point of almost stopping, in part stationary and unmoving. The ripples in the ocean smoothed as they took on the unexciting appearance of the rooms polished colourless floor covering. Ben looked back at the occupant one last time, as he made his way over to the only other piece of furniture in the room, a blue leather settee. Ben sat down on the futon, stationary, eyes fixed on the glass walls. Waves logically rolled up to the shoreline, almost immediately slowed their momentum becoming still; Ben focusing on the now unchanging events. Had it not been for the activities of ten minutes earlier, the occupant of the pod would not have noticed the waves having stopped, becoming lifeless, unmoving, then as if by a mechanical means started a slow ripple, gathering in momentum. Ben's mind cast back to different times, as the waves outside started moving again. They continued their rolling motion but this time away from shore, as if being dragged back into the ocean. The occupant of the pod had seen the waves start to roll down the beach not up; it confused them as they looked over at Ben who had now settled back into the futon. His eyes where shut and the room's purple glow now dimmed, as he entered into deep sleep, his final conscious was that of his life story and how this moment, and that of the occupant's inevitable passing away that needed to be "distorted"; he had remembered that phrase from his youth. The room with time slowly dimmed, eventually devoid of any light, Ben's conscious soon became aware of his unconscious and although he now looked comatose, Ben had prepared his mind and state to enter his past, Ben was to anyone else, now lifeless.

******

Ben was still yet to understand the room as he woke. He had seen many parts of Old Morley Hall both period to the time of its build and this room, the coffin room. Strange as it was to be built hidden, and for what purpose and by whom. All Ben knew was if he could think it from within the room, or even outside for that matter, he somehow could live it, or so he thought. He used both Marshall's similarity of "The Sector", and his own of, simply "The Coffin Room". He had a little chuckle to himself and thought how silly it sounded, when Marshall expressed it with a little more professionalism; well, either way, it was strange how it did happen. Real or not, fact or fiction, imagination or a dream, something he would hope he eventually would understand.

What was confusing was the realism he would never quite know where he would wake. He remembered the first time, and that of falling asleep behind the hanger and awakening here at Old Morley Hall, but then confused as to the museum with Emily. He had lived in a time of war and quite possibly twice, well so he assumed, as he knew about Operation Hydra but what of the USS Trilogy? In addition, his return across the channel, and finally how he was with Emily in 1953 in the park and unquestionably after that. He never did ask her when they were at the museum what year it was; perhaps it had little or no significance. He had to agree on one thing, and that was whatever year it is now he would have to accept anything beyond that, had not happened yet, and for that to have not happened what would he do, as he knew what would?

The last time he had those science fiction thoughts was from his favourite book, *Armageddon*. He remembered Emily had said once something about logic of life or fact or fairy tales that do not exist. Well, apart from the beliefs of the book he read as a child, he now knew they did.

He made his way up the stone stairs toward the cellar as the hissing sound of the coffin room cavity door shut into its opening, sealing the room off. He strangely felt into his pocket for the gilded key, something he wondered why, and for what reason it just crossed his mind. The small-elongated shape of the key was felt as he entered back into the cellar.

******

Yellowish-brown leaves were falling from the silver birch trees. It was cold outside, and had a slight breeze to the air, chilling it even further. This was a positive thing, and Ben thought to himself it was abnormally wintery and presupposed it was around August, so that was a good start. Now that he was halfway there, he did not really know what his next move would be, or how to approach it. He eventually left the pastoral grounds of the Hall and guessed it was best he returned to the base. Would it be there? In addition, what year, something he guessed he would soon find out.

Ben started to get an understanding of when he had returned. He could hear a familiar sound of overflying aircraft, perhaps only a few miles from his location. He tried to pinpoint their direction, but to attune to, it seemed in itself a task he was unable to achieve. He continued to walk to the base, when a voice common to him and perhaps him alone called out.

'Ben, what are you doing?' questioned the voice.

Ben slightly turned toward the sound and before he cast his eyes upon them, responded, 'Heading back to the base.'

The voice spoke again, 'I suspect you are wondering in what year?'

Ben completed his full turn toward the voice and was now fronting a recognisable face, one he did welcome, and one he suspected he would happen upon first.

'Well Marshall, something tells me I have probably been here before,' suggested Ben.

'Before, being the operable word, yes you have,' said Marshall.

'Well, if I have,' questioned Ben, 'tell me what year it is then?'

'Ben, it's not a matter of what year, its why, simply ask yourself why you are here?'

Ben thought about that notion for just a minute, and as much as he tried to provide an answer, he first had to understand the question, so he repeated it in his own mind.

'Why am I here, why?'

He debated for a few moments, and could only conclude, he didn't really know why, and turned back to Marshall for help.

'Marshall, I can only understand that you seemed to have been part of my adult life as far back as the base; well, when I first arrived that is, Marks even when I came back from 1953, questioned me over who you were, he, well, I didn't get a chance to go into it too much, but nonetheless he didn't seem to know who you were. I have seen you in the strangest of times, you seem to just turn up. I don't think I have truly understood any of that reasoning, suffice to say why, or better how is that just possible?' questioned Ben.

'Ben, think about your past dealings with everyone at the base, their reactions when you spoke about Peenemünde, or Operation Hydra, ask yourself about what happened after your loss of memory when returning to the base from Operation Night Owl? Your headstone, Emily and how she didn't remember you.'

'Emily explained that she, well, she made me up, and I was just her imagination.'

'Her imagination, Ben do you know how silly that sounds?'

'Well yes, about as silly as what this all is, I mean you, me, here, now and what year, it's about as silly and not even thinkable as all of this now.'

'Ben, your entire life up to now unexpectedly changed? You are looking for some answers as to how this has happened? You have met Emily and she had no recognition of you or her life before? What if everything has now changed and you are alone in this world that is not known to you. And what if this world is real Ben, and your past was just your imagination. Finally, what if you have a choice, a choice for you to determine which world would now be your life? A past which you had only just begun or a future which was still yet to happen.'

'What good is my future if I don't have Emily in it, she is dead, and my past, well, it does appear I am MIA, so that would mean supposedly I am dead also, and that as well as your statement is sounding more ridiculous by the minute.'

'As silly as it was when you told Marks about Operation Hydra,' suggested Marshall.

'Well, you got me on that one Marshall; you certainly have got me on that one.'

'Ben can we agree, you don't know if now is real or your past was?' questioned Marshall.

'Yes, I agree,' said Ben. 'That being said, if I don't know my past, or don't know of now, assuming it's my future, how can I remember both times.'

'That's the thing, you have a choice to make your own destiny,' said Marshall.

'Let's just go with that for a moment, my past, then, at the base, I meet a beautiful woman, fly a mission and don't return, mmm that's a hard one Marshall, I would be better off here, but wait, I am here whatever the year, with someone who is now dead. It doesn't sound like my options are actually that hard to choose from when in both of them, I don't end up with the girl.'

'Ben, let's assume she did make you up in her mind, and you did or better were able to see that of which she had dreamed up, how was that possible? Or better, you returned back to 1943, after you had first met me in '53. Just go back to your life, think about some of the strange things that have happened.'

'What do you mean, strange?' enquired Ben.

'Well, strange as in meeting Emily in '53, your return to before the mission, that of Operation Night Owl, and how you knew of Peenemünde. All these things add up into defining your reality from fiction. Start with you, you know that's real and move on from there. It will all come together and you will know what path to travel down, then or now. You have a choice; you can determine what happens from now, a past or what is still yet to happen, your choice'

'As I said Marshall, it is not a very welcoming selection I have,' finished Ben.

'It is Ben, remember you have the "The Sector", use it as you see fit.'

Ben, recreated events so far and that of his exposure to the room at Old Morley Hall, Marshall just referred to it as "The Sector", what an unbelievable thought, a room in a 700, 8 possibly 900-year-old building and he and Marshall perhaps had the sole use of it. Why, and for that matter how did Marshall even know about it in the first place. If Ben still had "The Sector" as Marshall put it, how was he to use it, could he simply go back into it, think of a time, a date, lay in the pod, wake and start over? Why him, why Marshall? It didn't make any sense at all.

'Marshall, who are you, answer me that?'

'This I will guarantee you Ben, that is, choose wisely, trust your instincts, and you will find out much more than who I am, you will find out truth from reality.'

'Marshall, please answer me, who are you?' pleaded Ben, drawing the words out in a lengthy sentence.

From above came a thundering and conversant drone. Ben looked up in time to see a Liberator flying low and erratic, battling flight, unable to sustain a controlled descent from its torn and twisted control surfaces. Its battered body shape, traumatised from war doomed the plane's flight path as wavered and undecided, the pilot was just able to fly in a direction of Buckenham base. Smoke billowed out of its inner starboard engine, propeller feathered and was wind milling in the breeze as it flew over low, almost scraping the tops off the trees in its path. There were scattered bullet holes down its port wing damaging the aileron control mechanism making it stiff, almost unusable. The starboard wings undercarriage dangled limp looking, swinging in the breeze like the perpetual arm of the clock tower near his old school, the port main gear still safely stowed.

The plane passed overhead, Ben could make out the stowed undercarriage finally lowered the locking strut holding it secure, the starboard still wavering in the slipstream in back and forth movements, indecisive and uncommitted. He then saw the belly turret was not stowed safely nestled inside the fuselage, he could almost make out the despair in the young man's expression knowing he now faced imminent death. Ben was going through the motions of the pilot; placing himself in the same situation and deciding what he would do if he were up there. It felt real to him, that he almost stepped out each process, as would the pilot; real to the point to that what was happening in Ben's mind was happening as he thought it.

Another B-24 flew over, it too leaving a wake of smoke blooms in its path. Its antediluvian silvery aluminium colouring of the fuselage and the familiar tail insignia, that of J-25 now instantly recognisable to Ben. Ben searched his thoughts and that of how the reputed events what he presumed happened only days ago, was this very same event that was just happening now his crash and loss of all souls on board. Was he was just witnessing his own impending demise? The plane descended low past the treetops, Ben recognised it was his plane, and was he now going to witness his and that of his crew's death.

He stood motionless; he was rigid in form unable to interchange by way of hand movements or words with Marshall. He listened for the sounds of explosions and searched the skies for smoke blooms knowing the Liberator would soon collide onto the runway. This thought was now vivid in his mind, he knew it was actual, he knew it must have truly happened, then turned to Marshall for some sort of support or explanation how he just saw himself fly over, not understanding how this was even possible.

'You have just witnessed something unusual Ben, a plane you are piloting,' said Marshall.

'Therefore, I did crash then, and I am here now and this is just a fading memory of what has already happened.'

'No Ben, you think it has happened, and only you can fix it. Remember what you read on the note, you and your future is still yet to happen, and only you can decide how it will be.'

'So tell me, explain to me if I am here, how is what I just saw thinkable?' questioned Ben.

'Do you know where here is Ben, or better when, no you don't, so just go with it, you have been allowed the privilege, if you will, to alter, even revise your own destiny. You can make good a bad situation, as you know now of your past, present and pending future, who would not want that. However, I suggest you choose wisely, do not be avaricious or materialistic, just want for what will make you happy and it will be. My one last piece of advice is this, if you change your past, alter it in any way, it will affect your future.'

'But if my future has happened, how by changing my past will that effect it?'

'Well only, you can decide that,' advised Marshall, 'only you.'

Ben turned back toward the base and searched for any signs of smouldering blooms behind the treetops that J-25 could have left; there was nothing. He could only assume it was J-25 and still found it hard to accept he was conceivably even the pilot. Was this in fact him returning from Operation Night Owl and was not MIA.

He placed his hand into his pocket, and felt for the gilded key, then turned back toward Old Morley Hall and that of the coffin room. As the two strolled across the park common, and back into the grounds of the hall, there were no words or any argument spoken by Ben, and Marshall never volunteered any conversation, or further comments, it was silent, it was tranquil, it was unreal.

Chapter 8

Coffin Room – unknown year:
Ben did not truthfully pay that much attention to his surroundings and that of people socialising at the entrance to the museum. He could just make out with his peripheral vision some movement by way of shades and obscurities he had to agree were in fact people, people that would by all accounts once again ignore his presence. His focus was on that of the coffin room and his assumed link to returning once again to Emily. Was the room really going to be there, and would it allow him to re-experience perchance his past? Something he could not comprehend was at all even possible, by simply entering the coffin room, nestling into the pod, thinking of a past life, falling asleep and waking back in 1943. He never discussed this with Marshall, nor he [Marshall] offered any such conversation about returning.

They walked by the two guards at the museum's entrance through the grand hall and passed the entry to the kiosk. Ben briefly paused as if an occupant seated at a one of the tables had noticed him. This he found had it actually happened, rather odd, when up to now nothing like this had occurred before.

The occupant was consuming a pumpkin scone, whilst reading a newspaper and sipping a hot drink from a white china cup. Ben now noticed the occupant, who while reading his tabloid was acting in a sort of nonchalant manner, possibly trying to avoid their presence. They both stood fast and stared at the occupant, who by now, no matter how he tried to continue to act casual and mix with the crowds seated at the café, only became more visible to the duo. The newspaper slowly lowering off his face exposing the soberness in his eyes now seemingly fixed on Ben. He placed the remaining piece of scone in his mouth and washed it down with his tea. The man stood, wiped his face clean, and then delicately placed the napkin on the saucer of the china cup. He stood what appeared to be ever so slightly taller than Ben. He had on the attire of someone perhaps noteworthy, someone important, someone very focused on a given task. His featureless face pallor in colour and looking anaemic and animated, yet he gave off a verve of authority.

Ben was now aware the man imaginably had noticed him. The two were as if drawn to each other and walked simultaneously toward the entrance of the kiosk. They remained wordless, their bodies inches apart, their gazes noneventful and the two remained taciturn for what seemed minutes.

The man's face looked familiar to Ben, perhaps it was someone he had seen in his life, and possibly, he was at the base, yet improbably imparted to Ben's self-assurance, as there was something very odd about it.

Ben lowered his head for a moment and dwelled over the anomalous happenings over his past few weeks. He did assume "weeks" and could never accept that it was anything less than that. Yet those weeks, by all accounts, equated to apparent actual years, years that had seen the passing of his much-loved Emily. His need to get some clarity, some simplicity back into his life, back to a world and time for him that was real, back to 1943. He, through Marshall, perhaps would get a better understanding on how he could return, and the coffin room seemed the only logical path to do so.

Ben regained his poise and again faced the stranger having digressed about his past and need to return to it. His confusion in actually trying to assess any certainty from doubt, was becoming harder to gauge, and needed to remain positive.

The stranger had a thinning expression, and eyes slightly recessed into his face. His skeletal features and weathered looks were not a sign of a man in poor health, but of a man infinite with discernment, awareness and somatic strength. His ostensible gesture and posture were seemingly similar to that of Ben's yet strangely unalike. Ben thought back to the time he had met Marshall at the base, and how he remembered he was similar in posture and comparable in looks to himself. There were of course times in Ben's life when he had not remembered his meetings with Marshall, and he wondered if it would ever become clear to Ben or better understood.

The stranger oddly had the appearance to that of Marshall, but his senior and Ben put him at a young-looking dynamic 50 something, perhaps even older. Why Ben even considered the similar appearance did not make any sense, so to satisfy his intrigue looked nonsensically for a scar across the stranger's eye.

His weathered look and aged face blended appropriately with the many creases and furrows and any scar would blend with his facial features making it, if it were there, simply obscure. Ben again lowering his expression away from the drawing stare of the stranger, perhaps feeling somewhat intimidated.

'Ben...BEN,' Marshall raised his voice to get Ben's attention, 'Let us move on.'

Ben tilted his head back, widened his eyes and focused on the stranger.

'Ben, let us go,' reiterated Marshall.

Ben confused, from not being able to understand how the stranger had just suddenly reclaimed his seat, it was as if he had never moved. The stranger's poise was idly inelastic and as if was mechanically automated and rewound, possibly spooled back, he had returned into his original spot. He continued to read the newsprint as if nothing just happened, briefly looking around, quite possibly in search of that devout awareness by some sort of preternatural manifestation feeling he just had. Ben could now only presume that the stranger had not noticed him and that of Marshall, and this was all part of his abnormal and unconventional past few weeks. The man looked up over his newspaper one last time just to put at rest the presupposition he had seen some kind of apparition. The waiter had bought him his usual pumpkin scone and pot of tea and sat it on the table next to his brown leather satchel bag.

'Is everything all right?' he asked, having noticed his attention was erratic and not in line with his normal unbroken devotion he had when reading his newspaper.

'Yes all is just fine,' said the stranger, but asked confusingly, 'Why another scone and cup of tea?'

'Another, why it's what you always have, every day without fail, your scone and tea…is there…some… something wrong?' replied the young man.

It was just then that the stranger realised what he had just said and so not to look like an old fool, suggested he was just tired. He looked up over his tabloid as he sipped on the tea, then placed the cup neatly back on top of the saucer. The stranger continued to dwell for a few minutes longer on just what had happened. Did he witness, something he knew to be the truth at the time, and that of his past incarceration was then unjust?

The stranger had been imprisoned for a crime, and beliefs he had at time that were well a little unconventional. Interrogation by doctors and psychiatrists took weeks of deliberation and finally in the last 10 days of examination, diagnosed him with a simple mental illness. They concluded he had impaired relationships with that of reality, so they hospitalised him. They had said he was unfit for war when it eventually erupted, and he had remained hospitalised for over 13 years. He had at the time lost touch with reality, and he was now living this once again, was he simply psychotic. He had searched his mind and read books, and articles hoping he would one day discover the truth that had cost him his career, his family, and part of his life. All those years were wasted, and he now needed to find the truth.

He folded his paper neatly by half then half again, and with a small piece of leather twine tied it together in a neat loop then placed it into his satchel. He stood after giving considerable doubt that he had just seen the boy he investigated 13 years earlier. He was now a young man, and from months of waiting for him to show, stood, pushed in his chair, and followed Ben, and the man with him, out of the kiosk.

Ben and Marshall wandered off towards the coffin room, having now forgotten about the stranger. Ben's past few minutes unremittingly subjugated his thoughts with crushing beliefs of how uncanny it was that he and Marshall were so much alike. Apart from the age difference and the scar over Marshall's eye, were the only dissimilarities. All that has happened to Ben, this thought alone did not now seem that strange? The man reading his paper took on a similar presence to that of Marshall, even to the point Ben looked for the scar. It was the eccentricity of them both, the irregularity of how they together appeared to him. Both Marshall and the man seemed to portray themselves as if they had somehow lived this moment before. He passed on the thought as quick as it entered his mind, then thought to himself, *Scar, if only I had a scar.*

They walked down the passage of the great hall and towards the arched opening of the cellar stone stairs. He shook his head at the thought of the stranger and Marshall and himself as being so comparable.

The familiar musty smell of the mossy growth on the walls drifted up the spiral stairs. The aroma, malodourous and foul smelling throughout the cellar, made Ben's eyes watery and enflamed from the stench.

Bottles of wines were still arranged on their sides, lining the walls in their little neat rows, still covered in dust and debris. Cobwebs blanketed the walls still giving the room an ancient and prehistoric appearance, almost a primitive feel. Marshall stood motionless for a moment as if he was waiting on Ben's next move, Ben, the same, if he was waiting on an instruction from Marshall.

'Well, my boy what are you waiting on, insert the key', announced Marshall.

If Ben was to write a story about himself at this very point in time of his life up to now, he could certainly write a novel. It would be like his character hero in the book, *Armageddon*, that of Anthony Rodgers. It would have strange events of his seemingly unusual ability to be in differing worlds, in different times, with opposing outcomes. He thought of the concept behind Marshall having just said 'Insert the key', what if it was that simple. What if without thought he had done this very thing for all his life; well, part there of anyway? Furthermore, what if this imaginary place was just that and invented in his mind?

He reached into his pocket hoping the key would not be there and he would wake and find all this just a dream. His heart raced now knowing it was not a vision made up in his mind, as his fingertips felt the irregular shape of the key wards. He lifted the key from his pocket, placed it into the slot and turned the bow of the key, and the door opened as it had probably done an infinite number of times before. He walked down the stone stairs, and through to the coffin room's entrance opening, turned and faced looking back up the stairs.

Without thought, Ben inserted the key into a slot adjacent the opening, and once again turned the bow. The neatly fitting door slid silently out of the hollow cavity and securely filled the entrance. It was devoid of any motorised sounds and only made the noiseless 'ssssh' sound, telling him once again the room was now impenetrable.

Ben stood still for a moment, not knowing his next move. He had witnessed the Liberator fly over, not knowing if indeed it was himself at the wheel or not. Perhaps it was himself returning from his mission and deliberated this in his mind. He accepted that it was a possibility, and moved on from that, then focussed on the strange man who had seen him at the kiosk, one that actually noticed him. As quick as that happened it was as if it did not, he turned and went to speak with Marshall.

It was at that precise and exact time; a strange occurrence had happened. It was a fissure, a flaw in the otherwise predictability of a set past. It had happened at a time when Marshall had thought he had now repaired all the wrongs. From Ben's age of eight, Marshall had influenced, corrected, and been able to somewhat sway Ben without Ben's knowledge he was actually doing so.

The opaque polished surfaces of the coffin room now illuminated and the faint glow providing sufficient lighting to see that Marshall was no longer in the room.

Ben oddly felt relief from this, he felt that he had prepared his own mind to make rational decisions and any judgements he would make from hear on in and decisions here on in would be his and his alone. It would be a decree without influence, deprived of guidance and devoid of thought. Marshall for whatever reason, purpose or whatsoever influence he had, would now remain absent from Ben's life. He no longer would be a part of it; it would be as if in every practical sense, he never even existed.

The stranger from the kiosk had just managed to see a door like partition slide across the face of the stone and then shut as if it were an integral part of the wall. A few seconds later, he could just make out a slight hissing noise coming from behind the partition, then it went silent. He composed himself for a moment, and it was to be this composure, his thoughts and intent and subsequent now likely coming of events that had just caused the alteration of any actions Marshall had set in place. It was this reason Marshall had gone from Ben's seemingly fabricated existence, having believed he had set things right, as he had said to Charlie all those years ago when Ben was eight.

The stranger smiled and happily shook his head in agreement, then spoke out loud to himself…

'I was right about the boy I knew it, Vermont, you old fool, you were right'. Ben's mother at the time spoke of Ben's visions, and Vermont had just witnessed something advanced, something unique, it was ahead of its time. His days as a detective were now overriding his otherwise stagnant mind, flooding back with strength and concentration. His acute attentiveness absorbed the situation and took over controlling his body as he turned without thought and hastily headed out of the building.

******

Old Buckenham Airfield England, 1943, that day:

The Liberator pilot reduced his throttle control descending the B-24 low over the treetops of St Peter. The conifer tree tips were darting and froing from the wake turbulence as the bomber glided low over Old Morley Hall, in preparation for landing. The uninterrupted droning of the Pratt & Whitney radial engines raised the heads of spectators below that searched the direction in which the approaching solitary aircraft was coming from. The engines resounded overhead in almost orchestral synchronisation, droning with complete unremitting unanimity. The odd eruption of exploding exhaust gases could be heard as they expelled from the innermost port engine. It caused it to pop and misfire, breaking from the rhythmical sounds as the aircraft descended even lower. The sustained approach by all accounts, was representative to how these monumental bombers performed; as box like as they were they were still almost as nimble as the Spitfire or the Hurricane.

The spectators below could almost taste the richness of the petroleum fuels as the yellow liquid detonated, triggering off the little controlled explosions within the cylinder heads. The two outer engines slowed to an idle; the innermost still alive as the exhaust blooms twirled and spiralled off the trailing edge of the partially extended flap surface.

The singular Liberator unremitting in its landing approach, continued at a low level towards the field. The silvery aluminium hull still shimmered even though there were now dull light levels of the impending rain as small droplets were exploding on the windscreen of the bomber. The pilot nestled into his seat, just pulling on his harness a little tighter, his fists firmly placed on the control wheel as the nose of the aircraft aligned effortlessly with the runway thresholds centreline.

The Chief and Marks stepped out of flight operations as the bombers crossed the threshold and flared onto the runway. The B-24's nose wheels setting down safely on home soil, after a successful mission into enemy territory. A mile or so behind the squadron and still on its final approach was the shiny fuselage of the new bomber. It was low, possibly to low but being un-laden, remained aloft with agility and without effort; the new Liberator had finally arrived.

Approaching the base, Vermont could see a pathway leading up to a single-entry gate. A military guard stood trying to look very important at his sentry point. He was reading perhaps a memorandum of sorts that Vermont guessed had been handed to him by the young man who stood rather awkwardly in front of the guard. Vermont had remembered this area when he was a child, where he would play amongst the pastoral grounds, but could not quite remember when it actually became a military airfield.

The guard's station had that horrible sickly yellow paint; it reminded Vermont of his time at the Norfolk Lunatic Asylum, the walls too were this distressing colour. He wondered how that alone would help in the rehabilitation, when it was to him rather confronting. During WW1, the asylum was used as a military hospital up to 1920. It had a name change thereafter to Norfolk Mental Hospital, and in 1923, until its eventual close, was renamed, St Andrews Hospital. Vermont always referred to it as the Norfolk Lunatic Asylum; it was after all how he remembered it as a child. By reminding the doctors of this, was perhaps the main reason for his early release in 1942 and subsequent self-emancipation of his past imaginings of Ben.

Vermont became absorbed with the thought he was now witnessing Ben, a young man who he had by all accounts had just seen at Old Morley Hall. He convincingly now knew the man with Ben at the hall was perhaps that of Ben's father, well to the point that's how Ben at the age of eight had referred to him as. To see this as an actual event was still very hard to understand and actually believe, yet during his incarceration he had some very self-same conversations with patients who had similar stories to tell. This he had kept to himself perhaps to remain on the rational side, and slowly worked out if he had made the stories disappear about Ben, he would eventually be released. Vermont didn't allow himself to be swayed by anything he was now seeing, just another trait of his training as a detective.

He watched the two; the guard's stance became a little more relaxed. He picked up a greenish coloured telephone hand piece and cranked the handle a few turns, then appeared to announce the arrival of the young man. Vermont was motionless as he concealed himself behind a shrub, just out of view to them both. He crouched even lower from hearing the sound of an approaching jeep, it stopped just short of the entry gate. Its passenger was a tall man over six-foot in non-uniform nor did he have any insignia. He didn't really appear to be military, except for flight wings and a pistol stowed neatly in its holster. Vermont kept hidden as the two eventually drove off toward the military base. 'That's enough for today', he whispered and decided to head home to compile his thoughts after all he was getting a little damp and cold from the rain anyway. His crouching position had stiffened his legs and his knees cracked as he stood, they worsened as he staggered off towards home. What made his knees worse was the fact it was also chilling down, and his old bones didn't go that well in these conditions.

His mind suddenly drifted back to his police days, and the unforgettable words he would use when chasing down someone on the run, 'Stop,' he would say, 'STOP or I will shoot.' Those were the last words he now remembered as the sentry guard placed cuffs onto his wrists and led him off for interrogation, inside the base of Old Buckenham.

******

Vermont was in the main hospital wing away from other patients. He had a bed close to a pair of swinging doors that lead into some type of laboratory. He had been evaluated from both doctors and nursing staff to gauge his sanity. It was more of a cross-examination than an assessment of his mental state, Vermont keeping his composure throughout. He knew only too well this process and would probably then have the advantage over his captors, if he ingenuously just remained focused. He watched intently how the pair of swinging doors opened and shut relentlessly, and if anything, that action alone actually almost sent him crazy. A few personnel were being treated for minor injuries, some were still with flight gear on, but ultimately, the hospital was just like most and that was, simply intimidating.

Vermont had seen Ben enter the room for his medical. A young nurse, the same nurse who had checked his vitals only moments before, had kept her equanimity during Ben's health check. Without showing any volatility, her self-possessed and confident calmness had kept Ben perhaps on the vulnerable side. Her beautiful auburn hair matched her cheeks as she blushed and tried to be professional in her behaviour, yet she still showed a slight vulnerability in front of Ben. He could hear the banter of Ben toward her, she kept things formal. His silhouette could be seen behind a standalone makeshift curtain that had been wheeled around her station, enough to provide some dignity for his medical and that of Ben's view to anyone else in the ward, including Vermont's.

Vermont had seen the repartee develop between them, and how unsophisticated and ingenuous Ben was perhaps without knowing it, and she remained composed and unruffled, yet the two seemed to develop a bond. He had a little laugh to himself when he saw her shadow of an arm raise high then jab him in quick succession, it indisputably would have hurt, and Vermont certainly felt the young man's pain.

Over the next few hours, Vermont became trustworthy to that of the young nurse. He, if he had to get any clarity over Ben's life before now needed her on his side. Vermont had little understanding for what he had seen at Old Morley Hall, yet knew from Charlotte's words of Ben being visionary, there was something about this young man, and the mansion.

Charlotte had told Vermont back when Ben was eight that he was quite visionary and told of a bomb that would end an entire city in seconds. When incarcerated, Vermont had limited access to the outside world. He was only able to get restricted news bulletins through staff or partial newspaper articles or listen to some BBC broadcasts over the radio from within the hospital. He had heard that the Germans had at around the latter part of 1938 or early 39, he couldn't quite remember, been experimenting with uranium, and they had managed to eventually split the atom. There were fears at the time that Nazi Germany scientists could utilise that energy to produce a bomb of unspeakable destruction.

Albert Einstein had fled Nazi persecution and moved to the United States, and he and Enrico Fermi, who had also escaped but from Italy, both agreed to tell the president of the dangers of atomic technology if it got into the wrong hands, that being Germany. Einstein had written a letter to President Roosevelt, urging the United States into the development of their own atomic research programme. At the time, Roosevelt didn't see the necessity to develop a programme, and Vermont almost conceded with himself that he probably was a little crazy in thinking Ben had foreseen this, so he agreed with himself he perhaps did belong at the Norfolk Hospital.

A turn of events in late 1941 eventually saw America develop the Manhattan Project, whereby they were to design and build an atomic bomb. Most of the research was being done at the University of Chicago, and eventually they had a breakthrough in December of 1942. Led by Fermi, a group of physics scientists produced the first controlled nuclear chain reaction. At that time Vermont then felt relieved that he had convinced himself these visions from Ben where in fact now real. It would be around another two years before America would get their breakthrough and on the 16th of July 1945, scientists of the Manhattan Project would test the world's first atomic bomb. Around 20 days later on August the 6th 1945, America flew over Japan in a B-29 bomber, named Enola Gay, they would drop a five-ton atomic bomb on the city of Hiroshima. Ben's vision of 15 years earlier would eventually then come true.

August 11, 1943, Operation Night Owl, post briefing 14:40 hrs:

Vermont looked across at Ben, as Emily was adding a powdered medication into a glass of warm water. Marks stood a little off to the side whilst Emily prepared Ben's treatment, Marks had settled a little knowing that the sleep Ben was about to have would indeed help the situation. Ben seemed erratic, non-coherent and seemingly ignorant to that of Vermont, even when their eyes met, there wasn't any response. Ben gulped down the liquid, Marks appeared satisfied then left, Vermont could see Ben almost look straight through her as if she were not there also. Ben looked scared, defenceless yet somehow positively vigilant to that of his surroundings. Ben slowly drifted off to sleep, his inaudible words confused Emily even more even as he called out her name, and that of a Marshall Hartley. Vermont wondered if this was the man he had seen with Ben at the kiosk and tried to attune in even more to what he was saying. It was just then that Vermont heard what he needed to hear, Ben clearly spoke of "The Sector" and "coffin room"; it confused her but not Vermont. He immediately recognised this must be the room at Old Morley Hall, the one perhaps that was undisputedly hidden and purposely built behind a stonewall.

It worried Emily and she did not like to see him in this way and tried to keep herself occupied by attending to other patients, eventually confiding in Vermont.

'Are you OK?' Vermont probed Emily.

'YES, I mean yes, sorry for raising my voice, it is just the mission I, I mean all the…'

Emily had almost forgotten Vermont was a civilian and that the base was covert, but continued, she had to vent her anger with someone, she thought.

'…I mean all the war and fighting, I just wish it will end, and we can get on with our lives in peace,' finished Emily this time in a more restrained tone.

'Emily, I need to tell you something, but are in fear you may be able to influence my return to Norfolk Lunatic Asylum.'

'Norfolk Lunatic Asylum?' enquired Emily.

'Sorry, the St Andrews Hospital, I was a patient, and that does explain my hanging around the base.'

'Why did you not say something before, we, I mean they could have perhaps released you, or sent you back, I mean back to the hospital, why are you, were you ill?' sympathised Emily.

'Well, how much time do you have to hear my side of things?' said Vermont.

'We are planning a mission but would prefer to stay around here just until Ben wakes, I guess, so what is your side of things then?'

Vermont took in a deep breath, nestled back into his bed, still partially restrained to his gurney. Emily wheeled over her Goodform industrial office chair; it had a dull reddish leather not the drab dark brown colour like her father's. Its roller wheel casters squeaked across the linoleum floor tiles loud enough to startle Ben. He murmured something about the halls, kiosk, then drifted back to sleep, Vermont told his story.

******

'It was around 1930. I was at Banham police department as one of their detectives and had been assigned to a case of a missing boy. There were a number of more missing boys, after that, I think seven or so, I can't really remember but nonetheless there were some concerns that they were all linked somehow. This one boy in particular, had turned up at school five hours later thinking he had only just got off the bus. The school had searched the grounds and surrounding bush land for him and there was grave fear for his safety. We at the department didn't come to the school straight away and elected to visit his home and speak directly to him and his mother, away from all the probing questions from teachers and his class friends. She seemed nervous at first and he could be, well more so would be taken from her. She told me stories of his visions, visions of future events, events still yet to come.

'At that time between my partner and I, we just put it down to the imaginings of a young boy. I became a little obsessed about the story that his mother had told me, and I stupidly at the time kept a diary of his and the other boys disappearances looking for any similarities. I ultimately ended at the hospital, tarnished as unfit for duty, mentally unstable and subsequently incarcerated at the asylum; until the war broke out, well a little after that.'

'I am not following you Mr Vermont; I mean how, did the missing boys have an influence on you being incarcerated at the asylum.'

'Well, this is where it will get a little hard, you see the boy who went missing but returned was Ben, and he at the time had no knowledge of where he was, and made some sort of reference to his father, sorry it's a bit vague but I believe the man he was refereeing to as his father is Marshall Hartley., I now believe he is real and I saw them both at Old Morley Hall just before they bought me here a few days ago. I had a belief that it could have been Ben's Father but am unsure now.'

'Well, Ben has only been here a few days, so that does not seem that strange; he could have been there before he came here.'

'Emily, there is a room there that is a bit peculiar…'

'Peculiar, what do you mean peculiar?' she asked.

'I saw Ben and Marshall, um sorry I have to presume it was Marshall, enter a room that was, hidden behind a stone wall.'

'Mr Vermont this is sounding a little childish,' Emily then regaining her poise.

'There is one more thing,' whispered Vermont.

'I truly don't believe there will be anything you will tell me that will change my mind, I am not convinced with any of this mumbo jumbo talk,' insisted Emily.

'Charlotte had told me of Ben's visions and that of a bomb that would end an entire city in seconds. Emily that bomb is or has been in the development stage since 1941. I fear Ben will be right, there will be a bomb of magnitude, one that will end lives, thousands of lives in seconds.'

'Mr Vermont, suppose there is some truth to your story, then why hasn't he said something?'

'Emily, I don't have any reason to doubt the truth behind Ben being visionary, he somehow had predicted, well, it hasn't happened yet, but the development of the atom bomb, and that must count for something.'

'I, are'…Emily hadn't time to finish her words…

'Emily, will you do something for me, and if I am wrong I will say no more of this, but if I am right, and I know I am, Ben, when he wakes must not know.'

'All right I will play this game, but agree with me that if you are wrong you say nothing more, and you agree to some help, as I will recommend you return to St Andrews Hospital?'

'Alright I do, I agree I will sign anything, do as you say, return restrained if I have too, but please, Emily, you must agree with me that Ben is not told of this.'

'Alright I agree with you,' said Emily, 'So what is it you want me to do?'

'I am hoping Ben has a key or some sort of unlocking device on him somewhere, perhaps I am wrong but if I am not, something tells me it will be better for Ben if he does not know.'

'Mr Vermont I will do what you want for my reasons not yours, you may need some help of which as a nurse are concerned for your welfare. But more so there is something odd in what you say, and that is this morning when I left Ben, he had the same cloths as he does now, but look at them, they appear aged, soiled and worn as if, well as if…'

Emily could not quite bring herself into saying what she was now starting to think, and that was what if Vermont had some truth to his claims, she would never know unless she did this simple thing.

She reached into his pocket, the odorous stains of gasoline and oils, stung into her hands.

Vermont had hoped he was right, and trusted Emily would find the key device. Vermont had played her off to his advantage, and if he was right and there was a device of some sort, perhaps it would allow him access to what was behind the wall.

Emily's face turned white and she felt faint. Her arm muscles were burning from the adrenaline flow of blood in her veins as her hand touched what she made out to be a small object. It was cold against her burning fingers, the knuckle joints tightened on her thumb and forefinger as she clasped what she preserved to be a small metallic object.

She pulled out what appeared to be a tiny gold coloured type of key. It was very inconsequential she thought to herself, something that if it did what Vermont said it would, appeared very simple in its making. She had envisaged a device with a mechanical type appearance, that had those complicated little cogs and wheels that turn the hands of an old grandfather clock. Her analogy of what she had in her mind was probably over thought and too complex but as overwhelmed as she now was by these entire circumstances, she allowed herself that way of thinking.

Ben mumbled again, this time partially opening his eyes, then instantly drifted back into a deep sleep.

'Well Mr Vermont you are right,' as she held up the key into the light of the room to get a better look at the device.

'So tell me, what now?' Emily asked nervously, knowing if she were asked the same thing from Vermont, she would have nothing to suggest feeling somewhat relieved when Vermont offered the same.

'If I had that answer, I truly would let you know, but I don't. I am guessing when Ben wakes up, we will know; he will either say something untoward thereby not helping our situation or entirely profound. May I look at the key, Emily?' asked Vermont.

She handed it to him, as Ben stirred.

'All I know is that Charlotte had told me some strange things about Ben being as she put, "unconventional". She did sound rather vague at the time and did change that view later when she came and saw me at the hospital.

'What do you mean?' asked Emily, 'She changed her view and saw you later, I am not following you Mr Vermont, when did she see you?'

'I am unsure of the exact date but strangely when I was in hospital, she just turned up one day, out of respect I think for had happened to me, being looked at, at the time as a suspect.'

'How later sir, tell me,' she pleaded.

'Well, I think it was just before my release, around a year or so before, if I recall correctly, so the latter part of '42, yes, around September or so, yes that's it, September, 1942.

'That is not possible Mr Vermont, you either are being very cruel or in fact truly in need of some help. Charlotte died in December two years earlier, Mr Vermont, two years; your story is what it is, just a story…'

Ben slept for a further 50 or so minutes, Vermont somehow convinced Emily to stay so as to gauge Ben's reaction on waking.

When Ben woke, he simply got up as if nothing had happened and went off to the showers.

******

The strange occurrence that had happened two days ago at the kiosk of Old Morley Hall, is something that does surface in our everyday lives. This occurrence could have little consequence and even go unnoticed, yet can never be truthfully explained how or even why it happens. We exist as individuals, living uniquely as one without influence or living concurrently parallel with another, almost synchronously. Unquestionably, there are some individual's paths that do cross and cause catastrophic sequences of events, unbeknown to them both, without warning or reason and as a result, those individuals' lives are then changed. Then there are those whose lives cross with intent, perhaps manipulated maliciously or for one's own personal gain. Our lives arguably could already have been planned out, perhaps plotted in such a way that if any input, any involvement, or simple participation from an influence could cause an unimportant change. It could also have a radical effect on the course of events that led up to that moment, and then if altered slightly or have the possibility of change from the influence, could this undeniably modify the previous path that got those all to that point in time in the first place? If two paths cross the already travelled or that of the intended, can this then cause a different outcome of probability? For a single path then to continue be it the past or the future, they cannot happen concurrently, one path must be terminated, it's opposing path must then cease to happen for that single change then to continue.

Vermont had that intent instantly when he saw Ben at the kiosk and without Ben knowing it at the time, had radically set himself on a path of an otherwise different result, both now and from his past. Should he not have or intended to change it, things would be as they are, and Ben was well more or less setting his own course of events, one he could assume would happen, had happened or through his own influence will happen. Perhaps Ben's life had never been mapped, until this very moment, perhaps it was never set before this influence had occurred, or perhaps it was yet to be and from here on in as it was always intended. Ben would live a phase of his life, a juncture of a passing moment before it even happened, and this very strange occurrence to that of Vermont had subsequently set Ben on a tangent, a digressional path to that of his deliberate and pre-planned past. This premeditated mapped out course of events that had and was already set before his meeting with the strange man at the kiosk, had fundamentally now changed Ben's future events that were still yet to happen, this in turn had also changed without him knowing it, his past.

August 12, 1943, Operation Night Owl, flight preparation 00:39 hrs:

Ben stepped out from the shower and buried his reddened face deep into his dowdy coloured bath towel. At that very moment, he became aware that the intense heat of the water about his facial features, so gently patted dry off any remaining droplets of the steaming water vapour about his cheeks. He had suddenly become conscious of now, with only sketchily indeterminate memories from the flight briefing up to the shower.

He partially remembered being at the ward, well to the point he slept or better woke there, but for what reason was just a mystery. Why had he been at the hospital, and without warning been sent there by Marks, was not only unknown, but very much out of the ordinary to himself. As he focused in on that alone, small pieces of the sickbay and his time there were coming back. He remembered the glass of paracetamol in warm water, Emily, and mumbling to her something about his rest on the grass outside Hanger 5 before the briefing. He could not quite evoke anything of substance, apart from the many confusing things that were now swamping his mind that happened before now.

He was able to produce only vague snippets of Emily at the ward doing her duties and preoccupied about something as she always did. He guessed it was the mission and possibility of the non-returning of some of the crew, maybe in particular, himself?

He continued drying off while searching his thoughts, and bit by bit they began burgeoning back in ever increasing and amassed detail. He would then get a glimpse of something he thought would help, then as soon as he attuned into that, it would ebb back like a receding tide, he could not just focus to some degree, on any one thing. His mind twisted and turned similarly to that of pilots of The British Empire Air Display. Their Jenny's performing aerial tricks, such as "wing overs" then falling uncontrolled in a spin, then to regain attitude before careering into the ground. His peculiar thoughts of unidentified places, unknown times and unfamiliar people, passed in and out of his mind. His concentration was trying to focus on something that he just could not seem to grasp. As soon as he got the memory, it would weaken whereby he become convinced that these fascinations he was now having, were just that of an improbable dream.

Oddly, he had a voice in his mind, one he was able to paint a picture of, enough to form a face, a person he would refuse to believe that they were not real, and part of this, whatever this was. This was his only true thought that seemed tangible and that was that of Marshall, Marshall Hartley.

He tossed his towel on the floor and began to dress into his flight gear, pulling first up his bib-front trousers and fastening his bolero style jacket. He lent forward to the footlocker and grabbed his A-3 parachute harness and booties. The lid of his footlocker provided some respite as he sat on its top and restored his thoughts for a moment. His booties that were always hard to pull up over his ankles, soon nestled comfortably about his foot, securing them like a warm woollen mitten he would wear on his way to school in winter. He pulled down the leg part of his bib front trousers and secured them about his booties. As he stood and closed the locker lid, the comfort of the clothing stretched and moulded to the shape of his body, providing a sense of security, refuge perhaps from the pending danger of the mission.

He leaned forward one last time and opened the locker lid pulling out his B-8 goggles, oxygen mask and gloves, which finished off his attire, then slightly hesitated before closing the lid. He glanced down into the locker and its contents, knowing he was fated to do one last thing. This thought, unaided as if inscribed into his mind, possibly something etched, told him to pause at the sight of his book, *Armageddon*. He grabbed at the comic book without thought flicking through the pages almost knowing exactly where to stop. It was choreography at its finest as if he had practiced this manoeuvre a thousand times, then looked at the floor to a spot he knew would be the place a small envelope would fall from the book. It fell, as he knew it would, at the exact place he was looking at, he picked it up as he knew he would and tucked it neatly into his pocket of his bib-front trousers, as he had done once before.

Rain started to fall when the crew were being ferried out onto the tarmac. Ben, sitting silently on the bonnet of Marks' jeep not saying much as he gazed at the droplets of rain falling like little snowflakes, illuminated by the floodlights, they looked unnatural as they fell toward the tarmac. Strangely, they looked almost like miniature soldiers, descending to earth, the lit silvery droplets, their tiny parachutes. "The Mule" was strategically towing the remaining floodlights into their pre-determined positions and the crew began arriving. Ladders were up against the engine cowls, men finalising their checks, bombs and ammunition loaded and petroleum fuels by the gallon were added.

Since his shower, the last hour or so seemed to have taken no time to tick by. Ben and crew had mulled about the main gear of their respective bombers and were just chatting about nothing when the 15-minute flare gun shot a blast up into the murky skies. The blaze ascended high above the field, like a rocket, Ben knew the enflamed blooms would sparkle and flicker about the night sky providing a phantasmagoria almost dreamlike appearance of varied dissimilar colours. He knew the flares spent residues would fall back to earth amid the rain drizzle, and turn the night sky illusionary, unreal and imaginary almost fantasy like. The crew's eyes looked up into the heavens at the still glowing effects of the flare, perhaps making peace with God or a loved one, as the last of the flames and burning embers descended back down to earth. The cinders of the flash making that "sisssssss" sound as the final little bit of heat they had, was draw from there lifeless existence from the precipitation.

Few words were spoken from the aircrew and most had scrambled into their aircraft. Personal were moving in all directions, like balls after the "break" on the Burroughes & Watts billiard table, a favourite in the mess hall apart from the Rock-Ola jukebox.

Ben stood idle and waited knowing he would soon see a lone figure walking toward him, similar in size, posture and appearance; it would be that of Marshall Hartley. Facing toward the huge tail fins of the B-24, he wiped clear the driblets of rain off his eyes then blinked trying focus at the person now standing before him.

'Hello Ben, how are you, ready for your flight?' whispered the figure.

Ben instantly became incapable of words, something was wrong, he tried to speak but his tongue almost felt anesthetised, unresponsive to any words he frustratingly could not put together or say. The night was still its pale purple colour almost lilac and the stars were still visible just as he remembered, however the voice wasn't right. He momentarily looked up at the night sky hoping to get clarity, focusing in on the glistening lights of the stars that he had likened to the runway markers he would see on a night landing. It was the same analogy he remembered as he said before, yet the voice, was erroneous, it was another, it was not Marshall's as was prophesied. The rain abruptly stopped, there were no puddles, no ponding and no sound, just the tranquil stillness you would get when flying through a thunderstorm, and into the "eye". His flooded back memories of when he was eight, at the school bus, still vivid in his mind. There nothing about this moment and the few hours after the shower that had changed, apart from the voice, the voice then spoke again…

'Hadn't you better get into your plane and fly this mission Ben?'

Something wasn't right, something he didn't understand, it was untrue, flawed in its exacting precision as was this moment before. He looked and focused on the image before him. Nothing would come from his mouth, his voice still silent.

'Well, get on board and fly said the voice…oh don't forget to…'

It was then Ben was able to speak, his words came out strong, unblemished and oblivious to the confusion he just had from the voice, yet able to finish off the words precisely that previously were spoken by Marshall, 'Oh, don't forget the read the note,' was all he could say.

Everything came together at once, his entire life, from eight to now, sped past in an instant. He hadn't time to understand fact from fiction, had he simply dreamed up his past, had it never happened and was this the first time he had done what he was now doing.

'Ben, BEN, I am getting wet, I need to go, hurry and get into your plane.'

Ben's mind was in a rush, the numbness in his concentration shot into his entire body like little convolutions, little tremors as he savoured their embrace and that of the familiar figure before him.

They then turned and headed back toward the rear of the aircraft, Ben as if in harmony with them, also turned and headed toward the underbelly hatch of his Liberator. He hadn't realised that the rain was once again falling, and the night sky was no longer a pale purple colour, and completely indistinguishable to that of the ground. It was ominous, it was wintry, it was without disagreement an unwelcomed night for flying. The underbelly hatch was latched, and Ben climbed up to the flight deck of his B-24, J Two Five, as Emily walked under the tail fins of the Liberator and back towards the base.

******

Emily arrived back at the entrance to the main building facility and had one last look over her shoulder in time to see Ben's Liberator taxi up to the runway threshold. Its bulky fuselage in the distance looked almost insect like, slowly crawling over the tarmac, bobbing under the sheer weight of the bombs held inside its aluminium abdomen. The nose wheel housing likened to the mouthpiece of the gargantuan creature swallowed the flattened and protuberant tyre; the hull instantly rebounded and coiled back as the Liberator came to a stop at the threshold marker of the runway.

Ben toggled the switch that extended down the landing lights from the underside of the wing, providing illuminated beam like spears that impaled the disconsolate early morning unlit darkness of rain and miasma. From inside the facility, Emily could hear the engine's resonate and rebound about the corridors, in metrical harmony. Ben's throttles fully forward the motionless Liberator, sat back onto the shocks of its main gear, the nose gear strut extended as J Two Five started its journey down the runway towards Germany.

The thunderous roar of each of B-24's four engines could be heard as communally in groups of three aircraft they careered down the runway following Ben on the way to their mission. By the time they were wheels up, the next three were already rolling down the runway, and so on. It was the 451st's standard formation departure under these limited visibility conditions. The squadron leader first and he would track out on runway heading setting manifold pressure at 2,700rpm for take-off, gear up, then slightly reducing to 2,650rpm at or around 300 feet. The first three would remain at 2,700rpm as they sluggishly caught up to Ben, then remain on his centre line reducing rpm as required. The next three would fall into formation on the port side, followed by the starboard side for the next three. This would happen four more times, so three left, three right, three left, three right, the final three would then be centred. The formation was never any more than four aircraft wide, so it was tight, effective, and it worked.

By the time Emily arrived back at the hospital ward, all aircraft had almost departed and the sound of the rain on the ironclad roof at the base drowned out the reverberation of the engines to an almost non-existent low rumble, as each plane in turn, entered cloud.

She had time to think about what Vermont had said in particular about what Charlotte had told him of Ben arriving at her doorstep as a child. It did seem rather odd that Ben simply got up and went off to the showers without even a "hello", or a "what's going on" type question, not even a simple acknowledgment of her presence. The more she thought of Vermont's accusation of the strange events at Old Morley Hall, the concealed room, nothing of anything made any sense. She provided Vermont an explanation as to why Ben could have been there, but when Vermont mentioned Charlotte telling him of Ben's visions, and she were still alive put an entire new perspective into all of this; it simply didn't have any truth to it.

There was no indication from when she saw Ben at his aircraft just prior to departure that there was anything strange apart from him looking almost right through her, as if she were not even there, and perhaps he expected someone else in her place.

She looked out a small hallway window in time to see a waning shadowy image of the last B-24 swallowed up by the amorphous layer of nimbostratus cloud and drizzle. It reminded her of her youth when she threw stones into the lake and how they slowly faded from view as they sunk into the bottomless and murky depths of the water.

Emily had to focus and get some clarity from what Vermont had said. She needed to see her father and find out why he had sent Ben in for some rest. It was not like him to be involved in her nursing duties or do something like this and to be there with Ben at his check-up, was and is something Emily in all her time with him both here and at home as a child growing up, had never seen before.

Emily without knowing it had now become part of this strange occurrence. She innocently had set her own self on a course of differing events, than that of her past. It was an ever so slight of a change, something very much innocent, and quite possibly without any effect on her future. She had only the one disconcerting question, and that was Ben had explained his mother had lost her life in the bombings, Vermont had said she had visited him at the asylum – what was the truth to this?

She started to piece together the events of the past few hours. If she was to believe Vermont, then Charlotte was alive, yet Ben had told her otherwise. Her father attending Ben's pre-mission check-up, and then to show up at the ward, odd by all accounts. Ben abnormally just getting up from his rest and heading off to the showers without any acknowledgment to her, not even a wink or a smile, not like him. She began to reflect on what if Vermont had just the smallest amount of substance in what he claimed. She would question Vermont one last time, and then go and see her father.

******

Flight operations was now in mission lockdown, Operation Night Owl had the count of plus twelve minutes. Halverson was on the Radio checking the progress of each plane as it crossed the oceanic waters of the North Sea. It was his own particular way of doing things, not normally done of course when a mission was underway; perhaps it was his way of just being fatherly to the crew. Marks had called Billy B on the radiophone and notified him of mission commencement at 01:58.

Marks had his secretary filing the aircraft load sheets, fuel weights and crew titles in rank and aircraft call signs, just as a formality. It was not that it was a requirement and truly needed, Marks only asked for it, to keep a little order in an otherwise informal base.

Marks and Halverson kept an eye on the squadron as they flew on toward Esberj, and into enemy territory. They continued to watch over the mission, as the planes flew deeper into rival terrain, Marks calmly lessened his concerns over Ben as the planes with each minute, neared Peenemünde.

Operation Night Owl, 04:40 hrs:

It was at this defined and precise moment that Ben had impetuously become more aware of his past. He too, like Emily, had slowly been putting things together in his own mind, trying to understand any reality in what or was not happening. The respite he had in sickbay, telling Marks of Peenemünde, departure at the base without seeing Marshall and then unpredictably seeing Emily in his place. He still knew about the footlocker and his book, *Armageddon*, deliberately opening the book at an exact page, then the note, and where it would precisely fall on to the floor. He had lived almost all of this moment, and perhaps the minor dissimilarities he was now seeing were in fact from his want of a change. He had done this before and as much as Marks thought he were crazy, and sending him to the infirmary, being checked by Emily was and is part of what Marshall had eluded to, that being Ben had the opportunity to set his own path.

Ben focused in on this alone; he had probably seemed distant to his crew up to now, but needed to take control of this moment. He knew exactly what was going to happen during the mission, when, and the outcome. He had tried to tell

Marks after the briefing, when he first woke from falling asleep outside Hanger 5, about Peenemünde. Marks without question found that totally implausible. Perhaps up to that point in his rather diverse past, Ben had not lived the life he had intended to or supposed to.

He had trouble in piecing together when or exactly where he had met Marshall for the first time. It had always crossed his mind, was it at the school bus, in the coffin room after the first time he ever woke in it, or in 1953 at the park when he met Emily and the boy? He kept going back to the words of Marshall, like "fissure" and "correct it" when he came to house and spoke to Charlie as being the reason for all his confusion. Ben's mind arranged these times, and he started to see how a time then could have been relived a second or third time perhaps, so it was then eventually corrected, or set right? Ben thought if it was that simple, re-experience the moment of then, now, this mission, alter only what he needed to and get back to base, get back to Emily. He swallowed the bulging lump in his throat, then called Wilson over the intercom, for a position fix.

Wilson seemed a little nebulous, that Ben had asked just as he was about to give a location, after all he was the navigator and he directed when position fixes were given.

Wilson took control, 'Um, I have a few position fixes of Amsterdam and Bremen, so am happy for you to fly this track for another six minutes at this speed,' Wilson finished feeling back in control of the situation…

Ben was smiling under is oxygen mask, as he mouthed the same words totally synchronised with that of Wilson's.

… 'Then, turn right onto a track of one one five degrees, and that should take us directly somewhere toward Peenemünde… I can get a fix off Denmark and keep us clear through the Femer Belt, over the water,' finished Wilson.

'Will do,' said Ben, 'will do,' placing Wilson once again at ease that he was most definitely in control of navigation. This placed Wilson at comfort allowing Ben to consider perhaps he had without knowing it, been successful in altering his future, and now back in control of his present, and will now be able to re-experience that of his past.

'Sir, Micky here, I have just received a cryptogram from base, telling us to avoid Peenemünde, and head down to Hamburg there has been heavy casualties in Poland, and we have received word they are aware we are coming.'

It was just how Ben remembered, but still much to do, he thought to himself by avoiding the attack of the ME109 he would save the lives of his crew. He would have to fly the channel avoiding the USS Trilogy not flying through it as before, and get back to base with his squadron, intact, and without loss of life.

******

Emily wheeled over her Goodform office chair to the bedside of Vermont's gurney. Its casters still squealed and made a rattling sound as she pushed it across the linoleum floor tiles. She laid back into the stool, her auburn hair out of place from the rainfall, her uniforms coronet falling off to one side and not placed with its usual gracefulness.

She nestled into the armchair positioning herself to face Vermont front on, the two looked at each other with thorough determination.

'Mr Vermont, I am going to make this very simple, and can get myself in a great deal of trouble over this, but something tells me you are without any explanation at the moment, somehow meant to be here. Something tells me there is some small amount of truth and I say very small amount that what you are saying, well with the key and how you knew it would be there, could be credible. However, Mr Vermont I find it hard to understand the untruth, which is Charlotte'

'Charlotte is alive,' interrupted Vermont, and have no explanation as to what this is either, and is all I keep asking myself. From way back to when Ben was at school and his disappearance, something I witnessed, and the entire school fraternity for that matter is a mystery to me. I have watched something very extraordinary at Old Morley Hall, and the concealed room, the man with Ben, perhaps his father, and the proof of the key, is that not worth some sort of investigation. You saw how Ben was vague when he woke, and before that for that matter.'

'If you are wrong about Charlie then that is cruel to both me and Ben, she did die in the bombings and that is that, but there is a little substance and unsure yet of the truth in what you are saying, and the key is what is giving you this opportunity now. So, before you say another thing, answer me this, what proof do you have Ben's mother is still alive?'

Operation Night Owl – Somewhere over the English Channel:

The strange occurrence that had set the path of differing outcomes had now strengthened. It dishevelled, and twisted at an ever-increasing expediential rate, unbeknown to Ben. The fissure that Vermont had opened altered past events that were going to happen to Emily and almost certainly, to Vermont, yet Ben strangely remained almost analogous to his past. Ben oblivious to Vermont being the main reason the fissure had occurred, presumed it was Marshall who had influenced him enough so his returning to a life with Emily would be imminent. Ben could only presume Marshall who was not at his plane before departure was all part of his altered future which Ben had assumed he had now set for himself. Both Ben and Vermont's lives were without reason running concurrently, and this was unexplainable, perhaps it was meant to be?

The complications of a path in life whereby two lives run synchronously yet with a differing outcome was by no means possible. How this was happening was due to a past event that perhaps did not occur, and did so only in thought, and by whom? If the strange occurrence was looked at in a likely and possibly way of actually happening, it could only be that is it completely and likely to be improbable.

******

The English coast was almost visible as J-25, descended through 25,000 feet at its nominal 100 feet per minute rate of descent. Ben knew he was nearby where he would encounter the lone ME109. He had planned out the encounter bit by bit in his mind knowing when and at almost what point.

Safety was less than 30 minutes away, as his eyes repetitively scanned the coastline's horizon for the first sign of the fighter plane. This was indeed common practice for all the crew, even though they were almost over allied territory.

The flight crew quickly became aware of a recognisable whirr sound, that of a Messerschmitt 109. Crossing the nose of J-25, and pitching high, the fighter plane barrel rolled sharply to the left, and Ben saw the familiar underbelly of the aircraft. The squadron at Ben's lead, held fast their formation causing the fighter to take evasive action and avoid their inexorable flight path. The 109 turned sharply back in hope for a line of site shot at the lead bomber, that of Ben's. Its 20mm nose cannon and two wings mounted 13mm machine guns spat bullets unswervingly at the cockpit of the Liberator, Ben's B-24 taking instant evasive action. It was at that precise moment the windscreen of the Liberator should have shattered. A piece of cockpit fuselage section would then have been ripped from the 24's aluminium structural ribs causing the Cap to be sucked out. But the Liberator wasn't hit by the 109s machine gun fire, and Ben's pre-planned outmanoeuvres had successfully altered a past event. The unwieldly Liberator effortlessly regained its flightpath back onto the incoming 109, its pilot confused at the rapid change of Ben's plane from formation.

'Fire those cannons Spot!' yelled out Ben, 'Give him everything you have, this one's for Emily.'

The order seemingly prophesied, as the nose gunner of the Liberator without hesitation or thought, instantly ended the life of the 109 pilot.

Anyone would have seen this moment as being, almost foreseen. It was a precisely executed flight manoeuvre in and out of formation, with the utmost of exactitude. The crew had witnessed something extraordinary; it was as if it were prepared ahead of time, almost rehearsed and the ME109 attack witnessed as incredulous. Should they have known it at the time that Ben would also deliberately avoided the USS Trilogy, would identify him perhaps as a deity or seer. To him, he was just simply reliving a past event, and making it better, making it right, well to the point he perhaps would live a full and fruitful life with Emily.

Ben's concurrent path was now running with Vermont's, and as coexistent as it was, Ben could not have foreknown or expected any change happening from Vermont's influence on Emily. Vermont at the time Ben had knowingly avoided the Messerschmitt attack, was in deep conversation with Emily and thereby unknowingly altering a path Ben had assumed he had just corrected. It was without warning and at that exact moment in time just as Emily had asked Vermont the same confusing question, Marks entered the ward.

'Mr Vermont, I ask you again please tell me of what proof you have that Ben's mother is still alive.'

'Emily, you are starting to sound as crazy as Ben was before he left.' The second Marks had just said what he said, he realised what he had said, and tried correcting his unpropitious words.

'I mean, as crazy as Ben was with the mission —' Marks adjusting his impulsive line of questioning.

Emily interrupted, 'That IS NOT what you mean Father, tell me, please tell me what you are saying,' implored Emily.

Marks quickly retorted, 'The squadron's only 10 minutes out Emily and we have a few damaged planes, so let us expect some minor causalities and get —'

Marks didn't have time to finish when Vermont, sat up in bed and spoke openly to Marks.

'He said something to you didn't he, he said something that is unbelievable,' questioned Vermont.

Marks didn't have time to think when he looked back at Vermont, with a belligerent look in his eyes.

'Excuse me sir, you are a civilian and under house arrest, you are not entering into this conversation.'

'Dad, please listen to him, please and tell me that you are not keeping something from me,' pleaded Emily.

It wasn't that often that Marks had heard Emily call him Dad. He had recalled only a few, each of which was when she had unheeded her situation especially when in trouble, and needed him to focus on the question not the reason why he was disciplining her, she was very good at changing his way of thinking.

'Emily, what are you not telling me?' Marks asked just managing to turn around the situation of cross-examination from him back to her.

'Dad, I need to know something and it will, well, I hope not sound too senseless. And please don't think I am injudicious in asking it but something is not right with Ben,' she raised her voice just enough to show she was serious. 'Mr Vermont investigated Ben's disappearance when he was eight, it's odd but Vermont also is saying something about Old Morley Hall.'

Marks had no words for this moment, now more confused that he had ever been, he felt it best to be silent now, focus on the aircraft arrivals and have his staff see to the wounded.

'Emily I will discuss this with you later —' he didn't have time to finish when she turned and headed out of flight operations, leaving Marks in wonder about Bens pre-knowledge on Peenemünde. Emily slammed the door behind her and headed towards the airfield.

******

The squadron flew in low over the surrounding fields of St Peter in preparation for landing. With the field in sight, each aircraft lined up in sequence, planes suffering the most damage took the more direct path followed by a lengthy "base leg", then turn at an oblique angle onto final for the remaining bombers. When Emily had reached the field, she had almost forgotten her father's comments just moment's ago. The count was around 20 aircraft that had almost touched down safety when Emily arrived, and she and her staff concentrated on the injured flight crew, as they clambered, bloodied and torn out from their respective bombers.

It wasn't long before the needy had been ferried by waiting ambulance to the main facility for treatment. From flight operations, Marks now had the count at 23 safe on the ground, Halverson had called the 24th which tuned onto a similar very short diagonal final approach, anarchic and to low, but nonetheless, controlled.

It was though dragging its left wing with two of the four engines now feathered, yet the Liberator pilot kept a skilful and measured approach path. The port main gear extended and locked; the starboard dangling loosely, wavering, in small regressive movements from the slipstream of flight. The underbelly turret was not stowed, still extended, lubricating fluids spilling from the turrets motorised pivot casing, its victim locked within, facing imminent death. The ground crew aware of the looming fate of its crewmember, positioned fire trucks, and rescue vehicles close to the assumed impact zone, as the aircraft finally crossed the threshold. The 24's pilot struggled at the control column as best he could as the plane crabbed in on final approach from the loss of its centre line thrust due to its partial engine failure. The pilot held the Liberator in "ground effect", as the starboard undercarriage tyre squealed, rubber fragments being torn off the tread pattern as the tyre flattened and compressed. The strut and joints of the pivoting arm started to twist out of shape and lubricating material spilled out from the joint. The undercarriage strut pin suddenly "case" hardened, abruptly shattering causing the collapsing of the one good wheel. The underside of the bulky fuselage scraped on the tarmac, the turret and its crewmember becoming one with the twisted smouldering metal parts, and igniting shards of aluminium.

Marks looked on from flight operations, knowing his crew were safe, with doctors and nurses providing immediate treatment to the wounded, while Halverson had put a call through to the Trilogy, to check if they had had a position fix on the one remaining bomber, J25 that of Ben's.

He could see Clifford Cooper, or Coop, the head physician scrambling about, meticulous in every action he made, although from were Marks was looking, he did look rather chaotic in his movement. Coop's ancestors were the barrel makers of early England, the Couper or Coupers were strangely meticulous, unlike that of Coop. The other oddity of Coop was that he as a child had the misfortune of Metatarsus Varus, more commonly known as "Pigeon Toed" which was a rather fitting as to his epithet of Coop. His deformity was not that severe and later in life he happily grew out of it, but the name stuck, and he got used to it.

The crew with the aid of Emily had set up an improvised operating theatre in the 24's bomb bay area, to be close by to the trapped crewmember. They were able to fit the gurney through the opening with basic surgery instruments, plasma drips and wash cloths, despite the recommendations not to from the fire crew.

The ripped fuselage hull in which they climbed through was just forward of the turret, ground crew having only to cut off a small piece of aluminium to gain access. The imprisoned crewman within the belly turret, had hydraulic oils spilling into his beleaguered chest wounds caused from the ground debris and fragments of the planes body panels that had cut into his torso on landing. The ground crew had fought on despairingly putting out spot fires during Coop's and Emily's efforts to save him.

A small section of smouldering engine cylinder not noticed in the fire fighters efforts, continued to intensify in temperature, heating the leaking oil fluids, which effervesced and bubbled on the heated engine parts. Smoke billowed out of the engine cowl, rising high above the tail fins of the Liberator, some smoke had drifted toward a few silver birch trees at the southern end of the runway. Two nesting honey buzzards in the birch trees took to flight heading north as the smoke haze eventually engulfed the trees and their nest.

The pilot of last arriving bomber could see the smoke cloud rising from the damaged plane that had come to rest to the side of the runway apron. He flew awkwardly high above the threshold, and aligned his aircraft well left of centre line to avoid the debris strewn over the runway surface. His plane's engines thundered overhead, the sound echoing through the opening in the damaged plane below deafening the hospital staff as they fought desperately to free the entombed officer.

Exhaust fumes ruptured in small explosions as J25s throttle quadrant was set to idle from the co-pilot. Ben fought the weight of the bomber, desperately pulling back on the yoke, holding it in a nose high attitude as long as he could. He fought frantically to keep the weight off the nose wheel, the tyre became outward and flat, the shock absorber depressing as the plane abruptly came to a stop, just short of the runways full length.

Leaking oil fluids pulsed from the ruptured lines of the crashed Liberator, squirting outward as did the trapped crewman's damaged arterial blood vessels. Emily calmly applied pressure to the wounds, the yellowish blood spurted up through her fingers onto her tunic, the bleached white colour now bloody and stained.

Ben and his crew scrambled from their aircraft out through their belly hatch, and ran back toward the damaged bomber, knowing their help would be needed.

Pressure intensified inside the unprotected fuel lines from the residual heat still being generated off the engines, as the officer from the belly turret was finally freed and placed on to the waiting gurney. Marks had looked up from flight operations in time to see him pulled from the wreckage by the waiting fire crew. He focused his field glasses in on the aircraft's hull breach, searching for the remaining medical staff; his heart raced as Emily crawled out through the opening in the hull. A drip of oil fell on the now cooling cylinder heads, but the dull smouldering immediately intensified into a glow. Emily was looking towards flight operations, her back to the aircraft, as the leaking hydraulic oil kindled and sparked. Marks now with a sense of relief seeing his daughter outside the stricken B24, took over the conversation from Halverson, letting Billy B know J25 had reached base. He abruptly stopped fumbling with words as he noticed a flash about the smouldering oils, he tried desperately to yell. Marks dropped the hand piece of the radiophone becoming dazed and disoriented; no words would come out and his mouth it was parched and emotionless. The scorching oil trailed back to a cracked fuel line, Marks finally yelled out, but could only screech out senseless words. Standing helplessly, frozen, his arms lifeless, he was unable to warn Emily, as the entire port fuel tank exploded, burning petroleum, and fragments of aluminium mixed with the scorching oils from the blast were propelled in all directions.

An ambulance medic and Coop had managed to see the build-up of smoke instantly recognising it, so had prepared for the detonation. Emily had been driven forward from the force of the blast, as did pieces of fuselage parts, spent fuels and a control surface off the wing. As the smoke cleared, a section the wing flap lay on top of Emily, a metal hinge gusset off the flap had pierced her body and her white uniform was now red and bloody. She lay still; her twisted and broken body lay lifeless as Coop tried to free her from the wreckage. Her head had signs of trauma from a direct blunt hit, her face had been pushed into the mud, and cheekbone broken.

Marks eventually arrived at the scene and observed his daughter's lifeless body, lying amongst the wreckage. Ben was standing over her, yelling commands, whilst confused and disorganised. He, with Chips and Murph, took over from Coop and lifted slowly the wing flap off her body. Ben dropped to his knees and thrust his hands into his face, then yelled out.

'This is not meant to happen, it not supposed to be like this, how is this possible!'

She was turned over and placed onto a stretcher, her lilac flower she always wore as her lapel pin was mud covered as was with her now totally unrecognisable body. Ben held onto to her frail hand as he and Marks supported her motionless figure, and she was carried to a waiting ambulance.

******

The next few days after the explosion were critical for Emily. She had undergone lengthy surgery to remove any shrapnel, and loose bone particles and damaged soft tissue from about her cheekbone. Her facial wound; a deep laceration from just below her left eye gashed through the lateral sidewall of the nostril, to the top of her lip. The septal cartilage and part of the maxillary bone were also damaged, and would need post-surgery once she became stabilised. A small hole was left as a drain, just below her nasal passage, but Coop feared emollients in some part had penetrated the mussels about the face, which he said explained the swelling around the masseteric ligaments. Infection set in around 24 hours after her surgery from what Coop suggested, by a few small pieces of tyre rubber that were found lodged somehow behind the masseter muscle.

Marks and Ben had kept a vigil at her bedside and sat together with her without sleep since she was first admitted. They had had little rest over the past

24 or so hours, despite Coop, assuring them both she was in good hands, and they needed some rest before the next mission.

Halverson had taken care of the base, getting damaged aircraft back into fight ready mode for their next operation in around two days. The replacement B-24 would not arrive before then so to be down one aircraft would put a great deal of pressure on this mission. Halverson had finally convinced Marks and Ben to get some rest, the two simply closed their eyes and slept where they sat, Dover was at the foot of Emily's bed.

Operation Hydra as Ben had predicted, was set for the 17th of August and Marks had only found out the truth of it from Billy B when Ben was on his way back from Peenemünde. Marks at the time when Ben had told him did not understood how he had known.

It was around midnight and just one day before the mission, Marks and Ben had finally woke. It appeared Emily was now stable, so Ben headed down to the mess hall after taking a well-deserved shower, Marks changed his shirt, had a quick swig of whisky and met Ben in the mess hall.

'So tell me my boy, what's going on?' enquired Marks

'What do you mean, sir?' asked Ben.

'Son, now is not the time if you have something to tell me better it be now, than later on. I have a civilian under house arrest, a daughter who is delusional about your mother and thinks she's dead, and you, who knows about the next mission.'

'Sir, I uh, well truth be known, I'm totally not understanding any of this, and I, well, just want things to be as they were.'

'As they were?' asked Marks, 'what do you mean, as they were?'

'Well, sir I um, well not really sure were to start, it's like I am not sure myself what is real or not anymore.'

'Not real?' asked Marks, 'what do you mean, not real?'

Sir I, I mean this is going to sound strange but I um, we'll I have flown the Night Owl mission once before possibly twice and —'

Over the intercom, a rushed announcement was heard,

'Marks, Ben please come to sickbay,' said the voice.

The two, stood idle for a few seconds, knowing they both knew had to get to the infirmary, yet Marks seemed confused, then spoke,

'We better go son and see to Emily.'

******

Emily was sitting up on the ward bed, with Dover spread over her legs. She knew it was not allowed but to satisfy the dog's wailing, she broke the rules.

Marks noticed the puppy instantly on her lap as he walked through the ward entrance door, and simply shook his head at his daughter. Ben too gave a slight shake of his head in disapproval, but the two in all were just happy to see her sitting up. They both greeted her in turn, Ben providing Marks the courtesy of first embrace. Ben, very diplomatically, lifted the puppy onto the floor and signalled one of the nurses to take Dover out for a break, well precisely, a toilet break.

'Emily, you're up, you're supposed to be resting,' broadcasted Marks, in his most disciplinary tone a father and Chief of Homeland Security would.

'Oh, Father it's nothing, and besides we need to get ready for the next mission.'

'Hello Emily,' Ben said timidly, 'you had me worried there for a minute, I mean I thought the, well things were not —'

Coop had been close by when Ben was asking his questions, he interrupted, 'Ben there is nothing to worry about, it was pretty basic stuff, and apart from some swelling, a few scars and bruising, Emily will have almost unimpeded recovery.'

'I see Dover was misbehaving just a little, being on the bed and all, are you in pain?' asked Ben.

It was not long before Marks noticed Coop, shaking his head and pointing to his office.

'Come on son, the doc wants to see us by the sounds,' suggested Marks.

The trio walked out of the ward, and toward the consulting room. Ben was supposing the worse, yet strangely he hoped, well sort of knew he may now have returned to the time when he should have returned after Peenemünde, should he not have crossed paths with the ME109. He could almost hear the words to that of Coop before he was about to say it. If Ben was right he had not only anticipated what the Coop would say, but with expected outcome, and that Emily had or has partial memory loss, which would have explained her loss of memory in 1953. So that being said if this is the case, he must have now set things right, well as they were.

Marks and Ben made themselves comfortable in Coop's consulting room; Ben predicted his words.

'Marks, Ben, Emily has suffered some memory loss, we are unsure how much, but we noticed, that she didn't recognise Halverson when he came into the ward, she will recover though,' encouraged Coop.

'Will she recover fully?' asked Marks.

'I expect so,' said Coop, 'Well, yes I guess but these things can be as simple as hours, days and can be as complex as years, sometimes taking decades, and we can never anticipate how long. I noticed she looked right through you also Ben, so we will have to assume you as Halverson are gone from her memory?'

'Well I knew this would be,' calmly said Ben, 'Well, at least I am back with her, that's all that counts.'

'Ben, you are sounding rather unmoved by all of this,' suggested Marks, 'Where is your compassion?'

'Sir, as strange as this will sound, I know she will get better so that's the main thing,' said Ben.

'WELL, THAT'S at least encouraging!' yelled Marks. 'But REALLY, what is wrong with you Ben, why are you so, well ignorant of the fact Emily is still very much, impaired? She has extensive facial wounds, and you can just sit here without any empathy towards my daughter, well, your sweetheart if I dare say it, I am now concerned you are not really the man for her.'

'Can I please interject?' asked Coop.

'I am sorry sir, I didn't mean to come across this way, and truly, if you only knew what I have been through to get back here you would understand,' cried Ben

'Sorry Ben, to break the news to you, but that is part of war and it's expected. As for the compassion of the thousands of widows who won't see their husbands, you Ben on the other hand are very lucky to be in one piece, and you get to see the girl,' gestured Marks as he waved his arms about in aversion in response to Ben's comments.

'I am not trying to be impolite Sir, nor am I downplaying this war or those who are my comrades or the widows, it's just that I well, I can really say, I think I have said enough, I'm sorry and should get ready for the next mission.'

'If I could just say something else that may put this in perspective a little, Ben, unfortunately is not all good news,' said Coop. 'There is another issue it is not something that we should take dispassionately —'

Coop did not have time to complete his sentence, when Marks interjected.

'What do mean "not all good news"?' requested Marks.

'Well the main problem is her memory loss as I have eluded to but, well the cause, we think, is due to a piece of shrapnel that had lodged its self into the frontal lobe, which we would have to assume is the cause, but more likely is her blast impact to the face onto the tarmac.'

'Well what if, I mean you can remove it?' asked Marks.

'Well to remove it is recommended, as there is the possibility of some brain inflammation and progression of growth about the foreign object which could cause further damage, by way of infection or further loss of memory, so yes I think we should,' finished Coop.

'What damage?' interjected Ben.

'Well, bluntly, she could well, I don't want to speculate but it could and is better to remove it than leave it, let's put it that way.'

'What aren't you telling me?' asked Marks.

Coop swallowed, compelled himself then continued, 'The growth if it forms, which I suggest will, can and will decay brain tissue, that decay could in turn cause further issues.'

'Well we need to operate and remove it,' said Marks.

'Well,' said Coop, 'the anaesthetic will cause problems for the foetus, most certainly due to the early stages of pregnancy she will if anything, miscarry.'

'I knew the lad was mine, I knew it!' yelled out Ben, 'Doc, she is going to be fine, I have seen her in 53, she gets through this.'

It was then Coop, looked at Marks, then back at Ben, 'What are you saying, Ben, you say one more outrageous comment like that and I will have to ground you,' voiced Coop in the best authoritative dialogue he could muster.

'Ben, that is enough, I have heard sufficient tales, you can come with me. Doc, he is in need of a full medical prior to flight, possibly grounding if you like, and I will sort this out on my office.'

The two marched out of Coop's consulting room and towards the airfield tarmac. They passed the damaged ground surface still gouged out from the recent downed B-24. Ground crew were still busy cleaning up the twisted plane parts off the field, the main super structure of the wing spar and fuselage ribs could still be seen, about the runway. Marks continued out into the middle of the airstrip, stopped and turned towards Ben, then spoke,

'Ben, what I am about to say I don't want anyone else to hear, and I need honest answers.'

'How was it you knew about Operation Hydra, tell me straight, no lies, tell me the truth no matter what.'

'Sir, I don't know how this will sound to you, but she will get better, please sir, I am back and things are now right, I have set them straight.'

'Set what straight, what things.'

'Emily sir, she did lose her memory, and well, she remembered but it was too late, I didn't age, and she died,' Ben went on to say, sounding more confused than ever, and for Marks, it is was not tangible, it was simply outrageous for one of his best pilots to even think this way.

'Ben, make sense, what the hell are you saying?' demanded Marks.

'Sir, I first recall it was after the mission and 1953. I was at a park bench and a, a, small boy he, are, well he talked to me and then I realised it was Emily, she, well, but it's all good because I am back now and it's, it's all OK, I, are well have fixed yes, I have fixed it all and now it's OK. The boy was hers but I didn't ask, I should have that is why she aged without me, yes she did and I well I am back so it is OK, I have…'

Marks could see he was delusional, and he was not making any sensible comments, he was erratic, yet still consistent in his beliefs, he needed rest, and Marks needed him for the next mission, that of Operation Hydra.

'Ben, the next mission is in two days, we need to get you back and checked over, and that I am sure of.'

As the two turned and walked back to the base, Marks hesitated, stopped then faced Ben.

'Tell me, Hydra, I need to know one thing and have no idea why I am asking this, but tell me, when do we fly the mission? I will have some partial belief in you if you know.'

'Um, in, five, yes five days sir, we go on the 17th.'

'Ben, I don't know what's going on here, but how in the hell do you know that.'

******

Marks sat with Emily for most of the afternoon, prior to her scheduled surgical procedure. He tried to quiz Emily on things that Ben was saying or had said to her in his first few days at the base, just to satisfy his own mind. Her memory loss didn't help and Marks decided to leave it and focus on her operation thinking nothing more about what Ben had said.

Ben's medical check took the same time as it took for Marks to sit with Emily.

The procedure would take four hours or so depending on what Coop would find. Marks would attend, although Emily had said for him to concentrate on the mission, and she would be fine in Coop's hands. Marks was uncertain if Emily knew about her pregnancy, and did not want to ask, or even bring it up until she was in the recovery ward.

Halverson had things under control at the base during Emily's operation, which set Marks at ease knowing that the next mission and details would be well taken care of. Halverson and the crew of allocators of each aircrafts inventory, had started with the load sheets, for fuel and ammunition, and any last-minute maintenance issues. The track out from the base would be similar to Operation Night Owl, with the exception of the rendezvous point with the RAF Bomber Command. The total offensive involving 596 heavy bombers made up of 324 Lancasters, 218 Halifax and 54 Stirling bombers would bomb Peenemünde on the night of 17/18th August, 1943. History would document this as the total number and did not account for the elite 451st. The wave of inexorable and unrelenting attacks that would see a loss of life totalling 215.

Emily's operation lasted six hours, two of those Coop and another physician, spent scrupulous time removing over nine pieces of foreign bodies from above and about the eye socket. There was single piece of aluminium shard lodged deep into the frontal lobe that was missed by both x-ray and Coop. Her wounds needed closing early due to decreasing blood pressure that reached dangerous levels. Coop then had her placed in intensive care under full watch, by nursing staff and himself. It was a simple prophylactic measure but nonetheless needed.

Emily's first few hours in the ward were quite possibly the most dangerous. Still comatose from the operation and effects of the anaesthetic, Emily's blood pressure remained low then erratically elevated due to partial brain inflammation, and a foreign body left behind by Coop. The shard of aluminium and past wounds from the days prior to the operation had and was now setting a series of events not common to medicine practices in 1943. Coop had with all intensive purpose done perhaps all he could do, yet oddly the operation alone was never going to be enough. Even if he could, and were successful in providing her a full recovery, her pending outcome and that of decline was due to Vermont's intent.

Her condition continued to plummet; the brain swelling, and infection worked concurrently placing toxins into her blood stream that were totally unnoticed by staff, and blood pressure rapidly increasing exponentially. Her heart rate and condition erratically changed from normal to critical during her comatose state. Unobserved by staff and without warning she suffered a stroke, paralysing the entire right side of her body. Her blood pressure continued to rise to a critical level, when Coop came in to check on her. He noticed her dangling arm, and bottom lip hanging loosely off to one side. Coop called out to staff for assistance, as Emily's elevated heart rate sent her into immediate cardiac arrest. The brain swelling about the piece of shard burst causing a dense yellowish opaque liquid about the infected tissue of dead white blood cells and bacteria to stream into the skull cavity. Her torso hung limp, skin colour showing changes from a flushed pink, to a cerulean blue, as the already decreased oxygen levels in her blood depleted even further. Her dying muscular organ slowed down the circulatory flow of blood. Its once rhythmic and automotive contractions and dilations of the vital four chambers of the heart, slowed then stopped. Medical staff raced the gurney to operating theatre "one" as swiftly as they could. Coop had not foreseen this moment, Marks too, was blind to her vitals at the time, and Ben had become unmindful and insensitive. He was possibly deprived of his actions, all due to the strange occurrence that had and was setting a differing path, both past, and now present. Coop's efforts in emergency surgery on Emily were in vain and at 18:21 on 23 August, 1943, Emily Marks aged 20, had passed away.

******

Ben had rested in the hospital ward away from the operating theatre where Emily's body was in preparation for the base's morgue. Ben had been admitted as a precautionary measure after the death of Emily and prior to his flight back to Peenemünde. He had undergone a series of aptitude and physical tests, even the base's chaplin had spoken to Ben, quizzed him over religion, and to some extent touched ever so delicately on Emily's death.

Ben had presumed having arrived back from Peenemünde, without crossing paths with Trilogy he had set things right, he had set his new path, and that of a life with Emily both now and after the war. This was not to be, and for two times in his life had experienced the death of Emily Marks. He had spoken to the Chaplin over this, and for a pastor with an impartial look on life, let Ben have his say. He never doubted what he said, never condemned him over his belief just listed, and provided the comfort to Ben; that someone believed his story.

Vermont had been listening as best he could during Ben's check-up, trying to evaluate the situation to see if there was any irregularity. He listened for anything he may say that would provide a starting point for Vermont's hopeful conversation with Ben. Ben slept for a short time after the Chaplin had gone, and Vermont waited in desperation for him to wake as he listed in-depth at his mumbling during his sleep. Ben finally woke around 10 minutes or so later and was oblivious to the ward's emptiness. Vermont knew it was now or never that he needed to speak to Ben.

'Hello Ben, do you remember me?' asked Vermont.

'Should I?' answered Ben.

'Well perhaps not, said Vermont, you were only eight at the time.'

'Eight,' said Ben, he repeated it again, 'eight, at school, you came to the house, yes you came to see us at the house.'

'Ben, we quite possibly do not have much time before someone comes here, and I heard what you said about Emily. Ben I am being released and may never get to see you again, I am in fear they will incarcerate you as they did me, let me help you.'

'What help, what do I have, I am emotionally instable, I don't know what's real anymore.'

'You disappeared on your way to school, can you tell me what happened, I need to find out what happened… I listened in your sleep, you were mumbling about a person called Marshall, was he the man I saw you with at Old Morley Hall, wasn't he?'

'Old Morley Hall, yes it was, I mean I did, I remember now I disappeared at school the same as now it's coming back, he was there, it was Marshall.'

The memories of his youth started to rush back into his thoughts. His mind as he had recalled when he first met Emily, he also focused in on his past when he was eight. The time was if it was only yesterday and he could see the school bus, Nancy Belrose, the school yard, his teachers, the clock tower…'Yes, the clock tower!' Ben yelled out loud, 'the tower, I remember.'

He looked back at Vermont, and recalled him at the house, his mother talking to him, and Marshall…

'What is happening to me?' asked Ben, 'It is as if every time I get direction, I lose grip of it, and I cannot seem to get it right. I, I mean my mind is drifting between now and then, I get strange images, strange thoughts of the future. Something I have seemingly lived twice, and I am not sure if now or then is real. I can't quite seem to focus on what happened at school, yet I know I, well according to you went missing. My future without Emily now and before I fixed this, witnessed a future where she ages. I have flown the mission twice, and now, she doesn't remember me, well didn't remember, which is the same as it was in 1953, Marshall said choose and choose wisely, I, I don't know what I am saying,' confusingly finished Ben.

'Ben, I have had a whole chunk of my life taken from me also, my wife divorced me, I spent many years in an institution, and now I just happened to find you and if I only knew now, what I knew then. Even your mother played down the event; she was very concerned about your being found on a doorstep. She did feel a little bad later in life though she well felt rather a bit guilty about a few things so when she visited me at hospital, she did say that —'

'In hospital,' cried Ben. 'What do you mean, when were you there?'

'Well, I was there a number of years ago but released in 1942, your mother came late in that year —'

'That's not possible, she, umm, she died in the London bombings, in '40, yes 1940, December, you are, I mean it's not true Mr Vermont.'

'Ben, I have no reason to lie to you,' said Vermont.

'Mr Vermont, something is truly happening, I mean my mission, I did not return before but now I did and Emily well she did have memory loss but now she is gone, she is dead and I do not know how to fix this. Marshall would know how to fix this.'

'Is he that man I saw you with at Old Morley Hall?' asked Vermont.

'Yes,' replied Ben, 'he was, but for some reason he does not appear to me anymore.'

'Marshall who, was it Hartley, was it Marshall Hartley?' enquired Vermont, 'I met him in 1930 when you disappeared, he said something quite bizarre, he said my future had already been written, I had already lived it, and for it to change, a past event must not happen. I thought he was crazy and yet when he asked me to tell him something very few people new. And then he looked at me in the eye with an utter resolve, and then I told him.

'I told him, that I had lost our first child at birth. It devastated my wife to the point that she took it from her mind and she, well rather, blamed me. We both struggled with the loss and she had no one to turn to console with. Both her parents were deceased, she had no siblings and I, too, was an only child. It was found out she was infertile, and no one knows or will ever know that. She is now recluse in an institution locked away, sees no one, is frail and has become a self-same hoary, gaunt-looking figure of a woman, she lives with those that are twice her age; it saddens me how we both have ended up this way.'

The strange occurrence that had and was truly setting a differing path than that of previous events was and had set itself in motion. It would, in time, be recognised, it would, in time, be able to be controlled and it would, in time, be understood by Ben. For anything to work in life, be it aircraft of war, or a hospital drug, it first must be tested, that test, this test, was Ben's.

******

The laws of Quantum Progression were not yet recognised. It never existed as did once the atomic bomb, yet it would and so will the understanding of the physics of how it worked.

Scientists have this eccentricity about themselves that when they want to name something of importance, they invent new words. Some words have meaning, others just sound so genuine that we are led to believe they must exist, even if it sounds totally unrealistic. In 1943, if one were asked to try to understand the power of an atomic bomb, they couldn't, and even the eventual designers, and scientists at the time such as Einstein knew it would be evil to the world, but to explain this, was and would remain indeterminate even to his way of thinking, it was simply unknown. But in 1945, it would and did show the world something unprecedented at the time. Einstein was right with his equation of $E=mc^2$, which explains, that a tiny amount of matter contains a tremendous amount of energy; the atomic bomb on Hiroshima was just that.

Quantum Progression is simply the atomic bomb of a pending future. Emily had now become part of it, Ben's life was running concurrently with it and Vermont had only the intent of it. If a scientist of 1943 was asked to explain it, they would be wrong and it would take another millennium to be fully understood.

However, what if this next best thing, this very strange occurrence, this nameless phenomenon that these three people were a part of had already occurred. What if it had already existed on this earth but was unknown to them? Perhaps it was not intended for use by man, but one of those without their knowledge had and was progressively without any thought somehow correcting this wrong that had occurred. What if the wrong never did happen or happened after it was corrected. What if Quantum Progression had and was created almost 10,000 years earlier?

Chapter 9
The Conclusion...

Ben settled back into the well renowned park bench seat, pondering over how many times he had done this very thing before. He reminisced meeting Emily here in 1953, and her son, his son, and regretted not recognising the child back then. Would he be sitting here now should he have known then what he knew now? It seems to be that age-old thing how we all would have done things much differently should we have known.

He held on tightly to his one last possession in life that was real to him since he could well remember, that was his leather satchel. Ben's life up to now for an outsider was simple, for him at just 22, it was grandiose having achieved what he had. He had lived through the two same events in a single war, lost Emily two times in his life, witnessed the death of his mother, her subsequent rebirth, and visited his own entombment site. He let out the smallest chuckle to himself thinking no one could boast this in his or her life, even though it must be and sound completely implausible.

He had come to accept that for whatever reason he was unable to know exactly when or where he was, what year, time or place, there just had to be something that would either fix that, or someone or something to show him how to get things back to normal. *Normal*, he then thought, *what exactly was that? Well, normal to the point you live, you breathe, and you die. Normal for most that is, but for Emily and if Vermont was right, Charlotte, there was no such thing.*

Marshall, Ben then thought to himself, *What of Marshall, and why did he no longer appear to him?* It was a tangled web of confusion and total misperception; it had little or no clarity or transparency, just total abstruseness.

Ben asked himself if he had lived something, something wonderful and pure being a life with Emily from their first meet, to her eventual death at 71, why was she then taken again from him at her age of 20? What was the reason? What was real, that's something he just could not evaluate.

The coffin room seemed to be the linking factor, and the commonality in all of these varying times and places, and people's lives. He would either wake there, or rest there and wake elsewhere. The room did have something very unexplainable about it, in what was happening to him now. He quite possibly had not really given any thought as to how the room even got there and was built by whom. Perhaps it had crossed his mind once, when speaking to Marshall, but with all his confusion lately; it was unclear.

Old Morley Hall from his understanding was built by the Sedley family around 400 years ago, and the moat, a further 700 years or so before that; he guessed the Anglo-Saxon period. He somewhat figured that would put the moat being dug at or around 800AD. The coffin room was either build into the foundation depth of the stone when the moat was dug, or in the 16th century when the hall was built. Looking at the room in its entirety, how it was constructed and why, had no substance apart from the fact it was hidden. Quite obviously, the room had been used by a select few, Marshall being one of those and now himself; this was still a mystery to him. Marshall had always referred to it as 'The Sector' and that to Ben sounded ahead of its time.

******

Ben watched the sun gradually setting over the tops of the silver birch trees. An angry discouraging darkness of the approaching night cooled the air about his face, slightly numbing his cheeks as he watched intently the two nesting honey buzzards, soaring in ovate loops about their nest. They used the backdrop of the approaching darkness as camouflage while in search for any signs of nocturnal rodents. Ben attuned into their pattern, as they flew concentrically to the nest, soaring higher in rotation with each turn. The darkness hiding their body shape against the night sky stealthily, yet restlessly they flew on watching the ground for the slightest of any movement. Their mission was to destroy life just to save their own, and Ben thought of the war he had fought as the same. He wondered what it would have been like looking up and seeing a formation of bombers, dropping death upon people below. Would it be the same for a rodent who perhaps misjudged their own steadiness and looking up in time to see the bird's talons before they would feel the piercing pain ending their life in a microsecond.

He focused hard on the fear people in Peenemünde must have had in seeing the contrails of the exhaust blooms in ubiquitous analogous lines trailing the bombers high above their city. Or the whistling of the bombs as they fell to earth and boomed in loud unremitting rumbles on impact. He wondered if the noise of the planes would have even been heard, or he wondered if the people would have even known, before it was too late. He tried to concentrate on what they would have described in their own minds, the very first time the formation of bombers flew over, or did they simply hear the blast or feel the earth shake on detonation oblivious the squadrons above. He tightened his eyes and pictured this thought alone, gaining with each moment a more elaborate picture of how it would have been feared, how the outcome would have not been known. Strange pictures began to develop in his mind, anomalous to the point they were very familiar to here, yet distant. He could not quite hold onto a time or place that he was now seeing about him.

It now rained, as it rained on many occasions in his life before when unexpected and sudden changes happened. However, there was nothing, no change just nothing and he still appeared to be in the park, and the honey buzzards still flew overhead.

The darkness now an ominous grey, chilling the night air even further, his cheeks and jawbone both now ached. The honey buzzards soared even higher, and rain fell even harder, the drops beating down onto his face numbing his cheeks even more. He pictured the rodents looking up and seeing the danger yet their own instincts told them to keep on searching for food to survive. A rancorous circle of life, as was war, and both rodent and Ben did not have a choice.

It got darker, colder, and the noise of the rain hitting the ground then precipitately became silent, the cold developed warmth, and the night abruptly and knowingly turned into day. His mind was drained of any thought and increasingly he became fatigued, weary, whereby his mind needed rest. He knelt down on the ground then leaned over to his side, curling into a foetal position. He felt secure, yet vulnerable to the elements, and the warmth heated his body and soul, that drew his eyes and mind closed of any thoughts; he rested.

******

Ben eventually sat back up looking skyward and once again could see the honey buzzards still circling. His mind felt drained with all that had happened in the past few days. He felt he needed more respite, and from being unsure actually how long he had just rested for, would very much welcome more.

His surroundings seemed a little ambiguous yet strangely definite in a peculiar way. The woodlands were thicker, the parklands more dense; it confused him, was he dreaming, had he woken in a different place? Looking up, the honey buzzards kept encircling the dense grasslands in tighter and tighter circles. His mind began to fade of what was now, from then. He looked at the honey buzzard one more time and then could only digest a thought of, they soared in the skies, and strangely was now just like any other flying beast he would then have observed. The silver birch was thicker and appeared to forest with greater coverage; he focused in on that alone and did not think them as a specious of tree, rather than just well, he did not really have a thought.

What was going on in his mind? He vaguely knew of his surroundings and a past thought of where he was just at. It was somewhat like, knowing of something without actually knowing of it. The thought of Emily was slowly drifting from his mind, the base, the mission, Marshall, were all becoming cloudy in his thoughts. Had he been able to think about it, it would be seemingly as if his mind had been reset into a default thought.

He looked about, the only thing he could distinguish was now, this moment, and then as he tried remembering was quickly fading. He was just able to evoke the thought of the park bench, small details of the base at Buckenham, Old Morley Hall, some parts of common of St Peter, and could only just paint a very small picture partially in thought, but reality was now taking hold.

Imagining those thoughts of where the hall should be, was now simply an open field, and there were workers in abundance moving about in differing directions, each their own task. The workers he didn't understand as they were attired in what appeared to be a sort of animal skin, flocculent and shaggy. Ben was witnessing something that in light of his past hours, days, weeks and years, something very enigmatic, something unknowable, something that was only possible if you were there.

He looked up one last time for the honey buzzards to try to regain some sanity. He once again didn't think of the honey buzzard as that species, and yet again it was just another animal, this to him although strange, now felt right. Flight to him, was one that disobeyed all things known and it too now felt right. The birds spiralled up in the skies, of which he had no knowledge of how that was possible, and what now was, he in time was going to understand.

****

The Arrival

The underbelly hatch doors opened in flight, hanging squat almost diminutive compared to the bulky hull shape of the aircraft they hung from. Wide-open and exposed the inner fuselage cargo area now visibly displaying the many conduits and fluid tubes and motorised rudiments essential to the workings of the fuselage bay area. The bay doors quivered in the slipstream of perfectly unbroken air that flowed linear to the hull of the aircraft as it glided effortlessly, towards the coastline below. The rupturing air braking from its faultless flow, that now formed small pockets of vortices as the ruptured flow of air passed over the now exposed cavity of the aircraft's underbelly.

The hatch doors likened to the dangling talons of a honey buzzard, an indigenous bird of prey which was soaring just above the treetops, very oblivious to the aircraft 25,000 feet above. The buzzard, flew in low for a strike, the rodents scattering in all directions bar one in its line of sight. The russet coloured thighs of the bird retracted from under its flank feathers relaxing the leg shanks, hind and outer toes hung loosely under its abdomen as it flew in for the kill.

They too quivered like the hatch doors of the aircraft but in a controlled manner, performing as the bird's flight control surfaces, steering and turning the buzzard in an unstructured yet calculated flight path. The bird struck in hard at the rodent, the outer toe talons piercing deep into the chest cavity, killing its prey instantly. Prodigious amounts of blood and torn hide were ripped from the rodent's lifeless body as the buzzard's beak cut deep into the flesh as it flew off with its spoils.

The pilot of the aircraft's mission, although analogous to the birds, was not of destroying a life, nor was the cargo in which the aircraft held, and was here for a differencing reason. The outstretched wings of the aircraft were long and lengthy equal to the birds and kept the aircrafts outward shape aloft with the aviator needing only to apply small controlled movements likened to that of the buzzard's talons, keeping the aircraft on a predetermined set path. The fixed unbending primary wing shape, altered slightly as small surface parts, extended or retracted, moved up or slid out allowing the machine to follow an almost imaginary flight path of decent. The pilot continued to move his controls as the aircraft descended even further passing the bleachy white sea cliff face of the coastline below. Dropping even lower in altitude and verging off for small course corrections, the craft eventually positioning itself above a cleared plantation area directly below.

In the midst of a silver birch forest, workers were cutting the last few trees of a large open area. They had finally cleared the grounds in just over four seasons, almost reducing the forest by half. They were namely here to clear the land for the arrival, but also too for the rock that was being quarried out. The area mined would eventually form a deep excavation and with an unnatural shape, making it clearly visible from above. The quarried stone would be placed over part of the cleared grounds of the woodlands where it would be separated into colour variations. The stone portions weighed the equivalent to that of twenty men and were measured using a rudimentary measurement and weighing device, yet the 1,300 stone pieces quarried if each were weighed separately would be precisely 2,000 kilos each, or better, two metric tonnes.

The stone area dug out was not quite round, almost an oval ring in shape, and the depth of excavation below natural ground was equal to that of two men, and five men head to toe in width. The size of the excavation was comparable to and modelled around 2,000 men standing in a grid like technique, the amount of men was not critical just a systematic calculating device the workers used. The centre of the ring had been cleared of all-natural surface ground material thus exposing the underling rock that in turn was quarried flat. The recent rains showed no visible signs of ponding water, a clear indication of the exactness the workers had in excavating of the now totally levelled area. Centre to the sphere shape was a rectangular section gouged out like the outer ring. It was equally divided into two parts, the depth for the first half was the same two men in height, the next part was four men in height and both sections were five men head to toe in width.

The workers had followed a crude diagram of single lines, and cross shapes and forms of figure's, which had been carved out into a clay tablet, passed down to them from their ancestors. The tablet, again very rudimentary in its interpretation of what the workers had to achieve, possibly not something that needed to be exact in fact, yet the time of completion was.

The tablet had shown a fixed light in the skies, and the passing of another that was only seen every three generations, and this date, every 480 generations. For the tablet to have such an undeveloped arrangement of edifice, be it circles and oval shapes and lines, it was exact, it was precise, and to the very day it had shown the workers how to complete the cleared area precisely to the time of the arrival.

The levelled stone could clearly now be seen from the overhead aircraft, the rock ornate in colour, lavish with mauves and violets, its surface reflected from the enormous whitish yellow planetary sun. The aircraft that was seemingly now almost stationary in the cloudless skies above appeared unmoving, and motionless. From the ground, two of the workers looked up with reverence to the flying machine that hung from the skies like the honey buzzard. The area was to be a reference point, a final stopping place if you will, one of many that had been constructed over ages, and this portion of ground had its purpose, both now, but in time to come was built for a differing reason.

The remaining workers had all now stopped and each knelt, then leaned forward and placed both hands flat to the ground, foreheads placed on the levelled stone. A song low in tone, yet instrumental in verse had started in simple language. A single male upraised himself as he embraced the song then clinched together his hands, palms touching and fingers pointing toward the sky, toward the flying machine as he mouthed a chant.

The aircraft fell away from the skies dropping vertically straight toward the carved-out level surface of the stone. It abruptly stopped at the height the honey buzzard was only moments before, then it floated, it was noiseless and unmoving. The male's song increased in volume, his head now tilted back, and eyes wide shut facing the cargo area of the craft hovering above. A boxlike structure lowered from the belly of the aircraft and into the deeper rectangular void at the centre of the levelled-out stone. He unclasped his hands, waved his palms guilelessly in an up and down motion, as the hatch doors of the flying machine abruptly closed. The craft began ascending, slowly at first then at an expediential rate. His voice only silenced by the low hum of the craft as it increased its rate of climb, soon back at 25,000 feet. The male's chanting song abruptly stopped, as a gilded amulet, pointed at one end, was thrust into his chest cavity, his lifeless body fell forward into the void joining the cubed "offering" from the craft. The male's life was the workers gift, their offering; a single response, a written ruling if you like, perhaps a code as was told in tablets of clay from ancestral writings. The craft had ceased its assent, it stopped, rotated horizontally facing the path in which it had come, stopped once more then slowly moved off again reaching the bleached white cliffs of the coast line, then faced the heavens in a vertical position and was gone.

It was then and only then, the workers could rise up from the levelled stone surface and face the skies. The amulet that was thrust into the chest cavity of the fallen, was done by the only other mortal who was permitted to have witnessed the event, and he was then to be sacrificed at the end of the next four seasons, that person was Ben.

Sacrificial Ritual

The stone quarried was a gloomy purple colour, yet baroque with veins of none uniform shapely patterns. It was being re-stacked in close proximity to the excavated outer ring shape, and divided into colour variants of the common purple, soft delicate violets and the most sort after being lavender, all in the three lunar cycles after of the ceremony. As part of the ritual, the body of the sacrificed was to be gently lifted and removed from the excavation in the centre of the cleared ground. His bloodstains would be cleaned off and his deep wound sewn then dressed in a compound made of oils and clay. His burial communal clothing was to be without bracelets, talismans or even footwear so he was to be returned as he had once entered the world, but with dignity. He would be dressed in the self-same rudimentary fabric about his body he wore as a worker before his elevation in stature, that of the chosen mortal. His sacrifice as the mortal was as a walking spirit, to enter the world of the immortal, that of men who flew in the flying machines, the eternal, the divine beings, the Gods.

Days after the aircraft had left, the abundant honey buzzards had returned for nesting. The workers continued casting in place the box like shape placed there from the aircraft. A solution made of a type of granular lime chalk, a ground up grey powdery stone mixture, gypsum, some clays of varying textures and the chiselled pieces of pebble from the rock were all used. The fine mixture was then packed about the placed cargo covering most part of it and just covering the higher pointed end, then filled with untainted water.

The buzzards assembled their nesting material about the silver birch, similar in fashion to the workers who used the mixed materials to meld in the box shape, setting it into the excavation with their casted mixture of the stone like material. The mixture would in turn set harder than the natural stone and blend as if it had formed naturally. At the completion of the entombment ceremony of the chosen mortal, and after the hardening of the encased material about the box structure, a second excavation was done being two men in depth and again five head to toe in width. One end, the furthest part away from the box cargo had a dias of stone platforms laid 10 out from the wall and were arm's length in width. At the completion of the 10, more were laid on top but 9, then more on top, again with one less, until the dias reached the excavated cleared natural ground level with just one stone then laid. At the opposite end of the dias and near the box structure, the final section was then cut back exposing one face of the cargo that was still covered with a protection about its structure. Chosen rock from the quarried stone was then placed over the cut-out rock, like a covering that started at the box cargo then stopped above the 10th laid stone dais. A wall of stones was then built two men in height above the last stone and up the first. An opening was left, then the walls were again covered in stone, it formed a type of covering, and entry point to the encased cargo box. It would look when finished simply like a type of shanty, an entry point of the soon to be exposed tomb, below.

The clay tablets stamped and moulded with varying pictures and shapes telling stories of both old and new, were also to be laid at the base of the box shape, at the completion of the cut-out rock. The tablets would tell of the earliest arriving of the first deities and the flying machines they came in. The very early tablets spoke of the winged people likened to the honey buzzard, who could circle around in the skies and that they had come from the high above the grounds in which the workers lived. Over time, the tablet writing had become less complex and the language spoken more understanding. They had been shown of ways to harvest and been taught how to store and preserve foods. Their previous traditions and techniques still used, and now only refined over the ages.

After the covered section of stone had been placed over the final piece, the outer-boxed cargo protection was then removed. It was a type of covering, protecting the internal workings of the box structure, sacrificial in itself. Once removed, it revealed an inner shape, box like and upright and equal to, the height of a single man and wide enough for him to walk through but still appeared solid and impassable.

The next in line that was chosen to be sacrificed, was part of this ceremony, the ceremony that would help the mortal, become immortal. At the rising of the great orb over the land beyond and on the start of the fourth cycle of the moon, the ceremony commenced. The wingman had returned and helped with the mortal's body in carrying him down the carved-out sections of rock and to the upright shape. The young man, who was next to be sacrificed, stood just outside the line of sight of two pilots. One of the pilots had what looked like to the young man a charmed amulet in his hand, but more than half in size, and half again to the one used that he had thrust into the chest of the chosen. The pilot's amulet was gilded in gold, but not pointed, and looked more like a talisman that would be worn as an ornament. The young man watched on as one of the pilots took the golden charm and slid it into a small opening next to the impassable solid upright shape. The shape to the young man's amazement was suddenly gone, it seemed like it was swallowed up by the boxed cargo. The impassable solid wall fell into the upright opening and as it did, it made this strange noise, a hissing sound, like the serpents and asps the villagers would hunt. A space tunnelled out within the boxlike shape could now be seen. It was similar in size to the young man's shanty, and something he had never witnessed, something new, something as unnatural as the winged men's ability to soar like the honey buzzard. The pilots carried the body in and placed it on to another shape, not known to the young man. It looked like a resting place, quite simple in form, and the young man could not find the words that would best tell a story of what he was seeing. He did though find enough words to know this was a ritual or kind of ceremonial a rite of passing and this place, the tomb, was the burial chamber.

The chamber looked like the large yellow orb, the sun above that was raised high in the sky that would glow more vivid than the colourless smaller orbed moon at night. The chamber's ground reflected the light on its surface as if it were a still mere, a lake, like the ponds of water that reflected the images of surrounding lands and although it was a hard surface like rock, it felt like it should be soft and moist and he touched and fingered it, it was unnatural to stand on. His memory up to now could not hold onto anything he was seeing, it was if it would enter his mind, making some sense, and then gone, he was confused, and his mind became blank.

He unexpectedly awakened to his consciousness, assuming it was the next day. He felt uneasy, and above all despoiled from his otherwise pure self. He could not remember much of the ceremony other than small pieces of strange colours unknown to him. Colours he had to imagine must come from the moon at night and the sun from the day. It was not just the colours that made him feel uneasy, it was the shape of the burial chamber, the floor and walls seemed to be one, and felt soft, yet cold and hard, like rock. The thought it could be what it was, was something he could just not imagine. Something in his inner beliefs, told him he knew but every time he tried to speak it out loud, the words did not come from within.

It was not long before he could now understand his surroundings, and his accepting of what he did see, and oddly understood. His process of thought, the words to describe what he saw and assumed to that of his environment, slowly filled his mind. Perhaps a story from an elder, or writings from a tablet, and this day of the ritual, that of the chosen mortal's sacrifice.

He looked about as if a new world in which he now was, was it then, that ancestral dream, his made-up memory from stories told by the elders or something if at all possible could be. He looked about in his outlandish new world and it was then when a honey buzzard flew over, it was a gentle reminder he was where he was. He then cast his eyes back at the stacked rock over the carved out opening to the chamber, and settled on perhaps just some imaginings, he created upon himself. He turned away from the tomb and saw the two wingmen heading back toward the flying machine. The smaller of the two wingmen stopped, made some waving hand movements at the other wingman, then turned back towards the ritual area, they at the same time gestured the young man to follow. It was a simple waved-hand movement, the young mortal understood that the God's were somewhat of the rulers, so he obeyed.

As they both reached the tomb chamber, the wingman grasped up with both hands and removed their headwear. Their face looked like the chamber as he had remembered, their skin glowed like the moon at night, and pale like the chamber's walls and floor. Their hair was blood red like the sun as it would rise before a tempest, before the cold seasons rain, and floods. The young man did not understand the wingman he was looking at, as their features were small and delicate. They were youthful and sylphlike, with lean skin, yet the darkened eyes portrayed power, strength, it gave them a confusing stare, one that would equal a village pubertal girl, and yet had the strength to carry 10 men. Before him they now stood as he did and were without height as he was they now had a sense of weakness perhaps mortal, she then lowered her headdress to her side and called out in few words.

'Time, there is not, I must give this gold offering, this amulet, this you will keep at your side, tell not of this day, this you will do, when I am gone.'

She pointed to the small opening and held the amulet just from it. With her hand she pushed it into the hole and turned the charm, it made the hissing noise then the solid impassable wall had once again vanished. The young man's heart elevated in strength, his arm muscles tensioned as if, in the ready, to fight. His inner strength raised his senses, his fists closed, blood rushed from his knuckles and into his palms. Sweat flowed from his brow, down his cheeks; his eyes focused waiting for her next movement.

'Do not fear me, do this, I must go…'

She turned back the amulet, it made its "hisssss" sound then the wall again appeared as if one with its surroundings, she removed the gold amulet delectably holding it with two fingers then reached out, and gestured him to take it from her.

'Take this now, walk and keep at your side, tell this not, and return when I am gone, sleep in the chamber, sleep and you are to be immortal, sleep, dream and go to the new world, I must go…'

The wingman pulled back on the headdress, climbed up the carved-out rock and was gone.

He stood for a moment, looked at the gold offering the wingman had passed to him, and then placed it into his haversack that hung from his shoulder. He climbed up the carved-out rock then stopped and looked through the opening. He watched as the wingman's craft elevated slowly above the birch treetops, then effortlessly ascended into the skies, then was gone.

******

The young man rested in his bivouac, thinking of what the young wingman had told him. He peered out through a small hole in his bivouac at the dull night, then reached into his satchel. Fumbling through its contents, he eagerly felt for the amulet, instantly sensing its coldness between his fingers. He had removed the thought of the wingman having given him the gift, then pulled the amulet from the satchel. The thought of why him, firstly to be the chosen one, to be sacrificed and now the amulet, and the strange tomb chamber below ground. He understood the circular shape about the tomb, now having been filled with untainted water as the protection for the entombed.

The talismans yellow gold colour glistened in the moonlight, its shape, its corners, and its intent, statuesque and smooth, without delineation. He held onto it tightly as he did his haversack; then knew what he had to do.

******

The moon illuminated an ersatz trail from his bivouac to the tomb chamber. The light providing a way down the stone dais and to the chamber wall. Not thinking, he placed the amulet into the slot and turned it, instantly the rock wall moved away forming the opening. He rapidly remembered the unsoiled freshness of the flooring and sides of the tomb, they irradiated like the moon, making this moment dreamlike and unnatural. He could see the burial chamber as it now was, and he walked in through the opening and lay onto the bedding. Without understanding why he placed his haversack onto his waste, stowed the amulet inside the satchel, then closed his eyes, and dreamt.

******

9,600 years had passed from the very first time the chamber had successfully been used. The wingman knew for that to work in life, it first must be tested, and quantum progression for this chamber was the young man's unknown quest. It had taken him to indefinite times, a place he had been to in his dreams and had built in his mind from the readings off the clay tablets. This was to be the first time the young man would experience unfamiliar worlds, strange prophecies, and nameless places.

As he awakened, he remained in a somnolent state, yet alert enough to walk free from the chamber and out into an unidentified, and inexplicable world. His confusion had taken him from inside an unrecognisable large edifice of walls and openings, bewildering him even more. This alone had kept him in a state of torpor, mindless and confused as he wondered pointlessly through one-quarter cycle of the moon, and on the next rising of the great yellow orb. He happened upon a typical but very simple farm dwelling and his senses were drawn to it with a reassuring feel. He, without direction or purpose, stepped towards it, a glow from within assuring him of warmness and shelter. He continued his state of inactivity holding back any confusing thoughts he could determine from his unknown surroundings.

The primeval instincts he had instilled in him had kept him going up to this point. Strangely, he felt he could now rest, and it was as if his life cycle was now complete. His body parts began to slow, his mind was numb and he was without thought. The lifeblood keeping him standing facing the dwelling, slowly cooled, he could no longer stand. As he crouched lower, he could feel the pain in his body aching each joint as if he had just hunted and chased down a doe with young fawn from a herd. He curled his body up in a foetal position retaining any warmth he still had in his physique. His communal clothing scantly covered his body yet just able to retain any warmth he still had. He had removed his bracelets, talismans and footwear and placed them inside his leather satchel. Clutching tightly onto his haversack, he closed his eyes one last time allowing himself to be returned as he had once entered the world. The young man would now rest, and his body would soon shut down, and he would dream dreams and reveries, and imaginings of strange places, times and people. Was his short time on earth never going to be understood? Therefore, he simply let go of life, for the last and final time

It was at that exact and precise moment of his life's ending, a young woman knelt down over him covering his cooling body in fleecy woollen blanket. This very event is something he would witness and do many more times in his life, something he had already done but this was now his first. Had the strange occurrence of Vermont reset the young man's world before his past had even taken place? The young woman curled him up pulling the blanket skin tight about his body, and then carried him inside the cottage.

******

A few months had passed and the young man had learnt things at an expediential rate. His writing skills and reading had developed quicker that she would have ever imagined. She had decided education was needed and had made some more or less no question asked type of arrangements for him to attend

Spooner Row Primary School. She had just three weeks from now, to get the young man ready, whereby he would not feel threatened there, therefore protecting his past.

It was a traditional village school offering all aspects of primary education from five to eleven years and worked well with just a short bus ride from her farmhouse.

In the past two weeks leading up to her decision to send him to school, she sat him down assessing his ability.

She had thought of many names she would call him and used her Jewish background as the deciding factor.

'I have enrolled you into school and what I can't teach you, you will learn there, and it's very important we keep you our little secret,' she said.

'Mother, I will and my memory of old is almost faded.'

'I think the mother thing as of today can also go, it is sort of, well, a bit to formal for me, so can we keep it just mum?'

'I will, mum, and please tell this being my naming day, what have you picked for me?'

'My parents were Jewish, and have tried to keep that little tradition, so as you are not technically my true flesh and blood, you are and always will be my son, and "son of my right hand" and that in the Jewish tradition translates to Ben, well, Benjamin.'

'What does your name meaning come from?' asked the young man.

'Oddly, my father was Jewish, but mother was from France, and she chose, well more so insisted on Charlotte. My father wished I were a boy, but he was happy for my mother to have the girl. It actually has a French origin of "free man", and "petite". My father preferred the male diminutive of the name being, Charlot —'

The young man then interrupted, 'Dimmm-inn-a…dim-in-o tiv,' almost spelling it out.

'Well, it sort of means, well does mean, the male equivalent of my name, so Charlotte as a male would be Charlot or Charlie.'

'I like that, Charlie,' he said.

'OK, Mr Ben Walters, I am Charlie, your mother, pleased to meet, sir.'

The two shook hands, smiled, then Charlie rapped her arms about his entire body, squeezed him tight stopping his breath, he coughed, then the two went off for their usual afternoon walk around the yard.

It was not long before Ben had completely forgotten his past. Even when Charlie bought it up, he gave one of those confusing faces a boy of eight would give. Nights were the worse when he would have the odd dream whereby his past memories returned. When Charlie would speak to him over it, he would have difficulty in remembering some of those events, yet more confusing were the futuristic ideas he had.

One afternoon when they were returning from Sunday picnic, Ben suggest they go home a different way and strangely they happened upon a small fate of old wares. Sitting amongst the items and hidden under a mound of books, was one in particular; Ben as if drawn straight to it, asked if he could have it. 'Of course,' she said it was fine, and that evening, Ben became so engrossed in his book, *Armageddon,* he read almost half of it that night.

******

Ben eventually intermingled with the other children at school, with little or no concern from Charlie. She generally drove him more often than not and did her very best in letting him just be the boy with over-all independence. The leading question for Charlie was where did Ben come from, and she literally did mean that. She often thought the clothing in which he was found in seemed rather period to a sect or a cult of some description, perhaps a religious faction? Police were investigating some missing children but apart from them, there were no bulletins or notices of lost or missing boys Ben's age, so she had kept his finding of him to herself.

She always found it rather appealing, how Ben when he went to school on the bus, would trot off down the driveway as if on an excursion. His books slung over his shoulder likened to a backpack and he would kick stones away as if they were obstacles on his imaginary path and scrape twigs along the ground like little road maps.

He would often draw as much as he read; it was as if he disinterred the knowledge within disclosing a hidden prodigy. Some of his sketches did not make any sense, and, they to her, were like an assortment of new and old. She recalled an old village scene he had sketched, almost antediluvian and the villagers had hoary clothing, yet in the midst of the medieval like campfires and shanties, there was a flying machine. It was not boxlike as was the dusters and their Curtis Jenny's, it was "avant-garde", she would say to herself in French, modern almost aberrant. His imaginings were a mixture of both novel with innovation to childlike and primordial, in the end she just accepted it and put it down to his visualisations as a typical child.

There was one particular day that almost bought her world to an end. Ben had travelled his imaginary expedition path along the driveway to catch the school bus; he gave his normal goodbye by teasing her with a "mum" not the Charlie she preferred. Ben and his friend's arrival at school was quickly overcome with an unanticipated deluge of rain. His school chums ran straight into the grounds, but Ben could only focus on the man who stood before him. The man was around 40, smartly dressed and standing high above Ben's lesser height, he gestured inertly to Ben. It was his way of perhaps making Ben feel a little less overawed, scared perhaps as would a child his age. The man's eyeglasses sat low over his nose, enabling his calming eyes to look directly at Ben.

'Hello,' said the man, his soft monotone voice easing Ben's concerns.
'Hello,' replied Ben.
Off to the side of the school buses hidden from view, was a lone figure of a man, who was performing lascivious acts upon himself. He watched on intoning

loudly to himself the displeasure he suddenly got that the boy in his sights had just mysteriously vanished, seemingly into thin air. Was it the rain that just came without warning that caused reduced visibility that perhaps took the child from his sights? The sudden displeasure he got from this took his need to act upon himself in the way he was, and frustratingly he screamed out in annoyance, he fastened his trousers and furtively headed back to his vehicle. The man indignantly headed out of the school bus parking area and travelled back to where he left his work colleague.

'You're back early,' suggested Vermont, 'Did you get done, what you needed?'

'No, no, I did not, it damn well rained, I will try again tomorrow,' retorted Peterson.

As quick as what just happened with Ben and that of lone figure of a man Peterson was over in instant, and if one could analyse this alone is was as if it was over before it had even begun. The 40 something smartly dressed man without the knowledge of Ben, had just stopped the intent of Peterson and that was to have Ben as another victim. The well-dressed man had spoken to Ben thereby stopping his pending victimisation from that of the detective. He, the smartly dressed man had as if by textbook gone back to Old Morley Hall, corrected the fissure, the opening in time thereby stopping Peterson and his intent from happening in the first place.

Ben had now realised the rain had stopped without noticing when. He headed back to school thinking nothing more of it, nor what had just happened. He then walked by the well-dressed man as if it was his first time without actually even noticing him.

Ben's absence from class had caused concerns from the school so the principal had called Charlie to say he was missing from assembly. He had suggested she get down to the school as soon as she could.

******

Vermont had thought it rather odd how Peterson seemed to be excited in investigating Ben's disappearance. They had arrived at their home before Charlie did, Peterson was mumbling profanities under his breath, about punitive actions he would take if the boy was his sibling.

She saw the waiting vehicle parked in front of the farmhouse porch as she arrived, and two men were standing off to the side of the squad car. Smoke blooms from a cigar encircled the face of Peterson, while Vermont was writing notes, notes personal to his own verdicts on Ben's disappearance, and that of other similar cases. She parked her car adjacent theirs and was almost straightaway helped out of her vehicle by Peterson. He peered into the car at Ben as he helped Charlie out, making Ben intimidated, and he sensed the unnatural scowl from Peterson. All through the line of questioning, Peterson's behaviour around Ben appeared uncharacteristic to that of a detective who was focussing on a resolving a crime. He looked Ben up and down, overshadowed him, closely brushed passed him and this turned Vermont's attention to some commonalities of this behaviour each time the two investigated these disappearances.

Charlie was going over some things with Peterson when Ben strangely called Vermont to show him his toy plane out in the yard.

It was at the precise and actual moment, something inside of Vermont had triggered him into a sense of remembrance or in this instance a memory of an actual future event which was still yet to happen. It was the intent in Ben's future that had now caused that previous past event to alter before it even happened.

'Mr Vermont, I may only be eight but have seen much in this world. If you believe in me, you will do what I tell you. Mr Peterson is responsible for the missing children. You will be blamed; your wife and you will become separated in time and both of you will spend stages of your life in an institution and I am going to fix this. I will tell you something that no one else knows and that is you lost your first and only child, you cannot have children and she is blaming you for that, and in months to come, more children will go missing if you don't trust me.' Ben simply turned and went back inside leaving Vermont in renunciation of what just happened.

As Vermont and Peterson drove off, Vermont had thought much about Ben's imaginings and felt compelled to pull over off the road to discuss it with Peterson.

Vermont had listened to what Peterson had said and oddly believed what the boy had just said to him, why he did, he would never know, but in time, he would.

Vermont spent the next two months, building a case on Peterson and eventually had him arrested on charges of murder and child abuse. It would be another 13 years before Peterson was released from an institution, the very same time Vermont would have, should he not have just done what he did.

Vermont remained in the force and indecorously on the very day of Peterson's release, once again, had to investigate a missing person. It was quite ironic for the man that of Peterson, who had tormented children quite possibly all his life, be that missing person and Vermont only saw this as a good thing. It was in a way justice for those families who had suffered under the hands of Peterson, his body was never found and was said that he simply walked off into a new life.

Banham England May 1940:

'Charlie, I won't be gone long around a year with the preliminary training and its only 34 weeks, then I will be sent to an Operational Training Unit [OTU]. That will take around 8 to 14 weeks depending on how I go. I have asked if it is possible for you to visit and they are allowing this so why don't we make it a date when you come, in fact let us make a pact on it.'

'I need to visit London so that will take up most of my time,' she said.

'I really insist you do, please say you will come, make me that promise, tell me now before I go,' pleaded Ben.

'I will try, I promise…'

'Mother,' Ben said in an insistent tone; she knew he would not take no for an answer, 'let's make it in December, early December, make it the 2nd,' said Ben confidently, knowing it was at least a day before the bombings.

'Why the second?' enquired Charlie, 'Why the second?'

'I don't know Mum, just sounds like good day to me.'

She nodded in acceptance, then they both hugged. Ben had repaired the fissure, he had stopped the death of his mother from the bombings and now needed only do one last thing.

******

Ben had systematically restored all the wrongs and knew there was this one thing he had to now repair. He concentrated on that time, then this moment. He counted down the minutes then to the second in which he knew he now had to be. He pictured the rain, the shadowy and murky skies then focused in on the 15-minute flare. The hallucinations and displays of sparkles, became vivid in both mind and then gradually blended into the place that he now stood at, patiently waiting. His transitions between times and places had become almost instant. The controlling of quantum progression for him had now developed into just a thought whereby he couldn't remember even entering the hall, heading down the cellar stairs and into the coffin room. How that was achieved, without knowing was more likely he had done that same thing over and over never knowing how many times, when or from where.

His mind pictured perfectly the time and that moment when he had realised things had changed. It was when Emily turned up at the plane not Marshall, so he uncomplainingly stood without any preconceptions of how it was going to be and fixated on the point of needed change.

Ben's mind was in a rush, the numbness in his concentration shot into his entire body like little convolutions, little tremors as his heart pounded and he savoured the embrace and that of the familiar figure now before him. He held onto to her tight, knowing this moment would alter his and her future, and things would be back to where they should be.

'Don't cry Emily I will come back, I know this, and we will enjoy growing old together, you me, Dover —'

'Ben, I have something to tell you, I am —'

'I know Emily, I know —'

'How do you know what I am?'

'You're pregnant Emily, I will return and you need to trust me on something, will you promise me you will do it no matter how crazy it sounds and how improbable that I would even would suggest it.'

'Yes I will and was worried for a bit with Vermont and his silly things he was saying.'

'I will explain it all to you one day, I promise and as for Vermont, there is some truth in what he is saying, but now is not the time, so trust me when I say, don't go into the aircraft that lands before me on my return.'

'What are you saying…before you, land? What do you —'
'Trust me on this Emily, trust me please and I do promise you all is going to be fine. Don't asked why just trust me.'

******

Peterson had woken cold. He was and surrounded by deep unrelenting forest, it was dark, and his partially exposed body was scratched and broken. He had dried up blood over his arms and the little clothing he had on was torn and ragged. He was somewhere he was unacquainted to, yet the smell of the familiar silver birch was all round him. He looked about and both his surroundings and attire were something that was foreign, strange and unknown.

He looked up in time to see and aircraft fall away from the skies, and then abruptly stopped at the birch treetops. His senses began to attune, there was song all-round him it sounded primitive, the chant was unison, almost orchestral, hundreds of people were keeling down with their hands flat on the ground, the slapping of palms and thwacks on the ground and their instruments. Peterson looked behind him and could see another dressed like him with unclasped hands, waving his palms naively in an up and down motion, as the hatch doors of the flying machine opened. What was happening was his only thought, his years of training as a law officer were flooding back into his mind trying to quickly assess his now apparent impasse. The aircraft started dropping cargo from its large cavernous belly, Peterson looked on in amazement how the flying machine just hovered. The chanting continued, his fellow man behind him with eyes tightly closed continued in song.

Vermont reassessed his situation as best he could soon realising he stood over a deep void where the cargo was now being lowered into. He quickly started piecing together his predicament noticing all others remained with their heads to the stone ground except for the man who stood behind him. Peterson then saw what appeared to be a knife, a very ornate gold knife in the hands of the man who stood behind him. He again quickly reassessed his situation and could see something was not right; he stood in front of a void. That void was intended for him and instantly working out that he needed to be the other man. The chanting stopped, Peterson knowing what was next snatched the knife from him, immediately reversing the situation. The man then fell bloodied into the void.

It was then and only then, the workers could rise up from the levelled stone surface and face the skies. The amulet that Peterson had stopped from ending his own life was subsequently thrust into the chest cavity of his adversary, they now being the fallen, they were the sacrifice and Peterson would be the chosen mortal.

Old Morley Hall-August 1953:

It was a beautiful day, and Emily had told Francis to stop randomly tossing his ball to Dover and keep it close by and not to bother anyone. Francis then had begun to throw the ball on his own as Dover by this time had quite possibly had enough. He tossed the ball high; it bounced then sporadically went in the direction of an old man seated on a park bench. Ben constantly vigil on Francis's actions, remembered how this very moment, he too, sat on the very same bench with the activities of the very same boy. Ben unerringly did not think too much about the fact there was a man on a park bench, sitting there looking up at the sky. He didn't see the similarity that every time an aircraft flew over, and the old man looked up as being anything similar to that which he did at that very same spot. Something within Ben told him to watch over Francis, as he got closer and closer to the old man's bench seat.

The old man observed the boy, leered at him then demurely relaxed as if drawing the youngster toward him. The old man's entire life had albeit come to an end, he was infirm, fragile and desired rest. Yet his abysmal want for a child, a boy, a youth so young and innocent, was his hunger and it inexorably parched his throat, causing shortness of breath. He sadistically trembled, his palms sweaty and his bonce oozed fluids of profane malodourous perspiration.

Francis's ball fell just short of the old man's feet and as he leaned forward to pick it up, the old man salivated at the thought the child was within his grasp. He relished the moment, played with his own emotions, his excitement, and his hunger for the child could not be held back any longer, the old man trembled as he spoke.

'Hello,' said the old man.

'He-ll-oo,' said Francis, 'What... what are you doing?' he asked as if scripted in the same words that he had done, when Ben was in the very same spot, and the boy then had asked him the very same question.

'Well, just sitting here he said, just sitting, looking up at the planes and the people like yourself who come here and play.'

The old man's palms wilted, his fists tightened becoming almost lifeless, non-existent, yet coiled in close to his body ready to strike. His palms dripped sweat becoming dank and his frail body became unsteady and insecure. He felt the need, the need to reach out to the boy, but held his calmness, gaining the pleasure in knowing of the boy's vulnerability, his weakness, his innocence.

'What is your name?' asked the old man. A question he knew the answer to, yet was part of this gruesome and tasteless playacting.

'Francis,' said the boy, 'and that's my mother and my father.'

'Oh, what are their names?' he asked as he scrutinised and studied his surroundings, his inherent past haunting him, it called to him within.

'Well, Mummy is Mummy and Daddy is just Daddy,' he said.

Taking in what seemed to be his last deep breath; the old man held the oxygen into his expiring lung compartments, savoured the moment, and then exhaled his foetid reeking breath through his parted and desiccated lips. His mouth partly open, he quickly inhaled, smirked at the boy, then once again exhaled, expelling his malodourous breath past his taupe coloured decaying teeth, then spoke.

'No, I mean their proper names, like your name,' whispered the old man.

'I am not allowed to call them by it, but that is Emily, she is my mummy, and Daddy is just Ben. But, I am not supposed to call her that, but I do, and sometimes Mummy calls him benja…bennjanr —'

'Benjamin said the old man, it's Benjamin. Can we have a little secret if I tell you my name,' said the old man.

'Yessss,' said Francis, whispering back.

'Well, my name is Mr Wallace, and I am pleased to meet you, Francis.'

The old man swallowed the build-up of saliva in his throat, the drool partially falling off to one side of his withered lips and hung loosely from the stubble on his chin.

Ben looked over one last time, just before Francis threw the ball back to Dover. His concern for the old man was building, yet somehow did not see the danger, nor did he anticipate there was any. Dover galloped off to get the ball, Emily raced to for the ball crossing Dover's path to get there it first.

'Francis, our little secret can be, that you can be my friend if you like, but friends call each other by different names, so how about you just call me…'

Emily reached the ball first, but as she turned, her frozen state instantly told Ben something was wrong, she stood arms at her side, her tightened grip of the ball instantly relaxed, the ball making a thud sound as it hit the ground. Ben looked at her while shaking his head and miming the words, 'what is wrong.' She only had the energy to raise one hand and point over his shoulder toward Francis. Ben briskly turned in time to see the old man standing and leaning forward with outstretched arms inches from his son, their son.

The old man then placed both hands on the boy's shoulders, his fingers sadistically depressing the deltoid muscle; he leaned forward and whispered once more, this time in Francis's ear.

'Francis, you can call me Peterson and I am very happy to meet you.'

Ben and Emily's response was wordless; they both now were looking at a park bench devoid of both man and boy.

The image that together they had of their son now only a silhouette in their minds. The man and boy, their boy, their son had eerily vanished and had oddly now be replaced with that of another man. Standing analogous in height to that of Ben, was a lone figure of a male. He was a smartly dressed, surprisingly elegant looking with his dusky coloured bowler hat that kept the suns brightness from his face. He glowered too at the unoccupied place where a man and child once stood, the smartly dressed man had a mien of uncertainty. The vagueness in the lone male's face as to what was now before him, an empty park bench devoid of Francis, was suggesting something had gone terribly wrong. The elegant man removed his bowler hat, at the exact time Ben had yelled out.

'Marshall!' Ben screamed, 'You were gone, I, I mean I hadn't seen you…what, what's going on, you said I had fixed things…I had chosen wisely…'

'You had Ben, well you have, but something is not right, how did he, I mean, he was exiled I sent him too… he does not have the amulet…I have… well, you have it'

'Marshall!' Ben yelled again, 'You at this time when I need you the most is not making any sense…what is going on, exiled…what amulet…who are you, tell me who?'

'Marshall, I am Marshall, Marshall Hartley.'

Ben curiously looked deeper into his eyes, he oddly again saw the similitude but improbably this time he now noticed that the scar above his left eye was absent. *Who*? he again asked himself, who was this strange man who seemed only to be able to be understood, by himself, perhaps even seen only by him? He looked back at Emily and she appeared solid, her arm had not moved and still firmly pointing, she was conscious yet motionless, looking right through Marshall Hartley as if not there, desolation in her eyes.

'Ben, I am Marshall Hartley,' he said this time with buoyancy and self-assurance, 'Marshall, Marshall Benjamin Hartley.'

Ben, stood speechless, wordless to the point he only could think what was just said but not say it…Marshall would say it for him.

'You, Ben, have been setting things right all your known life, it was you all along, and only you, I am you, and only stand here in your mind because of you, you can fix this, you will fix this…